M000285532

ALSO BY CLARE SESTANOVICH

Objects of Desire

ASK ME AGAIN

ASK ME AGAIN

A NOVEL

CLARE SESTANOVICH

ALFRED A. KNOPF
NEW YORK
2024

THIS IS A BORZOI BOOK PUBLISHED BY ALFRED A. KNOPF

www.aaknopf.com

Knopf, Borzoi Books, and the colophon are registered trademarks of Penguin Random House LLC.

LIBRARY OF CONGRESS CATALOGING-IN-PUBLICATION DATA
Names: Sestanovich, Clare, [date] author.
Title: Ask me again : a novel / Clare Sestanovich.
Description: New York : Alfred A. Knopf, 2024.
Identifiers: LCCN 2023033253 (print) | LCCN 2023033254 (ebook) |
ISBN 9780593318119 (hardcover) | ISBN 9780593311202 (trade paperback) |
ISBN 9780593318126 (eBook)
Subjects: LCSH: Self-realization—Fiction. | LCGFT: Bildungsromans. | Novels.
Classification: LCC PS3619.E83 A94 2024 (print) | LCC PS3619.E83 (ebook) |
DDC 813/.6—dc23/eng/20230724
LC record available at https://lccn.loc.gov/2023033253
LC ebook record available at https://lccn.loc.gov/2023033254

Jacket illustration by Tyler Spangler; (eyes) Margarita Khamidulina and (hand) kyoshino, both Getty Images
Jacket design by Janet Hansen

Manufactured in the United States of America

FIRST EDITION

For Eddie

ASK ME AGAIN

WHAT'S IT WORTH?

In a courtyard behind the hospital, with cold metal benches and leafless trees strangled by Christmas lights, Eva came upon a doctor smoking a cigarette. He sucked on it hungrily. He exhaled out of the side of his mouth and glared at her—defiant, adolescent—as if daring her to point out his hypocrisy. She was the actual adolescent: sixteen years old. She could have told him that she enjoyed hypocrisy. No, not in herself; her own contradictions made her seem strange and ugly, like dressing-room mirrors that revealed angles of her face she couldn't usually see. But in other people, inconsistency was interesting—a mark of complexity, maybe maturity. She smiled at the doctor. He crushed the cigarette under his shoe, an elegant pivot with an inelegant sneaker, and went back inside.

You weren't supposed to like hospitals, but secretly Eva did. She liked being close to so many extremes. Birth, death. It was surely the cleanest place she had ever been—surgeons, she learned, scrubbed their hands for two to six minutes, all the way up to their elbows—and also the dirtiest: blood, shit, infectious disease. (She timed six minutes.

It was a long time.) People yelled in hospitals and people whispered. They limped or they hobbled or they sprinted from one emergency to the next. She had watched a man fall asleep standing up. There was good news and bad news. Miracles happened, but sometimes—a lot of the time—life simply dealt you a bad hand.

Whenever she heard an ambulance approaching, Eva went toward it, not away from it. She stood right next to the automatic doors of the emergency room, longing to cover her ears and willing herself not to. It would have been easy to block the sirens out, but she had recently adopted a new ethic, too new to be violating already: *Block nothing out*. If she listened long enough, close enough, the wailing of the trucks became an urgent pulse inside her body.

While her grandmother slept in a semiprivate room, a pale-green curtain separating her from a carpenter who'd fallen off a ladder and broken his back, Eva wandered the halls in search of characters. In the basement—radiology—she found a woman in a plastic chair clutching a jagged chunk of rose quartz in each hand. In her lap, a pile of other crystals: amethyst, obsidian, tiger's-eye. On a floor with a view all the way across Central Park—cardiology—she found a man singing union songs while wheeling an IV up and down the hall. "Which side are you on," he belted, then hummed, then belted again. ("Yours," a doctor rushing past assured him.) Through an open door in the pediatric wing, she found a toddler wearing a Styrofoam helmet. His parents argued loudly while he stared at the television: a soap opera on mute. Abruptly, his mother changed the channel, and a dour newscaster appeared. The child smiled placidly as grim headlines scrolled across the screen.

Then there were patients, like Eva's grandmother Adele, who seemed too empty to be characters. Vacant stares in the waiting rooms, haggard faces in the cafeteria. The elevators were packed with people who didn't want to look at you. But of course they had stories, too—all the more alluring for seeming blank, or being hidden. Eva was good at looking for clues. Everything could be a puzzle, which meant that everything could be solved. A man leaned over the water fountain, his gown gaping open to reveal all his moles and liver spots and gummy pink skin tags, and in her head, Eva connected the dots, drawing a constellation across his back. All the sounds in a hospital, she discovered, seemed like codes: the beeping of machines, the squeaking of sneakers on freshly mopped linoleum. They were probably all code for the same thing. *Hurry.*

She brought these characters, these puzzles, back to her parents. She meant it as a kind of comfort: someone else's story to distract from their own. Adele wasn't unconscious, but she wasn't exactly awake either, and no one would say when, or if, she might be. The doctors, with their unreadable expressions and their unknowable expertise, with sentences so complex they might as well have been secrets, blandly instructed them to wait, cryptically promised they would see. Eva's parents were not very good at waiting. They paced, they grimaced. They clenched their hands and jaws without noticing they were clenching. Her dad was better at it: he had his sketchbook, the rhythmic sound of pencil against paper, like an animal scratching plaintively at the door. Eva's mom kept buying things from the vending machine at the end of the hall, packages that had been there for too long: crackers crumbled to dust, chocolate white with age. She opened them and then abandoned them, forming a pile on an empty chair, as if stockpiling for some future disaster.

Adele was in the hospital because she'd jumped out the window at her nursing home. It was a second-floor window. She hadn't died, as she'd hoped she would. Her bones broke in lots of different ways: her right kneecap into many pieces, her lowest rib neatly in two. Her pelvis had somehow remained intact, spider-veined with cracks like the surface of a melting lake, but her ulna had pierced straight through the skin of her forearm. By the time Eva and her parents arrived at the hospital, it had been pushed or pulled back into place—reset.

For nearly her entire life, from Kraków to Boston to the assisted-living facility in New Jersey ("The Village," they called it), Adele had been a devout Catholic. She gave God credit for everything, beseeching him desperately, thanking him profusely. She had never insisted on anyone else's devotion—Eva's father (her son) hadn't been to Mass in decades, Eva's mother could be haughty in her nonbelief—but their ingratitude had worried her and brought her pain. Then, a few months before she jumped, all that had changed. With a suddenness that seemed biblical, her piety had turned into rage.

Why had everything been taken from her? Her husband, her driver's license, her bladder control, one friend after another. And then the house. She had given her life to that house. She had given other people lives in that house. Three children, six grandchildren. She raged instead of eating, raged instead of sleeping, raged into the phone long after she had accidentally hung up. The doctors had explanations for the anger. Tangles in the brain. Something called plaque. The explanations made her angrier. She was not one of those old people. She was not confused—she was furious.

She left a note beside a dish of spearmint lozenges before she jumped, dated in wobbly handwriting no longer recognizable as her own. December 3, 1906. (Later, the doctors used this against her: she was a hundred years off.) In the note, Adele's anger was not personal or petty. That might have made things simpler—that kind of rage might have been easier to refute, or at least to ignore. She didn't call her children traitors or cowards, which made them realize that's what they were. It was the world, she said, that had disillusioned her, God who had betrayed her. And not just her. She could have tolerated that; who was she, after all, to be spared grief and humiliation and incontinence? But what about the others? The young, the beautiful, the not yet disabused. What would happen to them?

Eva avoided eye contact with the nurses in the emergency room, in case they noticed her coming and going. Sometimes she acted like she was looking for someone, scanning the waiting room with a purposeful look on her face, but she felt guilty pretending. And she was not above superstition: pretend to have an emergency and eventually she might be punished with a real one. (She told herself this wasn't how the world worked. But how *did* the world work?)

One morning, Eva sat in the corner of the ER, reading a book. It was quiet this early—less to watch but more calm in which to watch it. Nearby, a bearded guy slept across two chairs, covered in a dirty coat that smelled so bad it almost smelled sweet. A few seats over, there was a teenage boy, skinny limbs and stringy hair, whose eyes were also closed, but his posture was too good for sleeping. Maybe he was meditating. Beside him, a woman sang something in Spanish to the baby in her lap, who started crying the instant she stopped, even just to catch her breath.

Eva's book was a book of poems, which she regretted bringing. She liked poems, or the idea of poems: their difficulty. She liked deciding what they meant. But when she read so many back to back, understanding escaped her. The first ones she had annotated eagerly, filling the blank space on the page with urgent notes; now, halfway through the book, all her circles and squiggles seemed like some made-up language, invented to try to decipher another made-up language—those opaque phrases, those brutally severed sentences, those connotations or denotations, she could never remember which.

She closed the book. She listened to the mother singing and the old man wheezing in his sleep. She opened the book again. She read the poem a second time and a third time, straining to unlock something, then waiting for something to be unlocked, then cursing the very idea of the lock. Why not just say what you mean?

When the teenage boy stopped meditating and started stretching—twisting in complicated, yogic postures that Eva would have been embarrassed to attempt in public—she finally gave up. On her way out of the ER, she slipped the book under one of the empty plastic chairs. This was a statement—*Fuck poetry*—but also a ruse. She would have to come back for it later.

In her grandmother's room, she found her parents discussing whether to summon a priest. Adele had renounced priests, hadn't she? It had been months since she'd gone to Mass. But what were months, Eva's dad wondered, in the scheme of eighty-eight years?

He did the math: "Three-thousandths of a lifetime."

"So what?" Eva's mom said. "The other nine-hundred-and-ninety-seven-thousandths were a delusion."

The truth was the truth.

Her father's cousin texted him the name of a priest. The last rites could be administered by Skype. No one liked this idea, but they couldn't explain why. If they didn't believe in priests, what did it matter?

When Eva went back for her book, the boy was reading it, legs crossed, back straight, mouthing the words. It was a short book, and she could see that he was already nearing the end, turning the pages methodically, not even pausing between poems. This was not how Eva had been taught to read poetry—to appreciate it. But that was the kind of thing teachers cared about and artists didn't: the right way to do something. Eva wished she knew more artists. Her dad had tried to be a painter, but he'd long since given it up as a profession. Now art was just a hobby, which was a ridiculous-sounding word, like something out of a children's story. It embarrassed Eva to hear him say it.

When the boy finished reading, he closed the book but continued staring at it, as if the cover had something to say—as if it might speak. The same poems that had said nothing, meant nothing to her. Was *he* an artist?

"That's my book."

She sounded more aggressive than she'd meant to, but he looked up calmly, barely startled.

"Thanks," he said, as if she'd lent it to him.

He held out the thin volume, which seemed thicker now that someone else had read it. Had he read all her notes, too? Had he seen them trail off, swallowed up by each artful, reticent page?

"How embarrassing," she said.

"What?"

Eva waved the floppy book. "My marginalia."

He shrugged. "I didn't read it."

Instead of being relieved, she was hurt. "Why not?"

"I wasn't trying to understand the poems," he said after a moment. "But I liked the sound of them. Or, you know, the sound in my head. Which isn't exactly a sound."

"Oh."

Eva sat down next to him. Across the room, in the chair where she'd been sitting a few hours earlier, a woman with a shaved head was holding her arm slightly away from her body, as if, now that it was injured, she realized it didn't quite belong to her. Eva turned to face the boy.

"Are you okay?"

"Okay?"

She gestured around the room, the strangers in different states of distress. "Are you having an emergency?"

He shook his head. "It's my brother. He gets drunk, falls down. More routine than emergency, really."

Eva watched him closely, waiting for something to change now that he had revealed these facts—wayward brother, sudden collapse, routine disaster. His hair was about the same color and length as hers: yellow and brown, skimming the shoulders. She was pretty sure they were the same age.

"I'm Jamie."

Eva herself had never been drunk. This was not a matter of principle, definitely not a point of pride. Did *he* drink? He didn't look like a loser, or a Christian, or like someone trying to get into the Naval Academy, which were all the reasons she knew for sobriety. Her own reason—fear—was not one that she'd ever spoken out loud.

"And who are you?" he asked.

Eva wasn't someone who blushed, her complexion more pallid than pink, but she often wished that she was. The straightforwardness appealed to her: to have your face speak for itself.

"Sorry." She held out her hand, then instantly retracted it—too formal. "Eva."

They went to the cafeteria. Eva filled a cup with hot water, because she didn't have any money with her. Jamie offered to buy her something else, opening his leather wallet with the habitual ease of an adult, but she refused. Eva still kept most of her money in a jewelry box at home, afraid of losing it. He ordered a salad (no dressing, extra croutons) and two cartons of chocolate milk, which he drank very quickly, his throat bobbing up and down. There were a few silky hairs on his neck and a trail of pimples leading up to his jaw.

They didn't mention his brother again, and Eva never brought up her grandmother. Instead, she told him about all the strangers: the crystal woman, the union man. Only hours before, Jamie had been one of them, but she knew things about him now. His name, his brother, his aversion to wet lettuce. (It was too soft and slimy; he liked food that crunched.) She couldn't say with certainty that she liked him. He didn't bother to wipe the outline of chocolate milk above his lip, and he didn't make jokes at his own expense, as many of Eva's friends did. When she made that kind of joke about herself, he tilted his head in surprise or confusion, as if to say, *You want me to laugh at you?* It was unsettling. She hurried on to other topics.

When she told him about the baby with the helmet, Jamie nodded. She had already told her mom and dad, but they had interpreted the story of the boy's parents arguing as an oblique message about their own arguing, and had seemed wounded. They didn't say this outright, so Eva couldn't apologize outright, and there had been a regrettable silence, in which they listened to the carpenter coughing on the other side of the curtain.

Jamie said there was a name for the baby's condition, but he couldn't remember it. The boy's skull, he explained, had probably fused too soon. In most babies, the bones were soft and flexible, with lots of space between them, so you had to be careful, cradling their heads like thin-skinned fruit.

How did he know all this? Was he older than she'd guessed?

"Do you have a baby?" Eva asked.

He smiled: no. It was a nice, gentle smile—not too wide. Softness was dangerous, he explained, but hardness was even more dangerous. It didn't leave enough room to grow. He knocked on his head, and the hollow sound of knuckles on skull, bone on bone, seemed ominous.

"Hear that?" he said. "That's the sound of being stuck in your ways."

It was a long subway ride home, from the middle of Manhattan to the middle of Brooklyn. Eva switched trains downtown, walking slowly through a series of underground passages, because subway stations were essentially archeological sites—full of artifacts. Shopping bags left under benches, gum left under railings, a dozen used-up fare cards scattered around a trash can that needed to be emptied, each one an irretrievable record of where someone else had been. She waited for the D train in front of an ad featuring a famous actor's face, a palimpsest of graffiti: Sharpied mustache, spray-painted initials, a glued-on flyer advertising the services of a piano teacher. SIGHT-READING IN 30 DAYS.

Her parents were still at the hospital, and Eva was glad to be on her own. Without them, it was easier to think about Jamie, to imagine him moving through the city alongside her. This, after all, was the point of meeting someone new: everything looked different when it could be seen—if she got the angle right and the mood right, if she blinked right and breathed right—as he would see it. Well, it had to be a certain kind of person. She was capable of falling in love with strangers, but that was something else entirely. If she had been attracted to Jamie, she wouldn't have wondered what he thought about the station manager flossing her teeth with a strand of hair, or the sneeringly handsome face on the movie poster, or the rat chasing its tail on the tracks. If she had been attracted to him, she would have wondered what he thought about *her.*

On the train, Eva listened to a song she'd forgotten about. A few years ago, she had spent a week listening to it nonstop. Now, when she reached the chorus, a climactic, ecstatic burst (it was just a pop song), she was transported to those days:

The beginning of spring and she is bare-legged, walking down the street. The weather is still uncertain. Some people wear coats and boots, others tie too-heavy sweaters around their waists. The light is weak, watery light, but at least one woman is already hiding behind sunglasses. Eva is looking down at her pale shins, wishing she had shaved them. The hundreds (thousands?) of hairs look like the legs of insects emerging from under her skin, which makes her imagine the bodies of the insects—but, no, she won't think about that. She can train herself to avoid thinking about that. She reminds herself to look up instead of down. At faces, at buildings, at the tops of buildings, which are easy to forget to look at. At the sky, which can seem like a hard blue wall or like infinity itself, depending on the day. She is turning up the volume, starting the song again, hoping to rise above or beyond or just out of herself.

Then the train emerged from underground, the darkness of the tunnel morphing into the darkness of the night, revealing that there are many kinds of darkness. Once every dozen times she rode the D train, Eva forgot that it went aboveground. Every other time, she wished she could unremember, because the surprise of it was such a simple pleasure, hurtling all of the sudden into the known world. The sky and the skyline moved past her methodically, the *ka-thunk* of the train like a metronome, the evenly spaced cables of the bridge slicing her field of vision into so many measures. Then the train plunged back underground, and the window revealed nothing but her own reflection.

At her stop, Eva turned off the music and coiled her earphones into a small bundle that she would have to untangle later. She had worn them without thinking, forgetting that part of her vow—*Block nothing out*—had been to break this habit: to listen to less music, to listen to more of her surroundings. You couldn't eavesdrop with your ears plugged. She maneuvered around a few slow walkers on the platform—an old woman, a high-heeled woman, a dawdling teenager—before telling herself not to rush, not to not notice. She climbed the first set of stairs deliberately, mindfully. At the base of the second set of stairs, she stopped.

There was a man coming down them, and she could see right away that something was wrong. He was listing left, one shoulder tugging him down, his hand reaching for something, but not in the right place. He was grasping air, losing balance. Eva stepped back and collided with the high-heeled woman. The woman cursed. At first, the man's fall was dramatic—he stumbled, pitched forward—and then it was pathetic: he crumpled. Just as the high-heeled woman passed him, he vomited between his knees.

The man's ankle was bent at an ugly angle, caught under his opposite leg, and his shoes were splattered brown-green. Eva didn't move. She wanted to help, but what would helping look like? She couldn't picture it. What she pictured instead was the scene at the top of the stairs: the bodega with its rows of glistening fruit and bins of flowers dyed too blue, the smoke shop with its brightly colored bongs and many-tentacled hookah pipes, the old brick church with its stately spire and heavy, noble doors. She had walked from the top of the stairs to her front door more times than she could count. She could have found her way home blind.

Just as Eva was about to shake off her thoughts—less thinking! more acting!—a guy wearing big headphones pushed past her. He looked older than her, though not by much. He was singing quietly, but when he saw the man, he stopped and bent down, putting his hands under the stranger's armpits, the way you would with a child.

"I got you," he said gently, almost to himself.

The boy helped and the man let himself be helped. One of them slumped against the wall, the other crouched beside it. A mouth speaking into an ear. Eva stood there for a second longer, then raced up the stairs. Something slick under her sneaker, but she didn't stop to see what. On the sidewalk, the world was just as she had imagined it. Her heart beat in her head. She took the tangled earphones out of her pocket, because the silence was heavy and accusatory.

When Eva's grandmother woke up, she wasn't angry or regretful or sorry; she was sad. The nurses spoke to her in cloying voices, simple sentences.

In the end, Adele got her wish: she never went back to the nursing home. She spent a week in the hospital, and then she was gone. She didn't say much in the final days, and when she did speak, it was without looking at anyone—her words into space. At night, she chanted Hail Marys until the words began to loosen and slur with sleep, as if she were drunk, but she was only dying.

Jamie had given Eva his phone number. Did he expect to meet her again? How often did his brother get wasted? That week, she kept wandering the hospital, but she avoided the emergency room. She wanted to see him, but she wanted to leave it up to chance. In a fluorescent, windowless hall, she watched doctors with grave faces go in and out of an operating theater. It was hard to believe that all of them had peeled back someone's skin and seen what was underneath.

Her grandmother died on a Monday, when Eva wasn't there. She was alone in the two-story house where she had lived for her entire life, on a block wedged between the park and the cemetery, near the highest point in Brooklyn. None of the buildings on their street matched: there were a few cramped, clapboard structures like theirs, a set of brick condos with built-in air conditioners and shiny chrome gates, some classic brownstones with American flags waving out front, and, most recently, a new apartment building—all smooth gray surfaces, with floor-to-ceiling windows. It was evening, and through the kitchen window Eva could see the many varieties of Christmas trees in the living rooms across the street. There were colored lights and soft white lights and harsh LED lights. Their own living room still didn't have a tree. Maybe her parents had forgotten, or maybe they had remembered but it had seemed too festive, too celebratory, given the circumstances. Either way, Eva didn't mind.

She had a book in her lap again, but it had been open to the same page for a while. The sky got dark while she sat like that, not bothering to turn on a lamp. It was better to look through other people's windows if they couldn't look through yours. When her phone lit up with an incoming call, it was the only light in the room. She flipped it open.

"It's Jamie."

"I know."

Across the street, the overhead switched on in a third-floor apartment, revealing a scraggly, blue-green Christmas tree in the corner of a room cluttered with abandoned toys and laundry drying on a rack. Until then, Eva realized, it hadn't really been a tree, just the outline of one, its shape defined by the loops of twinkling lights.

Jamie was calling to tell her that he wouldn't be at the hospital anymore, at least not for a while. His brother had gone to rehab.

"That's good," Eva said. "Right?"

"Good, though maybe not good enough."

Up until the very end, his brother had resisted. First, he'd said he didn't have a problem. Later, he'd said he could fix it on his own. It was only when the neighbor had found him curled up in the elevator, naked, that he'd relented. Even then, he hadn't been persuaded—just defeated. While two humorless women from the facility watched him pack his bags, he'd stopped and looked at himself in the closet mirror. His face was puffy, but his arms were skinny. "What do you think?" he'd said out loud, to no one in particular. "Will they turn me into someone else?" No one answered, so he went back to packing, then followed the women out the door.

"What *do* you think?" Eva asked.

"He's tried it before. They tell you the addict isn't the real you. That it's not about transforming yourself, just about finding yourself."

"Just?"

A woman appeared in the apartment across the street, checking the laundry for dampness. She gathered everything but a pair of pants into her arms. Her mouth was moving. Was she talking to someone in the next room? Was she talking to herself?

"I think people can change," Jamie said. "If that's what you're asking."

"Where would the real you be hiding? Out there? In here?"

The woman came back into the living room. For several seconds, she stood motionless in the center of the carpet. She might have been waiting for something, or she might have forgotten what she was doing there. Jamie was silent.

"And why would it be hiding?" Eva asked.

Her parents came home before he had time to respond. Eva hung up hurriedly, because it seemed too difficult to explain whom she was talking to. A stranger? A friend?

Adele, they said, had waited until she was all alone to die. Eva's mom had been arguing with the doctors in the hallway; her dad had been buying coffee in the cafeteria. When he walked into Adele's room, blowing into the hole of a paper cup, his tongue burnt, she was already dead. He put the coffee down without spilling. His hands were warm and hers were going cold.

Eva's parents didn't cry, so Eva didn't either, but they were all very solemn. Adele had cried often, without explanation or embarrassment, and Eva wondered if their composure was a kind of betrayal. The last time she had seen her grandmother, Eva had been sitting in a plastic chair among all the machines that distilled Adele's body into numbers: heart rate, blood pressure, temperature. The numbers were green or yellow or red. Green was good and red was bad. Yellow was not so good, but by then yellow was normal. Her grandmother said her name.

"Eva."

She would have reached out to hold Adele's hand, but she was worried about messing up all the tubes. The old woman's eyes were two wet stones in her face. They looked off into space, or at something Eva couldn't see.

"If you know you're going to fall," she said, "jump."

DID YOU SEE THAT?

Jamie fell in love with the tree behind Eva's house. It wasn't clear who owned the tree: half of it was in their yard and half of it was in their neighbor's. The chain-link fence that divided the two properties had to be built around the trunk, stopping when it reached the tree and resuming on the other side. Every few years, the neighbor, a middle-aged guy who lived alone and had a noisy tool for each season—a leaf blower, a snow blower, a lawn mower that roared early on Saturday mornings—would threaten to cut the tree down. Then Eva's dad would talk him around and they'd forget about the whole thing for a while. Still, they worried. They wondered if the man had a chain saw. He liked anything that revved to life.

What was there to love about a tree?

"It has character," Eva said tentatively, trying to see what Jamie saw.

He shook his head. "No anthropomorphizing."

It was a black walnut tree, a tree that caused problems for other trees. In its roots and leaves and the heavy fruit that it dropped every spring, there was some sort of poisonous compound. The fruit were walnuts, which didn't look anything like what you thought walnuts did: the size of tennis balls, but hard and dense. They made a loud thump when they hit the grass, a loud thwack when they hit the concrete patio. Eva was always a little afraid they might hit her on the head. The thick rind of the walnuts stained her fingers bright green, but as the fruit ripened, the skin turned yellow, then black. Dig deep enough (years ago, Eva had used her dad's old pocket knife) and you would find the familiar-looking nut at its heart. Most of the fruit went uncollected in the yard, first rotting, then slowly withering into dry, rattling shells.

One thing Jamie loved was the way the black walnuts smelled—sharp and lemony, a scent that you could feel at the back of your throat. Eva, who didn't like it, thought it smelled like furniture polish, or paint thinner, but Jamie said it smelled the way it looked: green. He wasn't the only one who enjoyed it; you could buy the scent in a bottle and wear it as perfume.

The tree's leaves were teardrops, uniform in size and shape, with one leaf always exactly opposite another on the stem. If you were lying beneath the branches, as Jamie liked to, head on the soft ground, feet on the hard patio, arms spread wide, this produced a kaleidoscopic effect.

"You look like you're in a movie trailer," Eva said. "Staring at the sky, pondering the meaning of life."

"When you're tripping, leaves are almost unbearable to look at."

"Unbearable how?"

He put his hands behind his head, cradling his skull. "You understand that leaves are miracles."

With most of her peers, Eva didn't advertise her inexperience. But with Jamie, who knew firsthand about weed, acid, mushrooms, and salvia, secondhand about plenty else, she was no longer afraid. Early on, she had confessed her embarrassment to him, hoping to get it out of the way. He could have tried to reassure her, could have said something nice and untrue, like *There's nothing to be embarrassed about*—but he didn't. She appreciated that. He told her that curiosity was the only good reason to get high. Maybe someday she would start to wonder about all the other worlds lurking behind the visible one. Maybe she would want to glimpse the secret lives of trees, to know the things—the truths—that you couldn't dig your way to with a Swiss Army knife.

Jamie lived on the Upper East Side. There were plenty of trees up there, but few backyards. His father owned a penthouse with a large balcony overlooking the city, where he kept trees in pots: a Japanese maple, a kumquat tree that never bore fruit, a trio of dwarf cypresses that a gardener shaped into perfect cones. Each one was replaced as soon as it began to show signs of decline. Jamie's mother used to live in the penthouse, too, but since the divorce, she'd been moving down in the world—literally. At first, she had a view of Museum Mile. Now she lived on the second floor of a building surrounded by scaffolding and draped in a gauzy black shroud. Not that there would have been much to look at anyway, just traffic and dog walkers, guys in suits. She owned a few indoor plants, but in the gray, filtered light, she struggled to keep them alive. They made her feel bad about herself.

These facts emerged slowly, reluctantly—a picture of Jamie's life beyond Eva's. It was a life, he admitted eventually, while the leaves kaleidoscoped above him, refracting blue sky and green light, that he often could not bear to return to.

He had arrived at Eva's house for the first time on a Sunday afternoon, without any explanation or excuse, even though it was a long way from home. He had no book to return or retrieve; he didn't pretend he was in the neighborhood. (Later, Eva wondered if he had ever even been to the neighborhood, where there were no penthouses, no landscapers, very few suits.) He simply asked if he could come, and then came.

To be a good host, Eva filled up water glasses at the sink and put pretzels on a plate. Jamie ate everything on the plate, then everything in the bag. He told her that he never craved sugar but always needed salt. Lately, he'd been growing very quickly, so quickly that it hurt. That sounded dramatic, but if you thought about it, it made sense: his body was being stretched out. Picture someone on the rack, or picture a piece of clay tugged and kneaded into a longer shape: the clay got thin and weak, then tore. Jamie towered over both his parents. One night, he'd woken up in the dark gasping for breath, and it turned out his lung had collapsed. That was the only time he'd been to the emergency room for his own emergency. They could fix the lung, but they couldn't do anything about the rest of the body—they couldn't slow it down.

On that first day, Eva didn't know whether to worry about the long pauses in conversation, awkward silences in which they could hear her parents upstairs: the shrill commands of an exercise class playing on her mom's laptop (jumping, panting), the Donovan album playing in the spare bedroom that her dad used as a painting studio. (*First there is a mountain, then there is no mountain, then there is.*) Jamie had no nervous habits that Eva could detect. When he wasn't speaking, he seemed simply to be thinking. She hid her chewed fingernails in her fists.

Soon Jamie was coming every weekend. He was staying for dinner, then doing the dishes. He never asked what to call her mom and dad. They were Gail and Nick from the moment they appeared: Gail sweating in sweatpants, Nick smelling like turpentine. They liked that—they couldn't bear being mister or missus. They thought some of Eva's friends were too polite.

Her parents had certain ideas about rich people, and Eva could tell that they were surprised to discover that these ideas could not account for Jamie—how he behaved, why they liked him. A long time ago, Gail had lived among rich people. Her father had made a small fortune off a medical patent when Gail was young, but old enough that she could remember how everything changed, seemingly all at once. She liked to tell Eva about it, a mixture of wistfulness and bitterness in her voice. They'd moved into a new house, with room for more stuff—room, as Gail's mother said, to breathe. The house was bigger, and so, it seemed, were they. Gail remembered how her father looked taller in an expensive suit, her mother looked fatter in a fancy kitchen.

But whatever they'd purchased didn't last. Getting rich was a sudden revelation, and becoming poor again was a slow awakening, the end of a dream that no amount of pinching could convince them would soon be over until it really was. Her father didn't gamble his fortune away or spend it all in one place; he had not entirely forgotten how to save. But he didn't know how to turn some money into more money—a loaves-and-fishes miracle that he assumed only extraordinary men could perform. Why wasn't ordinary hard work enough?

He didn't learn his lesson, but Gail did. By the time she cashed her first paycheck, she'd concluded that the safest way to live was never to have too much to lose. She became a teacher, with a steady, unenviable income. She didn't buy fancy clothes or take vacations or use her credit card. When she met Nick, she was wary: being an artist (that was how he introduced himself back then) didn't sound safe. But he had a steady day job, and he never stopped at the first gas station, hoping there would be a cheaper one around the corner. In Nick's family, a balanced ledger was a moral concern, not a practical one. They had never been poor—his father was a successful doctor—but his mother counted every penny and clipped every coupon. If at first Adele had been saving for something in particular, the purpose of it had long since been replaced by the pure pleasure of it, the empty-stomach satisfaction of doing without, the rumble of desire not for anything at hand but for something to come. For a religious woman like her, it was easy to wring logic from faith: all that saving must have something to do with salvation.

God was beside the point for Nick and Gail. They took pride in moderation because it got good results. A family with just one kid, a house with just two stories. Over time, they learned to take certain risks. They even took some trips, though nothing elaborate. No all-inclusive deals, no all-you-can-eat meals, no infinity pools. They repeated their warnings to Eva with reverence that had become roteness, fears rubbed smooth by so many years of believing them: never trust anything that promises you everything. Nick admitted that there was a brief period in his youth when he'd wanted what lots of young people want—high highs and low lows, the extremity of feeling. Then he'd learned (and he hoped Eva would, too) that being average wasn't so bad, that being exceptional was a luxury not worth wasting your money on.

But what about Jamie? He was certainly exceptional: rich yet humble, rich yet kind, rich yet strange, rich yet deep, rich yet real. How could that not be worth it?

Jamie was never rude, not loud or crass or insolent, but he was indifferent to unspoken rules. He made himself at home. He filled up his own glass from the faucet, took books off shelves, spent solitary hours pulling up weeds in the yard while Eva did her homework at the kitchen table. One morning, before it was even noon, he ordered a pizza to their front door. He tipped the delivery guy generously. "Help yourself," he said to Eva and her parents, not noticing their surprise, or else ignoring it. No one took a slice. When he was finished, he swept the crumbs into the cardboard box, flattened it, and took it straight out to the trash. There were good reasons for everything he did (he ate when he was hungry), but he didn't go around explaining them.

The truth was that Eva had wanted a slice of pizza as soon as it appeared: the oil pooling in saucers of pepperoni, the elastic ropes of mozzarella, the way the whole thing shone. But as she watched him eat, folding each slice in half, orange grease funneling onto his plate, she couldn't summon any of her own reasons. If she was hungry, what was she hungry for? The burn of too-hot cheese, the burst of salt and fat and meat? The rawness afterward, on the top of her tongue and the roof of her mouth? She envied his efficiency—five bites, a discarded crust—and she envied his appetite. He wiped the oil off his chin.

One afternoon at the beginning of spring, Jamie roasted a chicken. He arrived holding it under one arm like a basketball—no bag, just the see-through packaging, watery pink juice pooling inside the plastic—and offered to make dinner. Eva, who rarely cooked anything that didn't come in a box, a simple recipe printed on the side, tried to help. She rubbed salt all over the bird as he had instructed, but its loose skin, pale and pimpled, kept slipping back and forth under her fingers. The way the wings were pressed against its body reminded her of a swaddled baby.

Jamie saw her struggling. "Here, let me."

He finished the salt while Eva washed her hands, unpleasantly aware, now, of her own skin, her own bones. He chopped potatoes and carrots and onions and sprigs of rosemary that looked like miniature trees. He set a timer and let the whole thing cook, without once looking at a recipe. Competence made him seem old—much older than her. When he pulled the pan out of the oven, Eva, watching him from across the room, pictured him decades from now, with another bird, another oven, his hair shorter, his shoulders fuller. She smelled herbs, something charred. The pan went back in.

"How much do you value the life of a chicken?" he asked when he stood up.

Nick appeared in the doorway, wearing shorts and no shoes, his legs pale and nearly hairless.

"You mean, how much would I pay for a chicken?" Nick said.

Jamie wore an oven mitt on each hand.

"No, not to buy. Something more fundamental. Like, how does its value compare with our value?"

"Hm." Nick opened the fridge.

"Way less," Eva said.

"But how much less? Fifty percent less? Ninety percent less?"

Eva hated this kind of question, for the same reason she disliked riddles and trivia night and the last, long problem on a math test: it revealed all the unused parts of her brain; it made her feel dumb.

Jamie seemed to use every part of his brain. He knew the names of birds, the stories behind constellations, the etymology of certain words—why *interest* could compel someone to gain knowledge but also to lose money. He memorized subway maps, not only in New York but also in London and Hong Kong, because he liked the way they looked.

"Can't we just eat the chicken?" she said.

Jamie accepted a can of soda from Nick between two mitts.

"The thing is, you don't have to value any single chicken very much to put all chickens first." He removed the mitts and flipped the tab on the can, which gasped with what sounded like pleasure. "Let's say you can free a chicken from a cage for just one dollar. There are so many chickens that, even if you value a chicken only one percent as much as you value a human, you should put all your money toward saving chickens."

Gail came down the stairs. "So why are you roasting a chicken?"

"It's called effective altruism. I haven't decided if I believe it."

Eva clicked on the oven light and knelt to look through the door. The bird was a gold dome.

"But I'm trying to get my dad to believe it," Jamie continued. "At the very least, it's a logical argument for giving your money away. A lot of rich people like the sound of it, because it tells you how to be good while also being efficient."

When the chicken was done, you were supposed to let it rest. The irony of this—letting a dead thing rest—depressed Eva. Standing in the kitchen, listening to the meat crackle as it cooled, she felt suddenly restless.

"But can you be good if you don't actually care?" she said.

"What do you mean?"

Nick took a stack of plates down from a shelf and Gail opened a drawer of utensils, but Eva ignored them, not offering to help. She wanted to get the words right.

"I mean, you could save a thousand chickens because it's the efficient thing to do and still not feel anything if you saw a single one being killed."

"Does it matter?" Jamie asked. "The effective altruists would say that feelings aren't part of the equation."

The bigness of the idea—*Does it matter?*—was exciting. Unnerving, too.

"How can it be an equation? Like, forget about chickens for a second." Eva wasn't sure what she was going to say next, which made her feel like she was standing at some great height. Dizzying, thrilling, not obviously secure. "Say you have a kid, and you give the kid everything he needs: food, shelter, an excellent education. Maybe you give the kid what he wants, too. Presents, a trust fund, something like that. But even after all that, you never really give anything *up* for the kid—"

When she paused, Jamie didn't nod to encourage her. He never nodded like that—to prove that he was listening, that he was right there with you. He was and he wasn't.

"You're talking about sacrifice," he said.

Eva wavered. "I guess so."

"I can tell you what my dad would say." Jamie accepted a knife from Nick and turned back to the bird. "He would say that sacrifice is religious bullshit."

"But I'm not religious," Eva said.

"We're all a little religious."

Steam rose from a long slit in the chicken's back.

"I agree with you," he said after a little while. "But you're talking about the abstract kind of values. For some people, values only make sense in numbers."

"Like life insurance," Gail said.

Eva had forgotten that her parents were listening. She glared at Gail. When Jamie finished carving the chicken—thick, bloodless slices—he looked at Eva expectantly.

"Let's talk about something else," she said.

The chicken was taken apart on a platter. They ate early, while it was still light out. Eva watched Jamie chewing, thinking—about what? It was easy to pretend that the muscles in his jaw, clenching and unclenching, were the muscles of thought. The meat in her mouth was dry. Where had her dizziness—her fear, her thrill—gone? The vertigo of a new idea. Maybe Jamie felt it all the time. Jamie, who dropped acid and loved leaves and could draw a thick, clear line between his dad's ideas and his own. Jamie, who believed in the secret lives of trees.

. . .

That evening, Jamie left the house and two hours later he came back. Gail opened the door, wearing pajamas with an old bloodstain on the back, a splotch the color of dead leaves. Eva hovered behind her. All the lights were off inside, but she could see that Jamie's hair was wet, his face serious—grave.

"What's wrong?" Gail asked.

Then again, wasn't his face was always serious? Jamie didn't answer the question.

"Something's wrong?" Nick was coming down the stairs.

Still, Jamie just stood there.

"Come in, Jamie. Gail, let him in. He's—Is that rain? Is it raining out there?"

Nick herded them into the living room and sat down. He made an impatient gesture that meant the rest of them should, too. Eva listened for the rain, but she didn't hear much—a vague shushing maybe, or maybe not. It was the kind of sound you could hear if you decided to.

Jamie sat on the very edge of the couch and insisted that he was fine, that it wasn't important.

"Really," he said.

Eva expected her parents, enlivened by a sense of emergency, to match his insistence with their own: no, you are clearly not fine. But faced with Jamie's gravity, their energy seemed to falter. Gail nodded. Nick nodded.

"Really," he repeated.

The couch was a soft, deep couch, made for sinking into, but because Jamie leaned forward, the rest of them leaned forward, too. Eva had read somewhere that the more empathetic you were, the more likely you were to mimic someone else's posture. It probably wasn't true, but she wanted to believe it—to believe that all of them were copying Jamie out of something like compassion, not simply out of deference.

In the end, the only thing her parents insisted on was that he stay the night. It was raining harder by then, a sound you couldn't ignore and certainly couldn't invent. Gail tucked sheets into the couch. She plumped a pillow. Nick poured a glass of water and put it on the floor.

"I'm putting this on the floor," he said.

"Careful," Gail said.

Jamie smiled an abstract smile when the three of them retreated upstairs. From her bedroom, Eva could hear him moving around. She lay on top of the covers, lights off, clothes on, shoes dangling off the end of the bed. Maybe he had witnessed something terrible on the train ride back to Manhattan: a fight, or a medical emergency. Indecent exposure? Someone bleeding or someone raging, or an addict with a canister of dust remover aimed straight into their mouth. Or maybe something had happened at home. His brother, drinking again. Naked in the elevator again. His dad—did his dad drink, too? It worked like that, sometimes: fathers, sons. But there were more mundane possibilities, too. You could argue with your dad about politics or morals or chickens or all three at once. You could slam doors and say things you might or might not regret. You could take a walk to clear your head. You could keep walking until you found yourself in front of the building where your mom lived, where your brother would never have been naked in the elevator, because to get to the second floor, the unenviable floor, you always took the stairs. You could look at the scaffolding and experience the strange revelation of a body turned inside out, the skeleton extracted for everyone to see. You could look at all that and you could decide that, no, it was not fine, not fine at all.

An hour later, Eva was still awake. She had slammed very few doors in her life and she had never witnessed a real fight. She had certainly never had a revelation. The last time she'd slept at someone else's house, there'd been popcorn, movies, stupid games of Truth or Dare.

There was a kind of rain that seemed to convey a message in its subtle sounds, but this was no longer that kind of rain: no romance in its pings on the roof, no nostalgic invitation in its gentle collision with soft ground. It was relentless, monotonous—all form, no content. Eva got up and went to the top of the stairs, where she could see into the living room, fluorescence angling in from the street. Jamie was standing in front of the window.

The stairs made noise underneath her, but he didn't turn around. She was a few feet away when lightning cracked, and right beside him when thunder followed. He started speaking without looking at her, without even acknowledging that she was there.

"When I was a kid, I cried whenever anyone else did. The way yawns are contagious for other people, tears were contagious for me."

He said that for a while, people seemed to think it was sort of cute. It wasn't as if he was sad all the time—he was just crying all the time. But as he got older, his dad lost his patience.

"The usual cliché," Jamie said. "Dads who don't like emotions."

Outside, the rain seemed to light up the asphalt, white bursts at the point of impact, like flashbulbs clicking in a crowd.

"Sometimes I imagine that instead of rain falling, it's being dropped. As if the clouds lose their grip and have to let go." Jamie's face was almost touching the window. "Scientifically, that's actually not so far from the truth. There's a point at which water gets too heavy to hold."

"What about your mom?" Eva asked. "Did she lose her patience, too?"

For just a second, the whole sky was illuminated. It seemed cinematic—not entirely real.

"My mom? She tried to stick up for me. She would say things like

The world is too much with him." Now Jamie's nose was pressed against the glass. "She meant, like, I'm too porous. Like, I carry the weight of the world. Which is exactly the opposite of what the poem means. You know that poem?"

Eva shook her head.

"Wordsworth. He's talking about materialism, actually. He's saying we have too much stuff, not too many feelings."

"What do you feel too much of?"

"It's ironic, because my mom has so much stuff. She's a compulsive shopper, basically. Like a hoarder, except she's rich, so she doesn't mind throwing things away."

Jamie stepped away from the window, and this time when he sat down on the couch, he let himself sink into it.

"Is that why you came back tonight?" Eva asked.

"Because of the compulsive shopping?"

"No." Eva thought about sitting down next to him, but didn't. "Like, because you were—are—too porous."

Jamie stretched out on the couch, the light from the window slicing diagonally across his chest, his feet lit up, his head in darkness.

"Maybe."

If she had been brave, Eva might have asked the question again—more precisely, more insistently. If she were as porous as he was, she might not have asked it in the first place. She would have already known the answer, as Jamie somehow always did.

On her way back to her room, Eva heard her parents whispering behind their closed door, something urgent but indecipherable. The sound of concern, she thought, was universal—a language you could understand without any of the words.

In the morning, the clouds were gone and there was debris in the street. The neighbors gathered on the sidewalk, wearing sneakers and pajama pants, discussing the disaster. They knew this didn't actually count as one—they'd seen real devastation on the news—but it was a surprise, and that was enough. They were unusually generous or they were suddenly imperious. A knuckly branch had fallen on the roof of a minivan, and everyone wanted to help, putting their coffee mugs on the ground, rushing inside for gardening gloves. One man stood on the hood of someone else's station wagon and barked instructions: "On the count of three." The minivan, in the end, was unharmed.

What was shameful was that Eva and her parents didn't notice the black walnut until Jamie did. They'd made a pile of fallen branches in the yard and collected trash that had been whipped around by the wind and trapped in the holes of the chain-link fence. (Not *our* trash, Gail said several times.) They'd called their work done and gone inside. Jamie, standing by the back fence, pointing up at the far side of the tree, made them come back out.

The place where lightning had struck was a wound, a five- or six-foot-long gash where the bark had been peeled away completely. This made the tree sound human, but there was no other way to describe it. The bark was like a shell—weathered and armored, craggy in the way that made trees seem wise—but what was underneath was skin, pale and yellow and fragile. Eva couldn't not think it: naked.

They looked it up on the computer.

"When lightning strikes," Jamie read aloud, "the liquids inside the tree turn into gas instantly."

Eva had never thought of trees containing liquid. But of course. What did she think happened to all that water? Now she pictured it traveling in tubes like veins.

Nick called an arborist, a man with a business card that said Tree Doctor. There was a good chance, the man explained, that the tree was dead, that it had died immediately. But damage you could see was better than damage you couldn't. He spoke gravely—more kindly, Eva thought, than any of her grandmother's doctors ever had. There was reason to hope, he said circumspectly.

At the end of the summer, they ran out of reasons. The tree doctor said doctorly things: they'd done everything they could. Mostly, they'd watered it. Eva with a hose, watching the roots drink. When all the water had been absorbed, the ground sparkled. *More.*

Caring for the tree made Eva care about the tree. And so when the men arrived with their saws, she was the one who needed comforting. Jamie, who had loved the tree first, told her that this was the way of nature.

"It giveth and it taketh away."

She had to admit she'd never read the Bible.

"The circle of life," he explained.

The tree came down in pieces, the branches lopped off one at a time, the trunk cut into segments, which made it seem like the tree was being disassembled—deconstructed. That it had grown so slowly, so imperceptibly, that it had looked more or less the same year after year, added to Eva's sense of tragedy. Why hadn't they paid more attention?

When only half the trunk remained, a naked post standing alone in the yard, the men took a break. Jamie approached the guy with the chain saw.

"Can I have one?" Jamie asked, pointing at the pile of wood.

Wood, Eva realized, was like *meat:* a word that could only refer to something dead.

"They're not mine," the man said indifferently.

Jamie thanked him, and Eva wished he hadn't: he sounded too grateful, too earnest. He should have tried to sound indifferent, too.

"What do you want it for?" she asked.

Jamie rotated a section of the tree on its side.

"I'm not sure." The wood on the inside had never seen the outside: air, sun, the back and forth of Jamie's fingertips. "Art?"

Eva saw the workmen exchange smiles, but Jamie didn't. The neighbor stood on his back steps, looming over the yard. Soon, the tree would be as short as he was. He was smiling, too.

When it was all over, the yard was filled with all the light the tree had blocked. Another tree, in a different neighbor's yard, was visible now, reaching tentatively across the sky with thin gray branches that looked more like nerves than limbs. Eva wondered what would happen to it now that it had so much extra space.

Jamie had told her about something called crown shyness: certain trees, he said, refuse to touch each other. They grow and grow and then, just when they're about to converge, they stop. When you look up, you can see the channels of space between them, like a force field surrounding the entire tree, or a halo. There weren't enough trees in the yard to show her, but he found pictures of it online. In the images, the leaves looked like a sheet of broken ice, with sky instead of water flowing in between them. Shyness, he explained, happened most often between trees of the same species—like repelling like. There were scientific theories for why it occurred, but no one was totally sure: it might be a way to stop disease from leaping from one tree to the next, or it might be a matter of sharing light.

Eva leaned back so that she was lying flat on the ground, her head next to Jamie's sneaker. She looked at the bottom of his chin, up his nostrils. The hairs above his lip were so pale that she could only see them when they caught the light.

"What kind of art?" she asked.

He shrugged. He was still thinking, rolling the logs back and forth, and in the movement of the wood, the turning, the tilting, she could tell that it was transforming in his head—that what had once been dead was now alive.

WHERE DID YOU COME FROM?

Jamie was not her boyfriend. They rarely touched. He might, pointing to a cardinal in the branches of one of the remaining trees, take her finger and guide it to the right place. *There.* Jamie's hand over her hand. She was interested—*Where?*—but no, she was not electrified. And it made her wonder if that sort of electricity had been overrated. Like any feeling, it was a current that came and went and left you wanting more. Why feel when—*Look*—you could see?

It seemed to Eva that everyone she knew had at least given a blow job. There were rumors about who had what: lopsided boobs, herpes, an orgasm that sounded like a rabbit in distress. She herself had done little more than kissing. A boy had put his hand down the front of her jeans and groped around for a little while, both of them surprised that the logistics of this were not as easy as they had been led to believe (the denim was not very stretchable), but she had not reciprocated with exploration of her own. She had only ever encountered penises through pants, never underneath them. This was frightening enough, the hard outline of what until then she had been able to pretend might not really exist. It was only exciting afterward, when she was remembering it instead of discovering it.

She wondered if Jamie had had sex, but she couldn't bring herself to ask, and none of his friends were her friends, so she couldn't ask them, either. She didn't even know if he had friends. There was so much, when she stopped to think about it, that she didn't know about him.

When school resumed in the fall, the extent of her ignorance was harder to dismiss. Their schools weren't really so far apart. Every morning, the distance between the two of them shrank, as Jamie went south and Eva went north, then both went west, until there were forty, thirty, twenty Manhattan blocks between them—approaching but never quite converging. From Monday through Friday, their lives were separate. Her school (big, public) was a squat gray building, and his (small, private) was a glass tower. Jamie's was for boys who wore blazers and girls who wore skirts. Most of them were rich and more than most of them were white. Eva's was not just for anyone—you had to get in, it wasn't that easy to get in—but there was plenty of diversity the school could have bragged about, if it had been the kind of school that bragged. The dress code was technically extensive, but only the obvious stuff was enforced: no curse words on T-shirts, no belly buttons exposed.

Eva told herself that none of this was a big deal. Their daily orbits simply weren't drawn to overlap. But each weekend that she spent with Jamie made the weeks in between seem emptier and stranger. On a Saturday, they took the train all the way to the Cloisters, wandering through the museum's narrow corridors and cell-like rooms, the vaulted chapels filled with paintings of other vaulted chapels, then descending through the steep gardens until they were standing on what seemed like a precipice: history high above them, solid and stained-glassed, and everything else ahead of them—the West Side

Highway, the bluffs of New Jersey, the Hudson winding and shimmering like a snake in the sun. On a Sunday, they brought binoculars to Prospect Park, alert for flashes of color, flutters of wings. They looked for birds with illustrious names (raptors, kinglets) and listened for humble songs—the warbler with its little orange tuft, its ambient chirp. They never saw as much as the guidebook promised, but the looking itself altered Eva: the utter disorientation when she lifted the lenses to her eyes and was suddenly lost in a universe of leaves, all its details intimately, divinely revealed.

But then it was Monday again, a jolt that was not unlike the confusion when she dropped the binoculars and the rest of the world returned in all its pointless generality—a whole sky whose blueness she forgot to observe, blurry figures in her peripheral vision that she routinely ignored. She took the same trains every day, and sometimes she saw the same strangers, mysterious lives that could seem endlessly deep or cruelly opaque. Why did she keep meeting all of them, but never once step through the closing doors and see *him*?

She didn't want Jamie to be her boyfriend, but she might have liked other people to think that he was.

Other people. The bright line that now seemed to split her life apart (the Jamie part, the not-Jamie part) made certain contrasts impossible to ignore: to be friends with him was to understand what her other friendships lacked. There were girls she had known for years, girls she had liked, or at least never disliked, her connection with them sealed by rituals she hadn't known were rituals at the time: birthday parties, school plays, school sports, piano lessons in the same old woman's apartment—the one with huge stacks of newspaper and a dish of cat food on the table instead of the floor. At some point, this proof of compatibility—of knowing the same people and the same places—was replaced by a more complex set of requirements. It didn't matter if you knew the same sonatas. What mattered was knowing the same secrets. A friend was someone who knew your celebrity crush and your real crush, what your retainer looked like and what your underwear looked like.

Those were easy secrets, loose change that could add up to something valuable, but it would take a while. Over time, the coins got heavy and dull in your pocket. People wanted something better. A friend was someone who knew that your dad smoked weed and your mom walked around naked, who knew that you'd seen an old man jerking off in the park and, instead of running away, you'd watched out of the corner of your eye. A friend was someone who knew that you lived in fear that there was something wrong with your vagina—something wrong or weird or unchangeable that you would never find out until a boy found out for you.

Eva could see how the currency of secrets worked, how it was exchanged and hoarded and inflated. She knew that teenagers were supposed to hide things, or at least to try. Close the door, hog the landline. The more you concealed, the more complicated you could seem, and not just to everyone else: it was thrilling to contain all those multitudes. At school, the thrill produced an electric buzz every Friday afternoon. Who would buy the vodka, who would stash the vodka, who had two dozen whipped-cream canisters buried at the back of their closet? You could feel the static in the hallways, the impatience as the last hours of the day were exhausted. What would be revealed this weekend, when the head rush of nitrous oxide made them dizzy with the thought of all that they could disclose?

Eva had been to the parties. She had said okay to vodka (never more than one) and no to whippets. She was not a loser. People liked her—invited her, danced with her, teased her in the mean but not-too-mean way that meant she was neither popular nor unpopular—but they didn't know her, not really, and it wasn't their fault. She didn't know how to give her secrets up. Hers were all too small or too big. There were plenty of shameful things she might have revealed—she still ate her own snot sometimes, she had only ever masturbated over her underwear—but surely it wasn't the secrets themselves, these puny, private acts, that mattered. Surely it was the telling that really counted for something, the fear that you had to overcome, even as it bottomed out your stomach and surged up your throat and told you that in just a moment there would be no going back.

Jamie was the one person Eva knew who didn't seem interested in secrets or confessions, in reckless revelations that forever indebted you to whoever had seen what you unveiled. He listened to what people had to say, but he didn't dig for what they had to hide. Everyone else's curiosity had made Eva afraid to share—a little proud of not sharing. She gave them just enough and no more. And yet Jamie's indifference made Eva want to tell him everything, or at least made her want him to want her to tell it. Every weekend, they came together and came apart, and for five days in between, she wondered what he was keeping to himself.

Of the new teachers that year, there was one everyone noticed. He was young and handsome and passionate, and he said that they could call him Neil. Sometimes he wore ties and sometimes he wore old, almost threadbare T-shirts—extremes that kept everyone guessing. Mr. Henderson, as he was officially known, taught Latin, a subject the school had been threatening to cut. This was another exciting contradiction: the least popular subject was now taught by the most popular teacher.

On certain days (usually the tie days), Mr. Henderson was stern and exacting. He closed the door the moment the bell rang and wouldn't admit any latecomers. He spouted lofty ideas about the importance of learning the origins of words, the complex histories lurking beneath ordinary language. But on other days—wearing sneakers, stubbled—he never even opened a textbook. He'd tell them stories about graduate school or show them movies, then let them leave early. He gave out lots of bad grades, but somehow he made Cs and Ds and the occasional F seem like badges of honor—proof that he was treating them like adults. There were rumors that he let students who got drunk at parties sleep on his couch instead of going home.

Eva asked herself what Jamie would think of Mr. Henderson, and decided he would not be impressed. Wearing a fancy outfit, letting them curse in class, watching R-rated films on Friday afternoons—these were all cheap tricks, used to woo an easy crowd: they were just kids. Seeing through his act made Eva feel almost elated. She sat at her desk like everyone else, but she wasn't really in it, she was above it, watching the scene but refusing to play her part.

The boys called him Neil right away and one by one the girls joined their ranks. Eva had refused to use his first name on something like principle—the gesture of familiarity seemed like another one of his ploys—but there were times when she was tempted. He had a strong chin and good hair. He *was* smart. By comparison, the boys in her class seemed younger than ever: they took their shoes off under their desks, they guffawed at their own jokes.

By the end of the semester, Eva was the only one still calling him Mr. Henderson. Whenever she said it, someone would laugh. Neil himself would just pause and smile, which was worse than outright laughter. In the face of that tight, knowing smile, what had seemed like conviction now seemed simply like stubbornness. Eva wished that she had given up long ago, that she had joined the crowd, even if it was an easy crowd. But it was too late for that—if she said his name now, everyone would notice.

The final Latin translation was due the day before Christmas Eve.

Eva waited as long as possible to turn it in, checking her work again and again, each error that inevitably surfaced a confirmation of her larger, graver mistake. She stared at the page until the words blurred. The dismissal bell rang.

Through the half-open door to the classroom, Eva could see him standing at the window, back turned, hands in his pockets. He didn't move when she knocked, so she knocked a little louder. He ignored her. It was already dark outside, and she could see the reflection of their faces in the window, which meant that he could, too.

She could have said *Excuse me* or *Hello* or *Hey*. She could have said nothing at all, leaving the assignment on his desk, where she could see a stack of all the other assignments. She cleared her throat.

"Neil?"

This time he did laugh, as if he'd been saving it up. His laugh was cold—not cool—and yet when he turned around, Eva had the ridiculous thought that they were going to run toward each other, hold each other. He was going to grip her shoulders and kiss her hard on the mouth. She dropped the paper on the desk and fled.

Outside, it was snowing, but just barely—you could see it most clearly in a cone of street light, tiny specks being tossed violently in the air. Direction meant nothing: snow could fall up. Home was south, but now Eva walked north.

Neil. She imagined saying his name while they were having sex, and she imagined him saying hers back, even though she had heard him say it many times—in both his stern voice and his chill voice, neither of which she could be sure was his real voice. Fantasies like this one were indulgences. She did penance for them in the cold, lungs tightening, face prickling and then going numb. Desire, in general, made her want to undo things: unsay that name, unthink that thought, untouch what she had touched in the battered bathroom stall—through her underwear, but still. She walked for ten blocks, then twenty. When she was standing in front of Jamie's school, she stopped.

The glass building was completely lit up, floor after floor that she could peer straight into. The school day was officially over, but plenty of students were still inside, huddled in small groups in classrooms, moving up and down the halls. A cluster of them moved toward the front doors, jostling and pushing but never breaking ranks, bursting outside as a single unit. Eva, having hoped that Jamie would be among them, suddenly feared that he would be. She shrank back, flattening herself against the trunk of a parked car, where the snow was landing imperceptibly, melting on contact. The alarm shrieked. Every head turned toward her at once, but none of them was his.

The groups kept coming, amoeba-like forms that spread out onto the sidewalk, engulfing each other and ignoring her. Every now and then, an adult emerged from the building, a man with a mustache or a woman in heels or flats, the tops of her feet exposed to the weather. Some of the lights inside turned off. A few floors went completely dark. By the time Jamie appeared, Eva had stopped expecting that he would. Her hands were numb, her ears ached. The first thing she noticed was that Jamie was walking beside a girl—ponytailed, skirted, a studied look on her face. The clutch of jealousy was almost pleasurable: so that's what she had been feeling! But as they approached, Eva could see that Jamie wasn't really talking to the girl. A few steps behind them was a man with gray hair and several formal layers—starched collar, tweed lapel—visible beneath his coat. He must have been a teacher, but he looked somehow more like a student, leaning toward Jamie in the thoughtful posture of a supplicant. They were both wearing ties, which wasn't in itself remarkable (the school uniform required it), but Eva had never seen Jamie in a tie. He looked grown up.

At the foot of the stairs, all three of them stopped. By then, the girl had become irrelevant. That kind of jealousy was crude—the same urge that made a child lunge for whatever didn't belong to him.

Weren't there prep schools where everyone went by their last names? Eva had read about them in books.

Before leaving, the girl briefly put her arms around Jamie's neck, a hasty, casual gesture that probably meant more than it seemed to. When Jamie and the man said goodbye, they shook hands. The teacher grasped one of Jamie's hands between both of his, a gesture that managed to be both professional and personal, as if they were two old friends, years of experience between them.

Eva could have called out to him—she had planned to call out to him, she had come all this way—but she didn't. She would have liked to cry, but her face stayed dry. At some point, the snow had stopped.

Jamie went out of town for the holidays; she didn't know where. Eva's aunts and uncles came from Boston, with cousins half her age, who wanted to go to Times Square and knew every song from a Broadway show they couldn't get tickets for. Her dad and his brothers started arguments and never finished them. "Let's not," Nick said, though he hardly had to say it: there were things they had learned to avoid so long ago it didn't even feel like avoiding anymore. This time, it was something about Adele's will, which Eva had never heard anyone mention before. She was curious about it, but she wasn't sure if she was entitled to her curiosity. Among her relatives, it didn't matter that she was polite and mature and didn't like musicals; in their cast of characters, she was, and might forever be, a child. So Eva stayed silent, doing her part to keep the peace, because who wouldn't want peace? They didn't fight, but they didn't really enjoy themselves, either.

It was a new year before Eva saw Jamie again. They walked across the Manhattan Bridge, which looked flat from afar, but was actually a hill. The view from the top was a spectrum of gray: the buildings on either side of them, the water underneath them, the clouds.

"Is it distance between us?" Eva asked. "Or is it a divide?"

The question was vague and unafraid. They looked at each other instead of looking at the view.

"What kind of divide?" Jamie said.

She hesitated.

"Do you mean, like, class?"

She wasn't really unafraid, of course, but she was excited, too. It seemed like an adult conversation—or even better than adult, because adults didn't talk about money.

"I'm not actually poor," she said.

"But I'm actually rich."

When they started walking again, she felt winded, even though now they were heading downhill.

"Do you wonder what I do all week?" she said eventually. "Don't you wonder?"

"Of course."

"And?"

He was quiet. The river was behind them now. Most of the bridge was actually over land: highways, baseball fields, roof decks, crates of frozen food on the frozen sidewalk, waiting to be unloaded. Eva watched the tops of trucks and the tops of heads, but no one looked up.

"Is wondering the same as wanting to find out?" he said.

"I don't know what that means."

"Because I'm sure we could find out. We could talk about why we're friends even though you live over there and I live over here and your dad is an unsuccessful artist and my dad is a successful art-collector. Or we could talk about why we're only friends, even though you're a girl and I'm a boy and we've both at least considered the possibility of seeing each other naked."

Jamie spoke calmly and clearly, and then he stopped. Was honesty a relief, or a shock?

At the end of the bridge, everything rushed in front of them: cars, people, the urgent beeping of the sign that meant *walk* but sounded like *run*. Time rushed, too. Too much, too fast. Eva stepped off the curb as a bicycle rounded the bend, and Jamie's arm appeared in front of her just in time, pushing her back onto the sidewalk. Neither the bike nor the biker touched her, but she felt the tailwind in her face.

"Close call," he said.

She should have thanked him, but her words caught in her throat. She nodded.

"Maybe there's a divide between everyone," he said after a moment. The light was green but they both stood still. "Some sort of wall. You can try to tear it down, and I'm sure the tearing, or the trying, feels good. Thrilling, even. But then what? What's there to want once you've stopped wanting what's on the other side?"

Eva watched another, slower bike make its way onto the bridge. "You sound defensive," she said.

"I'm not saying just accept the wall."

He seemed nervous. She had never seen him nervous.

"You're not?"

"What I'm saying is, maybe we only get glimpses over the wall."

"I could meet your parents. Your friends."

"How much knowledge do you need in order to know someone?"

"I'm not asking for your deepest secrets."

"How much can you take on faith?"

The green light turned yellow, and the last pedestrians hurried across the street, all steely faces and firm resolve. For a moment, Eva hated them, hated him, hated his wall. She looked down where his arm had been, pressed against her ribs. He was afraid for her and he was afraid for himself, and maybe fear made him better—maybe fear would even make them closer.

CAN YOU FEEL THAT?

Eva's plan was to become a journalist. She had been told that she was observant: *You don't miss a thing*. (Who had said that? She liked hearing it, but she wasn't completely sure it had come from someone she could trust.) As long as she had a plan, she was able to think about the future. In a few months, she would leave high school, and in a few more months, she would leave home. There were countless ways to count down: twenty-four weeks, seven final exams, six full moons, fifty Mets games, two federal holidays. On the other side of zero was the rest of time—impossible to quantify, terrible to predict. Everyone said that the years flew by. Eva looked back on her own short life and both did and didn't believe them. That was the thing, of course, about time. It was always so fast and so slow; it was just yesterday and it was ages ago; it expanded, contracted, ebbed, flowed, elasticked its way from then to now, an instant of slack that was called the present, gone in a single snap.

So Eva took it all one day at a time. Every morning, she bought a newspaper and a banana at the bodega down the street. She could have bought a bunch of bananas all at once, but she didn't. When the man at the register handed her the piece of fruit and the morning edition before she'd even asked, he was saying, *Here we go again*. She read the front section carefully, studying how it worked. She flipped through the other sections, looking for important headlines. Presidential nominations, a prostitution scandal, four thousand dead in Iraq, everyone arguing about torture (what counted and what didn't). She didn't let herself read the frivolous articles—the wedding announcements, the advice columns—because she was embarrassed by how much she wanted to.

On an unremarkable Tuesday, Eva learned that she had been admitted to an excellent college. Her parents said she deserved it, and her teachers agreed. Her classmates, she could tell, had not expected it. She was not the showy kind of smart. She had not, actually, even been sure that she *was* smart—she was diligent, occasionally passionate, always eager to please. Now she felt surer. She hadn't realized how much she wanted proof.

Later that week, Neil announced that he, too, was going to a new and better school, a private academy in the suburbs that several famous people, including one president, had attended. Eva, who dropped Latin that year, had mostly managed to avoid Neil, but that same afternoon, as news of everyone's futures migrated through the building, she found herself walking toward him in an empty corridor. He stared at her and kept staring as they approached. She couldn't read his expression. She didn't know what to do with her eyes. Just as they were about to pass each other, Neil raised his hand for a high five, and instinctively Eva raised her hand to meet it—she wasn't in the habit of leaving people hanging. Their palms made a sticky, unsatisfying sound.

"Good luck, kid," he said.

By the time she opened her mouth, he was pushing through the doors at the other end of the hall. What would she have said, anyway? She looked at her palm, still tingling.

Eva had been surprised to learn from her parents that they could afford to send her to such a fancy school. Adele, they explained, had left behind more money than anyone had guessed.

"We're rich?" Eva had asked.

Gail looked offended. "Of course not."

"Well," Nick said.

"There's rich and there's rich," Gail said.

"It won't significantly change our lives."

"It's already changed my life," Eva pointed out.

She tried to find out more: where the money had come from, where it was going, how long it would last. Many questions that were all versions of the same question: how much? Her parents wouldn't give clear answers. No, they would not be retiring anytime soon. Yes, she would still need some financial aid. Her cousins, they reminded her, wanted to go to college, too.

Now that she really was going, Eva thought guiltily about how rarely she missed her grandmother. Adele was the only one in the family who'd ever talked about the afterlife. While she was alive, her piety had made her absurd, but now that Adele was dead, Eva found herself overwhelmed by the injustice of this arrangement. If she was in heaven and no one else believed it, was that the same, in some sense, as not being there at all?

The possibility that Adele had been wronged gave Eva brief spurts of desire to be the one who did right. She summoned vague, pleasant memories of her grandmother. Adele with a rolling pin, Adele pulling a blanket up to Eva's chin, Adele interlacing her fingers and giving Eva a boost. She remembered especially the moment just after launching herself off Adele's hand but just before grabbing hold of whatever it was she was reaching for—a fence, a tree—when she was neither jumping nor falling but somehow suspended perfectly upright, standing in air.

That no one in the family ever spoke of the dead looking down on the living was mostly a comfort (who wants to be surveilled?) but occasionally a disappointment. Eva was not yet too old for the childish demand: *Watch me!* It would have been nice, she had to admit, to be told that she had made Adele proud. Adele in the sky, smiling beatifically, giving her money not simply because Eva needed it but because she'd earned it.

Unable to imagine Adele watching her, Eva was left to wonder about everyone else who might be observing her instead. She worried most of all about Jamie. At the beginning of the school year, he had refused to apply to the best schools. Puzzled, his teachers had diagnosed him with a fear of failure.

"What's the worst that could happen?" the college counselor had asked him.

"That I'd get in."

His parents were more than just confused—they were angry.

"Don't be self-destructive," his mother had begged.

But Jamie pointed out that he was only eighteen: "I hardly even have a self to destroy."

"Don't fuck it all up," his father had said.

Jamie liked the idea of going to California. There was a college that was also an alfalfa farm, but it was too small—he wanted something big. He'd told Eva that a good education meant learning how to be anonymous. So many schools wanted to teach you the opposite. He'd gone out to Berkeley because he knew someone there (an unnamed friend who'd dropped out, preferring mountain biking to chemical engineering), and afterward Jamie said he couldn't stop thinking about the redwoods. Walking past them every day would give you an accurate sense of scale: among all those giants, there would be no way to believe in your own significance.

When Eva's acceptance letter arrived, Jamie had been out of town for a whole week, traveling across the country for debate tournaments where he won prizes he didn't care about. She had considered calling him right away, to get it over with, but she made herself wait. Tuesday, Wednesday, Thursday, Friday. Four bananas, four newspapers, four vows to start fresh. When Jamie arrived on Saturday, he sat down on the living-room floor, amid the discarded sections of the paper. He looked up when she told him.

"Isn't it great?" Gail said, poking her head through the door. "Doesn't she deserve it?"

The same thing she had been saying for days. Newsprint crinkled under Jamie's elbows.

"No one *deserves* it," he said.

He said it simply, not cruelly, which made the clench of anger in Eva's chest—or was it just shame?—seem unwarranted. He turned the page of the newspaper and there they were: row after row of happy couples, their heads tilted toward each other, their smiles mirror images of each other. None of them showed their teeth.

"Why not?" Eva tried to match his calmness with her own.

"Is *desert* with one 's' or two?"

"Why does no one deserve it?" she said, impatience slipping into her voice.

She considered the page of announcements upside down. Everywhere else in the newspaper, people hedged their bets and covered their asses—all facts, no predictions—but here was an entire page of promises to last a lifetime.

"It makes sense that you got in," Jamie said. "You worked hard, you test well, you're well liked." He was looking at her, and she was looking at a husband and wife who could have been brother and sister. "But there are other people who did all the same things, and it doesn't make sense that they didn't get in. The difference between you and them isn't who deserves it more."

When he stopped talking, he watched her carefully, waiting to see how she would respond. She was not the only observant one. And yet his observations were not the same as hers—the simple confidence in his voice made that much clear. They sounded truer. Eva grabbed the newspaper from Jamie and crumpled it into a ball: all those faces, all their happiness, all the coincidences that had worked like magic, turning a single moment—a look from across the room, a call out of the blue, the right place at the right time—into an eternity of commitment. Why couldn't she, for once, be the one with the truth? The newspaper collapsed obligingly in her hands, but she squeezed it tighter anyway, just to feel the pressure in her fingers.

"By the way, I didn't get into Berkeley."

Eva released her grip on the paper ball. Instantly it expanded.

"Oh no."

She started to say she was sorry, but Jamie waved away her sympathy. She uncrumpled the paper, penitently smoothing out the crinkles while he continued talking, as calmly as before. He said it was an important lesson in humility. In the end, only one school had let him in.

"Choice is a luxury," he said matter-of-factly, opening up the sports section.

Eva had thought constantly, anxiously about the prospect of her own rejection, but the possibility of his had not entered her mind. Failure, for her, would have been a just reward for caring so much about success in the first place. How could Jamie, who hardly cared at all, be denied?

The school that had admitted him was in a small town upstate. There were woods nearby—not redwoods, but still: a forest, some mountains, many ways to get lost.

"It's a place for good kids with bad habits," he told her. "Rich kids, mostly."

Kids who were going to be filmmakers or great novelists, but not until they'd finished going on road trips and doing expensive drugs.

"Everyone there is obsessed with finding a mentor."

"What's wrong with that?" Eva asked.

"What they really want is a champion. Like, a patron. They want someone to open all the doors and then push them through. But gently—nicely."

"So real mentors have to be mean?"

Jamie looked at her closely. His eyes were brown, with a gold ring around the pupil, like the blurry aura of the sun.

"They're all staring at the doors in front of them, wondering how to get through, but most of the time the doors are already unlocked. Nobody thinks to just turn the knob. If they wanted it enough, don't you think they'd stop waiting around to be shown the way?"

Eva was impressed by his metaphors. He could extend them forever. He could get into your head. Here she was, trying to conjure up an image to match the one he described: a long hallway of doors, at a hotel, say, with "Do Not Disturb" signs hanging askew on the handles. Or no, maybe a hallway at a storage facility, fluorescently lit, doors that were grates you had to open from the bottom. While he talked, Eva kept changing the picture, trying to find the best one. She must have made a sound—frustration, defeat—because Jamie stopped talking.

"What's wrong?"

She shook her head. She didn't know what. Who were her mentors? Did she even have any? There'd been a nice English teacher, an encouraging soccer coach, but they were not inspiring people, not really. Jamie kept talking, and in her head, Eva peered into a crowded storage unit: windowless concrete walls, boxes and boxes of everything you couldn't take with you, wherever it was you were going.

After graduation, Eva emailed every local newspaper in the city. She said she didn't want to be paid, she just wanted to learn. For weeks, there were no replies. She had accepted a summer job at a restaurant—refilling ketchup bottles, wiping down ketchup bottles, bringing little pitchers of milk to customers who rejected the plastic thimbles of cream—when someone on Staten Island wrote her back. A man named Robert, who signed the email *R*. His newspaper was small and getting smaller, but there were still tasks to be done: a supply closet to be organized, coffee pods and sugar packets to be ordered, phone calls to be answered. They were unimportant phone calls, but Eva could eavesdrop on the important ones. To learn the trade, the man said, all you really had to do was listen.

Jamie said it was illegal not to pay her and Nick said it was irresponsible not to get paid, so Eva agreed to keep the restaurant job in the mornings—breakfast was busy—and go to Staten Island in the afternoons. She rode a bus and a ferry and another bus. It took forever, but even so, she arrived smelling like ketchup.

Robert was in his sixties. He chewed nicotine gum and shouted into the phone, because it was clear he believed that his calls were the important ones—the instructive ones. There were a dozen people on the staff, who did or didn't show up every day. Robert didn't seem to notice. The only person Eva really paid attention to was Robert's son, Robby. She guessed he was between thirty and forty. He wasn't obviously handsome: his features were all a little too big, his hairline was already beginning to recede. She allowed herself to be attracted to him because it proved that her taste wasn't the same as everyone else's.

Robby rolled his eyes at his father. He sent Eva links to long exposés in other, better newspapers—articles about whistle-blowers, fraud, lead in drinking water. He'd gone to journalism school, so he knew people who wrote those kinds of articles, and though he never said outright that he wanted to be one of them, Eva was outraged on his behalf: why wasn't he?

The job was unglamorous, and yet every evening when she had returned home, the glamour of the idea of it returned. She pictured Robby working late at night, scrolling through documents. Maybe he was a smoker. Maybe he ate canned soup and dry toast, not because he didn't know how to cook, but because he was too busy. In the mornings, picking up the newspaper—the one people actually cared about—Eva let herself imagine that when she turned the front section over it would be there beneath the fold: his name, his story, in ink that would come off on her hand if she pressed hard and long enough.

In July, a heat wave descended without warning. The restaurant put fans in the windows and stacks of napkins went flying. A fly circled a table streaked with maple syrup. Sweat rolled off someone's nose and into their omelet. Eva got dehydrated, so she went home early, where things weren't any better. No A/C. She turned off all the lights because it seemed cooler that way, and gulped water until her stomach hurt. She was lying on the floor when Robby called to tell her that he'd found a story—a real one.

It had started out with a dumb idea. His dad wanted him to visit every public pool on the island. All he was supposed to do was paint the scene: "How One Community Beats the Heat." Robby hated that kind of piece. He hadn't gone to school for that kind of piece. He sat at home for a while, feeling sorry for himself, watching the temperature on the outdoor thermometer rise and keep on rising. When he took the thermometer with him, it was just an impulse, not a plan; he wasn't looking for anything in particular. The first pool was mostly empty, still too early in the day for crowds. He ate a King Cone for breakfast and watched toddlers in waterlogged diapers waddle around on the pool deck. The second pool was noisy, and the third pool was packed. He was taking notes halfheartedly. He ate another cone. He checked the water temperature because he was bored.

"It's an outrage," he said on the phone.

"What is?"

Eva had taken off her pants and her shirt. Her hair was fanned out around her head like a mane, so that none of it would stick to her skin, and the backs of her knees were itchy with sweat.

"It's not water, it's soup."

She scratched her knees, which made her want to scratch them more. What was a normal temperature for a pool? She wished the numbers he was rattling off—he'd gone back to the first pool, then to the second—meant something to her. His voice was urgent. He was on his way to buy pH strips.

"I'm sure there are more violations," he said. "I can just feel it."

She wanted to feel whatever he was feeling: certainty, intensity, a plan unfurling in her head. When she sat up, her hair fell down her bare back. He told her to meet him at the fourth pool, which was bound to be the most crowded pool, and she said of course.

"Wear a bathing suit," he added.

In the heat, it was almost unbearable to touch herself, but when they hung up, she did. Her hand was slick with sweat. She finished standing up, because the furniture was already damp from where she'd been lying down. She took a shower so cold her breath caught. *That* was urgency: something seizing, clawing in her chest.

From the ferry station, she took a cab to the pool, watching nervously as the fare ticked up. The ride cost more than a week's worth of restaurant tips. She got there before Robby and stood awkwardly in the gravel parking lot. Under her clothes, she was wearing her newest bikini, which wasn't that new, the bottoms already sagging. One lifeguard—yellow-haired and six-packed, exactly the way you'd imagine a lifeguard—stood in front of a chain-link fence looking bored, and another perched above the pool, a girl who seemed older and more severe, but maybe it was just her sunglasses. Everyone was invincible in sunglasses. She blew her whistle, and for an instant all the people below her—kids, teenagers, harried parents—froze, as if they'd been caught in the act. Fear flashed instinctively in Eva's chest, even though she was all the way in the parking lot and couldn't possibly have done anything wrong. Then the lifeguard shouted something indecipherable and the scene came slowly back to life. Kids who'd been running now walked; the ones who'd been shouting stayed silent a little longer. Even when released from their poses, they all studiously avoided looking at the sunglassed girl.

When Robby pulled into the lot, he nodded in her direction—no waving, no *hi*. Eva checked to make sure the strap of her bathing suit was out of sight. In the back seat of his car, they sat across from each other, the recently purchased equipment laid out between them. It wasn't much. The test strips were only a few inches long and came in a container as small as a film canister, but supposedly they could detect everything they'd need. Chlorine, bromine, pH. Alkalinity and hardness—whatever that meant. Robby seemed to know how to pronounce *cyanuric acid*.

Even with the windows open, the inside of the car felt like an oven. Sweat poured down his head. His shirt clung to his skin. Through the wet fabric, Eva could see his nipples and the soft slope of his stomach. This might have repelled her, except that Robby showed no trace of self-consciousness. He was thinking about something else. Perhaps he simply understood that the body was a small, traitorous thing, whether hard or soft; if his seemed old—well, it *was* old. Listening to the sounds from the other side of the pool fence, all that pointless shrieking, Eva pictured toddlers and teenagers. It was much better to be old.

"Your suit?" Robby asked.

For a second, they both looked at her chest. She nodded. Robby explained that it would be easier to do the tests if she was in the pool. The thermometer had been too risky.

"A grown man in dress shoes, leaning over the edge."

Was he still looking at her, or was he looking out the window behind her? He didn't make a lot of eye contact.

"I'll do it," she said, and he smiled.

"You can keep the test strips tucked in your—"

Instead of finishing the sentence, he reached out and pressed his left palm over her right breast. This was shocking, but Eva didn't go rigid with fear or guilt or the wish to disappear, as she so often did when faced with the shocks of ordinary living—the lifeguard's harsh whistle, that armored stare. Instead, her ribs expanded. Something pulsed behind her eyeballs. Was this desire? It wasn't lust, exactly—lust was a flood that pooled randomly, drained quickly. This was a swifter current: it was desire to do something, desire that made wanting and doing seem like almost the same thing. Eva closed her eyes and the pulse got stronger.

But then Robby's hand was gone and he was opening the door and she was alone—shocked in the old, familiar way. She didn't stand up right away, dreading the terrible squelch of her thighs as they peeled away from the leather seat.

The water was as warm as Robby had promised, but heavier than Eva had expected. Descending the steps in the shallow end, she moved slowly, laboriously. Bare bodies kept knocking into her. Next to her hip, a boy's submerged head came up for air, coughing, streaming water from both nostrils. Should she do something? But then the coughing suddenly stopped and the boy was laughing.

"Scared you!" His too-tight goggles made his eyes look huge and inhuman. "You should have seen the look on your face."

He dove under the surface again, frog-legging away from her. The water didn't seem heavy for him at all. He was gone, and so was the look on her face, which wasn't really hers—not when he could see it, laugh at it, and she couldn't.

Test strips bulging in her bathing suit, Eva glanced up at the lifeguard. Her own face was there somewhere, reflected in a stranger's sunglasses, but she was too far away to see it. She was half dry, half wet, half in, half out, slathered in expired sunscreen, pretending to care about the alkalinity of pool water. It was all ridiculous. She took out one of the test strips and did as she had been told.

When Eva returned to the parking lot, her shirt back on, the damp shape of her bathing suit seeping through the back of her shorts, Robby was on the phone. He looked at her and then looked away.

"It *is* an important story," he said. He was holding the phone in one hand and folding the car's side mirror in and out with the other. "No one else is on this."

Eva couldn't hear the other end of the call, but she could tell from the petulance in Robby's voice that he was talking to his father. With each rotation of the mirror, Eva appeared, then disappeared. Not her face, just her torso. Wet T-shirt, uneven breasts. She worried the mirror would break.

Suddenly there was a commotion on the other side of the fence. A whistle blew, but everyone was already climbing out of the pool, pushing past each other.

"*I* give a shit," Robby said, shouting now.

Kids shoved their way through the gate, shrieking again—the kind of shrieking that contains both fear and joy, disgust and delight. Robby let the hand with the phone drop to his side. A tinny, indecipherable sound emerged from the speaker. Maybe it was a question: *Are you still there?* A boy ran past Eva, not the same one who'd laughed at her before, but he might as well have been. For an instant, their eyes met.

"Someone pooped!" he shouted. He was barefoot on the gravel, each step sending a current of pain across his face. "Someone pooped in the pool."

Eva closed her fist around the test strips, letting the moisture of her skin spoil whatever results they had recorded. It was too far to walk to the ferry, but she left on foot anyway. When she glanced over her shoulder at the empty pool, it looked blue and cold and clean.

Eva didn't go back to the newspaper, and no one ever called to ask where she was. Not Robert, not Robby, not the woman who wrote the horoscopes or the woman who wrote the obituaries, who kept a list of people she was expecting to die.

The heat wave broke. *Breaking* really was the right word, Eva decided. Relief was like that—a loud sound, a hundred tiny pieces, the sudden freedom of no longer holding things together. On the first cool day, Eva stood in the restaurant gripping a glass pitcher of water. She held it steady, pouring one cup after another, but the idea of it breaking, too, thrilled her: it wasn't a pitcher at all, it was just a lot of pitcher parts.

In the last weeks of summer, when Eva began receiving regular messages from college administrators, Jamie came to the restaurant every day. Most of the other regulars were old people who'd known the owner for years. Eva had memorized their orders (two eggs, crispy edges; Lipton, extra lemon), but it was Jamie who really talked to them. He could talk about anything. About the mayor, about someone's grandchildren, about how the city—the country, the world—used to be. With an old man named Elmer, Jamie argued about the Mets all morning.

"You like sports?" Eva said.

Jamie shrugged. "Sure."

Elmer had wispy white hair and a belt over his ribs. Eva knew that he liked jelly, never jam. Jamie knew that he was born in Puerto Rico and had been a roofer until his joints flared up. The things Jamie learned were never secrets or scandals—they were just stories—but most of the characters in them were gone and most of the listeners to them were, too, which made telling them now an unexpected pleasure, like snatching something right before it dropped out of sight.

On a Monday morning that seemed like every other morning, Eva poured Elmer coffee, brought him toast, took his check. Jamie ordered French fries. All day, Eva was distracted, but not by anything in particular. The future? She remembered that she still needed to buy extra-long sheets. At the end of her shift, Jamie walked her home. They didn't say much while they walked. On the corner of Eva's block, a fire hydrant was gushing into the street, but no one seemed to have noticed; the sidewalks were empty, the stoops vacant. Eva stopped in front of it, watching the water disappear down the drain.

"His wife died," Jamie said.

"Whose?"

"Elmer's. Yesterday afternoon."

He said it matter-of-factly, while Eva continued to stare at the wide-open mouth of the hydrant. Weren't there supposed to be kids around—splashing, shouting? She could remember the thrill of it, closing her eyes and putting her head right there in the middle of the stream. Eva turned to Jamie with a vague sense of injustice.

"How old was she? Was she sick?"

"I don't know."

"Who was she?"

"Donna."

"But who *was* she?"

"I don't know."

Eva dangled her foot off the curb and felt the water seep through the toes of her sneaker. She'd heard Jamie and Elmer talk about baseball and arthritis and a City Council member whose name she didn't recognize.

"Didn't you talk about her?"

"There are things people don't want to talk about."

Eva put her whole foot into the water and watched the current split in two. It was colder than she'd expected.

"There are ways people don't want to be known," Jamie said.

"I don't understand."

Jamie said that Elmer wanted to be known as the Mets fan, the union guy, the jelly-not-jam guy. He hadn't wanted to be known as the sick-wife guy, and he wouldn't want to be known as the dead-wife guy.

Eva pulled her shoe out of the stream, her foot newly heavy. She tried to shake some of the water off, which didn't work.

"It isn't fair," she said.

"What isn't? Death? Life?"

She stared at her shoe. She felt like a child. "Never mind."

They started walking again, water leaking out of her sneaker with each step, the rubber sole bubbling. She was too old to want to play in the hydrant but not old enough to accept that she didn't want to. She didn't know Elmer and would never know his wife and couldn't accept not knowing. At her house, Eva went inside and Jamie didn't, which made her wonder if she'd done something or said something wrong. She took the shoe off but not the sock, and later, when she finally peeled it away from her skin, her foot was pale and wrinkled and reminded her of a corpse.

The next morning, Eva did it all again. Coffee, jelly, check. There were only a few days left. Her bags were half packed. She didn't offer Elmer her condolences, didn't even say goodbye when the time came.

Jamie ate mountains of French fries. He pushed his plate across the table and shared them with someone he'd only just met. The count-down continued. He never said, *I'll miss you,* and neither did she. She filled the pitcher with ice and water and wiped away the ring it left behind on the counter.

CAN I TELL YOU SOMETHING?

Eva said she was lonely, and there was a long pause on the other end of the line. Outside the third-floor window of her dorm, she could see a dozen smokers huddled together under a bright-orange tree. October had turned into November, and now it was cold.

"Are you there?"

"I'm here," Jamie said.

"Maybe you're lonely, too."

"Maybe."

There was something religious about the smokers. Heads bent toward each other for a light, hands cupped around a flame. Sometimes, a cigarette would be passed from one mouth to another—lips that never touched each other but that touched the same thing. The smokers came and went without speaking. Often, they just stared into space.

"But it won't help to hear it," Jamie said. "You think it might. Misery loves company, or whatever."

"I'm not asking for help."

"Two lonely people is just more loneliness."

The smokers dispersed. There was one boy left, with a denim jacket and a beard that didn't really grow. He wasn't actually smoking, just playing with a pack of cigarettes. The cigarettes were a sort of protection, Eva thought: aloneness that didn't need to be explained.

After Jamie hung up, Eva watched the solitary figure while the sky got dark. He stamped his feet in the cold. She had smoked a cigarette only once—her lungs recoiling in distress, her cough betraying her—but she could have gone down to the courtyard and sat next to the boy who was trying not to look boyish and she could have pretended: inhaling, exhaling, as if smoking was as natural to her as breathing.

Pretending took energy, effort. It took desire. She put her hand on her throat and felt herself swallow her own spit.

A girl named Lorrie befriended her. Lorrie was full of opinions. Among other things, she told Eva to stop saying *girl.*

"You're allowed to be a woman now," she said. "It's not about feminism. It's just a fact."

As far as Eva could tell, Lorrie didn't need another friend. Everywhere they went, she knew people, or knew of them: her mom had worked for his dad, her ex-boyfriend had dated his ex-girlfriend. She was from Los Angeles, where her parents were filmmakers. The not-very-successful kind, which meant that she knew everything about the extremely successful kind; her parents were more obsessed with other people's careers than they were with their own.

"The sad part," she said, "is that someday I want to make a movie, too."

She didn't look sad, though—she just shrugged.

Lorrie had a squarish jaw and her pale skin turned mottled pink when she got hot or cold or angry, but she was beautiful; she had not only style but taste. She had long since moved past the adolescent stage of clothes that were statements, and now her wardrobe made measured announcements: long skirts, no sneakers, jewelry that really was one-of-a-kind. She told Eva that school wasn't what mattered. Life mattered. People mattered. Books could help (for inspiration, she conceded), but tests couldn't.

"You're too responsible. You have to cultivate irresponsibility."

Stay up all night, Lorrie instructed. Skip class, or at least skip the homework. Drink too much coffee. But no lattes—lattes were a joke. Go to dinner parties, or naked parties. Don't go to frat parties. Wear black or white or autumnal colors, and every once in a while wear something outrageously ugly. Flirt with grad students, fuck grad students, but don't make the mistake of actually talking to them. They sound ridiculous when they talk. Stop eating tofu, stop wearing earplugs, stop going to the gym at the same time every day, stop calling home, stop talking about home, stop missing home.

This advice sounded simple. When Eva was by herself, she found herself wondering if it was too simple. (She drank an espresso after dinner and was so jittery she considered calling the doctor—her pediatrician in Brooklyn.) But in the presence of Lorrie and her friends, who forgot to eat regular meals, then ordered greasy sandwiches in the middle of the night, who failed tests but knew how to pronounce all the French phrases Eva avoided saying out loud, intensity seemed better than complexity.

When Lorrie invited Eva to a silent party, she said yes before asking what it was. Lorrie explained the rules: You had to arrive on time, and for exactly sixty minutes, no one was allowed to speak. No talking, no whispering, no music, no exceptions. Then the ban was lifted and you were free.

"It's like an experiment," Lorrie said. "You don't know how you'll react until you react."

The party was in a house not a dorm, across the street from a neon bar where students never went. The house was falling apart—shingles holding on like loose teeth, a light on the porch flickering on and off. Eva never found out who lived there. By the time she and Lorrie arrived, there was an orderly line waiting to be admitted at the front door. To get in, she gave up her phone, dropping it into a bag that contained dozens of other phones.

"They'll be fine with me," the girl with the bag said. "And believe it or not, you'll be fine without them."

Inside, the furniture was cheap and new or else old and ornate—stuff you ordered online or stuff you found at yard sales. There was a claw-foot table with cup rings, but no real cups. They drank out of the same red plastic they always did.

Once they had poured their drinks, there was nothing to do. They stood in the unfamiliar silence, accepting this. There were a few people, Eva could see, who avoided it. A girl in platform boots wandered restlessly back and forth among the rooms, the clunk of her shoes receding, then approaching, then receding again. A boy cut and recut lines of cocaine on the kitchen counter, even though no one else seemed to want any. Some people mimed or mouthed, but mostly everyone just watched. The silence was a substance, like a gas leak you couldn't tell if you were really smelling: you looked around the room, wishing you could see it, feel it, somehow be sure of it.

Eva recognized a few people—there were thirty or forty in all—but she had never spoken to any of them. And here they were, still not speaking. Most of the time, silence was effortless for her. She didn't speak up in class because she didn't have anything to say, she didn't call someone's name across the courtyard because she didn't have anyone to call to. She didn't say good night to the girls brushing their teeth at the next sink—in their pajamas, with their unbrushed hair, it was impossible to believe they were women—because she hadn't said it the night before, or the night before that, and it would be too weird, too hard, to start now. You couldn't change all of the sudden—just like that.

Unless you could. Eva took a drink from her plastic cup and felt the possibility burn down her throat. She wasn't invisible, because no one was: in the silence, everyone became someone to look at, someone who might become someone else in less than sixty minutes. All you had to do was watch and wait and then, finally, open your mouth.

The minutes passed calmly. In the living room, Eva leaned against the wall and watched two boys on the couch lean against each other. She made eye contact with one of the boys, and neither he nor she looked away. He had a big nose and chapped lips. She was not afraid of him, even though these days she seemed to be afraid of everyone. There was no special meaning in their eyes. They were not speaking through the silence.

A loud noise made everyone jump. A heavy book had fallen off a shelf at the other end of the room, the sound disappearing into the silence immediately, leaving everyone to stare at its source, as if it had come from some other world. The boy closest to the shelf picked the book up. He wasn't tall but he was handsome: dark hair and a narrow, twitching mouth. He considered the thick volume, turning it over, testing its weight, and then he dropped it—another smack on the floor. They were all still watching, still staring. He picked the book up again and dropped it again. He did this three more times, and no one looked away. Then he slipped it back onto the shelf nonchalantly, as if nothing had happened, as if it were simply a book he had decided not to read after all.

When he turned back to the room, he smiled faintly, another twitch of his mouth, and Eva's hands, holding nothing but a flimsy cup and its clear drink, felt empty. She wished—suddenly, desperately—that she could prove she didn't really belong in the audience, that she had understood something about his strange performance that the rest of them couldn't.

She left the room and wondered if anyone watched her leaving. She stood in the bathroom, not needing to pee. It was a dirty bathroom, with tiny hairs in the sink and a bar of soap rubbed into a flat disc by one pair of hands after another, but that didn't bother her—even a dirty bathroom contained certain mysteries. Behind a mirror edged with other people's fingerprints was a cabinet of things they didn't want her to see. Eva was looking at herself in the mirror's water-stained surface when music erupted in her head. That was how it felt: as though the sound were somehow coming from inside her.

The sensation only lasted for a second. Then someone was knocking on the door and then someone was opening the door. It was him. *Of course,* Eva thought.

"Oh!" he said. Caught off guard, he was briefly unmasked—his face young and fragile.

"Sorry," she said.

His face reassembled itself. A firm jaw, knowing eyes. "I think I'm the one who's supposed to say that."

He stepped back to let her through the door, and it was only when she heard the click of the lock behind her that Eva realized she had broken her silence.

The party never quite became a normal party. They got drunk and danced and talked too loudly, just as they always did, but whatever happened seemed to happen to them all at once, all together. Somehow the silence had connected them. It was as if they had arrived at the party from the same place—not from thirty or forty different dorm rooms, private worlds of clutter and drama that would never be revealed, but from one shared room, in which they had briefly surrendered something crucial.

Eva was trying to think about how to put this idea into words—could she tell someone? could she tell *him?*—when the speakers blew out. The huge, ear-pounding sound turned into the tinny music of one person's phone, all the discordant voices suddenly audible over the song. No one could figure out how to fix the problem, and the crowd began to disperse. People were reunited with their phones, scrolling hungrily through whatever they had missed. The girl in the platform shoes kept saying, to no one in particular, "What next, what next?"

When Eva found Lorrie, she was in the middle of an argument with him.

"Oh, come on, Eli."

Eli. The name settled over him, changing him, though she couldn't be sure how. As if he'd taken off his glasses, or put on a new shirt—the kind of obvious change that nevertheless takes a few minutes to notice. The argument continued as they were funneled toward the door, something about a class that both of them were taking. Eli admired the professor, Lorrie hated him. They spoke passionately and fluidly. Eva leaned toward them, as if to absorb the intensity of their opinions. Only moments ago, she, too, had felt lit up by ideas, but now it was hard for her to tell: what seemed like insight might just have been alcohol. At some point in the argument, Lorrie jabbed her finger into Eli's sternum, the soft tip of her finger pressing against the hard shield of his chest.

Outside the house, people were calling cabs. *What next, what next?* Lorrie and Eli were climbing into a car, and the door was being held open for Eva. She hesitated. Someone turned on the radio, and it was that song again, the very first sound of the party. She took a step back onto the sidewalk. If she went with them, she would lose sight of them at the next party, the music would trap her in her own body, the memory of the night would get altered or dirtied or flattened into a memory like all the other memories of all the other nights. She let the door close and the car drove off. She walked home, turning the events over in her head, happy.

Eva watched for him everywhere—didn't even pretend that she wasn't watching. The odds of finding him this way weren't good: it was the end of the semester, exams were looming, and most of the time she was in the library. Every evening, she went to the periodicals room, where the walls were lined with newspapers from all over the world, even though everyone read newspapers online now. *The Guardian, The Mirror*, *The Star*. Names with a lofty sort of comfort, names that meant: something to guide you.

The room made Eva feel studious even when she wasn't studying. Green banker's lamps and wood-backed chairs, graduate students and law students, who looked like real adults, whose seriousness didn't seem like a charade. There was a man in bottle-cap glasses and a woman with a too-tight bun, who pored over textbooks the size of pastry boxes and hardcovers in classic, inscrutable colors—navy, camel, crimson. Eva knew what time the man would arrive and what time he would open a bag of pistachios. She knew what time the woman's birth-control alarm would go off and what time she would finally close her textbook and leave. Watching them work hard, Eva could tell herself that she was working hard, too. Pistachios, strictly speaking, were against the rules; the man collected the shells in his chest pocket.

Eli appeared at the door of the periodicals room in the middle of the night. Later, Eva marveled at this strange feature of life back then—that so much happened after midnight. Midnight was when you drank a tiny plastic bottle of vitamin B and memorized the names of five hundred paintings from the eighteenth century. Midnight was when the party started, when the romance began, when tomorrow's deadlines became real, when you turned the page of a book you'd already read, had been rereading for weeks, and every single word was underlined. It was when the boy you'd been watching for, waiting for, appeared at the threshold of a room filled with today's news—no, now yesterday's news—and said, "*There* you are."

Every day for a week, Eli came with her to the library. She stopped paying attention to the bottle-capped man and the tight-haired woman. Eli studied for his exams and Eva studied him. Late at night, he drank black coffee and ate fistfuls of sour, neon candy. In the morning, he ate nothing at all. He knew German and a bit of Greek and something about every genre of music. He fought dazzlingly with his parents and his sisters (there were three of them), but no matter what he called them once a day. His mouth twitched when he was pleased or annoyed or deep in concentration, and Eva took pride in having noticed this habit from the very start. It was proof that she noticed the right things—the important things—and so it hardly mattered when, at the end of the week, she sat down to take her tests and discovered that she had not read the right things, had not memorized the important things. So what? She made her best guess. She left things blank. On the last essay of the last exam, she gave up. On her way out of the room, she looked back at all the rows of hunched backs and scratching pens and she stood up a little straighter. She felt certain—for so long, she had felt nothing but doubt—that she had learned something after all.

The night before everyone went home, it snowed for the first time that year. A procession of people climbed the closest hill, cafeteria trays tucked under their arms to use as sleds. Their excitement about this ritual made them feel at once younger and older than they were: it was a timelessness that they weren't supposed to improve on.

At the top of the hill, Eva asked Lorrie if she had seen snow before—she was from California, after all—and everyone laughed. Of course she had. It turned out they'd all been on ski vacations. Eli was there, too, his hand gloveless and raw, the swoops of his hair frozen in place and dusted white. Under the buttery light of a street lamp, he produced a bag of chewing tobacco. He'd bought it for five bucks off his roommate, a baseball player who'd vowed to quit.

"Disgusting," Lorrie said, and the others agreed.

One by one, they disappeared down the hill, instantly veering off course, barely balancing on the flimsy plastic trays. Someone thudded into a parked car but got up laughing, shaking off the snow like a dog. Everyone was shouting. Maybe it was because they sounded like kids, or because the pleasure of the moment was so simple—the cold night, the steep hill, the thought of home only a few days away—that Eva felt closer to them than she ever had before. The voices were the same voices she had listened to in hallways and in basements with sticky floors, in the next shower stall and through her thin bedroom wall, singing along to pop music, calling their parents, talking in their sleep. She didn't know which voice belonged to which person, but she had been hearing them for months.

Eli pulled his bottom lip out and stuffed it full of tobacco. He held the bag out to Eva, and the ecstasy of deciding and doing all at once rushed over her. She took the brown stuff pinched between his fingers and let him guide it into her mouth. For a moment she was aware of her head floating, and then she was on her back in the snow. Eli was holding her cold face with his cold hands.

"You fainted."

Eva smiled and he smiled and then they laughed together. They spat out the tobacco. They spat until their spit turned clear, and then he kissed her. Numb lips, wet tongues. A single strand of tobacco, like a tiny worm, passed from her mouth to his, and they had to stop so that he could fish it out. He held it on his fingertip, and for a few seconds they both just stared at it, as if it were something that had emerged from inside them.

WHERE HAVE YOU BEEN?

Eva went home in December and again in March, and she said nothing about Eli either time. She hadn't intended to keep him to herself, but she thought too long about how to say it, which made it too hard to say it. Most things didn't have to be revealed in this way. Other people's curiosity helped: her dad wanted to know about her classes, her mom wanted to know about her friends, Jamie wanted to know about her ideas. They asked all sorts of questions, but when conversation gave way to silence—silence that to Eva could only contain (could barely contain) one thing—no one asked the right question: Are you in love?

Eva didn't think of the answer as a secret, because it wasn't a possession. She was the one possessed. She knew that this was the universal condition of love, especially first love; she'd read the books, seen the movies. She even knew, in bright, painful flashes that could be endured only by being ignored, that the condition never lasted. And yet none of that mattered. Knowing had nothing to do with feeling. It was astonishing that she had spent so long not feeling. That she had never until now gone an entire day without eating (because of joy) and then an entire day without moving (because of jealousy), that she had once believed—modernly, pointlessly—that the mind controlled the body.

When her transformation went unnoticed at home, at first Eva felt powerful. Being in love meant being in two places at once. Out to dinner with her parents, she passed the bread basket and thanked the waiter for filling her already full glass, but at the same time she composed an email to Eli in her head, wondering which details would impress or amuse him. On the couch in the living room, she watched a car commercial on TV, the same strip of California coastline that was in every other car commercial, but at the same time she thought about Eli's face, which was always changing, always intriguing, which she could have watched forever.

Her power was thrilling, until suddenly it wasn't. Sometimes she was angry at her parents for not asking about her life, and sometimes she was angry at herself for not telling them about her life. She wished Jamie would pay more attention to her, or else she wished she didn't need the attention.

One afternoon in March—officially spring, though it didn't feel like it—she and Jamie sat on the promenade at the western edge of Brooklyn. They were both on vacation, but he'd come home for just one night. For the rest of the week, he'd been at a meditation retreat: five days of total silence. No speaking, no reading, no journaling, no checking the news, no improvised sign language, no eye contact, no texting.

"And no leaving," he added. "By day three, most people want to leave."

"Did you want to?"

"Of course."

"But you stayed."

Jamie nodded.

"Impressive," Eva said, even though she knew it was the wrong thing to say. Jamie didn't believe in impressing people.

They were sitting on a bench, ignoring the cold, because this was their favorite view: the rushing highway in front of the rushing river in front of the rushing city. Behind them, a playground released the exultant, momentous sounds of kids yelling, balls bouncing.

Eva herself thought about impressions all the time. She liked picturing it literally: the mark that you left on someone or that someone left on you. Like a fingerprint, the topographical swirls of identity, which, if you pressed—impressed—hard enough, could be transferred from one person to another.

Eva shivered. The colder she got, the less impressed she became. Yes, he had done a difficult thing, an unimaginable thing, an unimaginably difficult thing. But why did Jamie need to be enlightened? Wasn't he already the most enlightened person she knew? She considered telling him about the silent party—her own meditation retreat, she might have joked—but she wasn't sure if he would find it funny or profound or boring. Her own memory of that night was streaked with strange significance, and yet the scene, as she imagined describing it, contained too many trivial details: the boy with cocaine, the girl with platform shoes, the head-pounding music, the throat-burning drinks.

Jamie took a book out of his bag and started reading. Reluctantly, Eva did the same, turning to the first page of a novel she was supposed to have read weeks ago. Her professor had discussed the plot in considerable detail, and now Eva found her attention wandering. She already knew what would happen. After a few minutes, she gave up.

"I can't read."

Jamie didn't look up right away. Maybe he was getting to the end of a sentence.

"What do you mean?" he said at last.

"I can't focus. My mind's elsewhere."

He put his finger on the page, holding his place. "How did you get there?"

"Get where?"

"Elsewhere."

A blue rubber ball sailed over the playground fence and landed by their feet. When they turned around, two small boys, one a little smaller than the other, were pressed up against the fence, staring at them.

"Our ball," the bigger one said impatiently, as if he couldn't quite believe he had to say it. He stretched his arm between the metal bars and pointed.

Eva ignored them. "Elsewhere isn't an actual place," she said, irritated.

Jamie picked up the ball and considered it for a few seconds, as if it were a mysterious, unidentifiable object, then lobbed it back over the fence. The boys raced after it, the game's brief interruption already forgotten.

"You know what I mean," Eva said.

"I do and I don't." Jamie turned to face her. "Can you really be lost in thought? If what you're saying is that you're in your head"—he said this as if in scare quotes, incredulously but not necessarily unkindly—"then you know where you are. And you know the way back."

There was more shouting from the playground. A thump that was probably the ball hitting the fence.

"You're the *only* one who knows the way back," he said.

The conviction in his voice kept her from responding. In the silence that followed, she listened to the rhythm of a ball she couldn't see, envying the straightforward rules of a children's game, the ball sent back and forth, back and forth.

Eva picked up her book again. They spent another hour on the cold bench, not talking much. He was probably used to that by now. Maybe he preferred that now. It wasn't so long ago that she, too, might have been content to be absorbed in her own thoughts, which were almost all thoughts about Eli. That was its own kind of retreat, into private plots that no one else could spoil. The pleasure had been theirs alone: to generate their own suspense. She turned the pages of the book dutifully, without understanding what she was reading. She would have to reread them later. She would have only herself to blame, but she might blame Jamie instead.

When Eva went back to school the next week, Eli met her at the train station and she threw her arms around his neck, kissing him in the way she didn't usually kiss in public. He seemed a little taken aback.

The wintery spring continued: big crusted-over mounds of snow, soggy clothes and dry skin, gloomy afternoons. Eva started ignoring Jamie's calls. Missed calls. But she didn't miss him. For the first time, she couldn't think of what to say to him. She saved up the best things—a funny conversation she'd overheard, a perfect sentence she'd read, a fragile idea whose weight she was still testing out—to tell Eli. To tell them to Jamie was to give them away. Occasionally, when they did talk, she'd wind up telling him anyway, and those calls left her bitter and irritable, as if she'd been tricked into something.

On the first day of truly beautiful weather, everyone rejoiced. Eva drank coffee on a bench, warmth slipping down her throat and spreading through her chest. A boy walking past stopped in a square of light and turned his face up to the sun, eyes closed, like a cat in a window or a lizard on a rock. Eva wondered if he knew that he was being watched—if he hoped that he was being watched—but then he opened his eyes and smiled and she could tell that he was smiling to no one but himself. When he started walking again, she followed him. They passed a patch of not-quite-green grass where a girl in a bikini was spreading out a beach towel, her skin pale, her thighs lumpy, and Eva envied her for not caring.

At the next corner, Eva had the sudden urge to talk to her parents. The boy crossed the street ahead of her, but she hung back. She called their landline and it rang and rang, until the answering machine picked up. It was her own voice, a recording from many years ago, in which Eva, still a child, strained to sound as grown-up as possible. Gail always said that she couldn't bear to replace the message. When the old Eva stopped talking, the new Eva started. She imagined her parents replaying the message when they got home, when her voice would once again be speaking from the past. Standing on the corner, speaking into the future, she said that she was just calling to check in.

"Actually, no—there's a reason I was calling. I was calling to tell you I have a boyfriend. I've been meaning to tell you."

A middle-aged woman in gym clothes was walking toward her, and it took a moment for Eva to realize that she was one of her professors, an art historian. Usually, she wore makeup and some kind of blouse. Usually, she was up on a stage in front of hundreds of students, squinting into the light of the projector.

"Well, now I've told you. So. That's all, I think."

But Eva didn't hang up. Having told them one thing, she wanted to tell them more things. The professor was right in front of her now. Eva smiled absentmindedly and got a confused smile in return. She didn't expect the professor to have noticed her face among the hundreds of others.

"It's such a beautiful day," she said into the phone. It didn't count as news, but it was true.

The professor stopped right in front of Eva, her smile widening. "Isn't it?" She was practically grinning.

It didn't turn into a conversation. She kept walking and Eva said goodbye to her parents, or to the empty room that her parents would eventually fill, but for the rest of the afternoon, the professor's words kept her aloft. She hadn't said anything that mattered—there had been no reason for her to say anything at all. No reason except that the weather was perfect, that they had both smiled, that everyone was bathing in the same liquid light. When Eva's parents called back that afternoon, she didn't bother picking up. What else did she need to hear?

That day was followed by a string of days just like it: sunshine that wouldn't go away. At the end of the week, Eli broke up with her. They were sitting on a brick wall outside his dorm.

"I feel dizzy," Eva said, even though it was a low wall. Her feet were planted firmly on the ground.

"We don't want the same things," he said.

It sounded like something from a movie—a recycled line. Eva opened her mouth to object, but he kept talking.

"We're in different places, you know?"

This was generic, too, and yet because she had thought it so often—when he was in California and she was in New York, when he was in one library and she was in another, when he was sitting right there and she was looking down from up here—she found herself nodding. Of course. She had known all along.

Her love story, she reminded herself bitterly, was the same as all the others. The books, the movies. When her parents asked, she said never mind—the story was over. From the moment she had careened down the hill on the plastic tray, the snow clotting her eyelashes, the wind finding every sliver of bare skin, she had been blind to caution. There was so much to regret! The things she had said when she was drunk. The sounds she had let escape when his hand, then his penis, was inside her. Promises they had said out loud, predictions she had made in her head. All of it had seemed to emerge from the deepest, truest part of her, a part she had somehow never known existed, like the extra room that appears in dreams. But now she wondered if what had felt like discovery had simply been exposure, if the room was just a closet, filled with unexceptional secrets and a lot of dust.

Eva went back to the library, back to the gym. She became a vegetarian. Everyone else said it was hard to study now that the sun was out, and this made her even more determined to ignore the people playing Frisbee and smoking weed and doing all the other collegiate-sounding things, to read everything she had been told to, to study everything that someone else had decided she should. Her grades had not been bad, but now they would be excellent.

At the beginning of the year, she had enrolled in a class called Conceptions of the Good Life, because the course description was full of big questions. Back then—when she was in love—everything seemed big. It was an introductory course, but lectures began at eight o'clock in the morning, which meant that most of the students were philosophy majors: you had to be more than just curious to get up that early. In a dim, half-empty auditorium, Eva sat at the back, taking furious notes. She'd never read philosophy before. She'd been surprised to learn that professors of philosophy—in this case, a short man with unkempt hair, who wore black denim and old, squeaky sneakers—were themselves called philosophers. She had not thought of philosophers as being alive; she had assumed that philosophy was something you studied, not something that you could still invent.

For seventy minutes twice a week, the professor spoke without interruption, never once consulting his notes, and yet he always sounded as though he wasn't sure what he was going to say until he said it, as if he were saying it for the first time. This couldn't have been true (he'd taught the same class for many years in a row), but his ideas were truly momentous—they guided him instead of him guiding them. While he spoke, he paced back and forth in front of the chalkboard, ignoring the lectern entirely, and sometimes he even walked up into the aisles, seemingly oblivious to the sound of sneakers on linoleum that followed him wherever he went. Throughout the lectures, he asked questions that sounded rhetorical but weren't: Is death an evil? Is society happier now than it was in the past? What are the politics of desire? What is the function of intuition? Do we have our pleasures or do our pleasures have us?

People raised their hands right away and sometimes started talking before they'd been called on, as if they, too, had been building momentum—as if their thoughts had to be urgently released. Eva wrote down the philosopher's questions and the students' answers, and then she left half a page of space. The space was for her own answers, which she resolved to fill in eventually.

On Thursday evenings, she brought her notebook of questions and answers to a small basement room, where a graduate student named Sabine led a dozen students in discussion. The first thing everyone noticed about Sabine—Eva had to admit that she, too, had noticed the obvious—was that she was beautiful: almost six feet tall, with big eyes, the right-sized nose, hair that shone with good health. Graduate students were not known for beauty, not even for health. Undergraduates often asked Sabine on dates, and her polite refusals—she smiled when she refused—were taken as glimmers of hope; some boys had asked more than once.

For the first half of the semester, Eva had skipped many of these discussions, and when she did attend, she was an infrequent participant. Eli had taken more than one philosophy class, so she talked to him about the readings instead of talking to her classmates. But after the breakup, she started going every week, listening carefully, scribbling extra notes. Instead of sitting in rows, as they did in the auditorium, the students sat around a large circular table with laminate peeling at the edges. Occasionally, Eva found herself in a chair right next to Sabine's, close enough to read the notes in the margins of her book—some in English, others in German. She had a slight, elegant accent.

Sabine's beauty was obvious, but her ideas were dazzling. Unlike the professor, she often paused as she spoke, yet these silences merely added suspense. For a few seconds while she gathered her thoughts, her eyes narrowing, her mouth motionless, her face was perfectly impenetrable. Anything (that is, everything) might have been behind it. Then she would speak, and in speaking come alive again, all the muscles in her face enlisted in the effort of expression. This process would repeat itself for a few minutes, until Sabine resolutely cut herself off: the discussions, as she reminded the students each week, were meant to give everyone a chance to speak.

But Eva didn't want anyone else to speak. She glared at her classmates. They had good ideas but not great ideas. They didn't seem to need to take notes.

Sabine only ever brought one book—no bag—and she never lingered after class. She tucked the book under her arm and left. It was clear that she had other places to be, and why wouldn't she? There was a bar where all the graduate students went—college kids weren't allowed—and Eva pictured her there, sipping something iceless in a small glass, surrounded by a group that was not an audience, all of them speaking and pausing and speaking again, ideas passed back and forth, in and out. At last call, they'd look down at their glasses, finish whatever remained in one bold swallow.

Most of the students hurried out of the classroom as quickly as Sabine did. On Thursday nights, the weekend parties were already under way. Parties were recommended after a breakup—Lorrie had given Eva a long list of recommendations, titled "Get Over It"—but Eva discovered that it was a bad idea to leave the basement with everyone else. She'd tried it, emerging from underground and making her way to a dorm where her friends and sort-of friends would be gathered around a flimsy coffee table of offerings: half-empty bottles of alcohol, a warm carton of orange juice, a bowl of melting ice. They would talk about—what *would* they talk about? Afterward, she could rarely reconstruct the conversations. Once a girl had said, "I hate my life," which seemed unremarkable enough (everyone said that), but later she'd said, "I want to die," and then the school had to get involved. That was a bad party, but it was a memorable one.

Eva knew better than to complain about the parties. On another memorable night, she'd eavesdropped on a girl and a boy arguing about exactly this: "What makes you think you're different than everyone else?" A good question—practically a philosophical question. But no one had answered it. (Later, the girl left in tears, someone's beer on her shirt.) And so, every Thursday, Eva skipped the parties and stayed in the basement classroom for hours on end. A windowless, fluorescent room—that didn't matter. She opened up a used copy of whichever book Sabine had slipped under her arm. A single page could take an hour to reveal itself. She sat in the chair Sabine had sat in, and in the margins wrote words that were not her own. Some of them were German words that she had memorized and would have to look up later. The hours passed without her noticing. (Time was the one thing that it helped not to notice.) At midnight, right before she left, Eva read through her notebook a final time. She didn't dare read the notebook in her own room, but here, in a chair where someone else had sat, with books that centuries of other people had read, she looked at all the blank space and felt briefly unafraid.

On a Thursday devoted to Kierkegaard, the room filled up and emptied out as usual, and then, hours later, one of Eva's classmates reappeared in the doorway—a boy who, like her, was not a philosophy major. At the start of the semester, she'd briefly imagined they might be allies, but in spite of his ignorance, he turned out to be a frequent, confident contributor to discussion. (Eva wasn't sure if she approved of his confidence.) He was clearly taken aback to find her there, still seated at the table, but he ducked his head and hurried to the corner, where he removed a crumpled piece of paper from the trash can, crumpled it even tighter in his hand, and ran out of the room.

When he was gone, Eva went and looked in the trash. A paper coffee cup stained brown, a pen snapped in two, an apple core. She found a sheet of paper with the same Spanish verb conjugated over and over again. *I left, you leave, we will be leaving.* Or maybe it wasn't *leave,* maybe it was just *go*—she couldn't remember. She returned to her notebook and tried to write something, but she kept getting distracted by the thought of the crumpled-up paper. There was too much empty space on the page to fill. Ten o'clock became eleven o'clock, minutes she observed as they disappeared, fidgeting uncomfortably in her chair. She was not as interested in what she would write as she was in what the boy might have written.

Suddenly it seemed essential that she escape the basement before midnight. She packed her bag in a hurry. Too many books, wedged inside at odd angles, the spine of one pressing sharply into her own spine. Aboveground, she kept hurrying, though out of habit she took the long route home, which passed the graduate student bar. She peered through the window, also out of habit, and as usual there wasn't much to see: the glass was grimy, the lights were dim. Two blocks later, she turned a corner and nearly collided with a baby stroller.

Eva was so disoriented—a stroller made no sense in the middle of a college campus, in the middle of the night—that she didn't immediately recognize the woman pushing it. Sabine wore glasses and shoes that looked more like slippers. But she didn't seem surprised to see Eva. She just seemed tired.

"He doesn't sleep unless we walk," she said.

The hood of the stroller had been pulled all the way down. Eva could see a lot of blankets and the mounds of two feet, but no face.

"You have a baby," she said, neither a question nor a statement. A hypothesis.

Sabine laughed. She leaned over the front of the stroller to peer inside.

"I can't risk showing you," she said. "One wrong move and he's wide awake. But another time—we'll have you over."

Eva had imagined Sabine's apartment, of course. In her head, it was filled with books in towering stacks, grains in jars, a real kettle on the stove, whistling austere commands. She hadn't pictured a *we.* Did *we* mean two, or three? She hadn't pictured plastic dishes or splattered food or everything sharp kept out of reach.

A sound inside the stroller startled her. Sabine pushed the invisible baby back and forth, back and forth. They had to get going.

"Someday you'll meet him," she said as Eva stepped aside to let them pass. Then she paused, one of her perfect pauses, and smiled. "You'll tell him all your ideas."

When Eva arrived in the auditorium the next morning, the chalkboard was still covered in notes from the previous night's class—some kind of physics. Eva didn't understand any of the equations, but at one point in high school, she'd learned some of the concepts. She remembered the easy stuff. Acceleration, inertia, free fall. She remembered that before there was real energy there was potential energy. While Sabine and another graduate student erased the board, Eva walked past her usual seat in the last row and chose a spot in the middle of the room. There were half a dozen people who could see the back of her head, and one person right behind her, close enough to read over her shoulder. She opened her notebook to a new page, which bore the faint impression of what she'd written on the previous page. At the front of the room, Sabine was standing on her toes to reach the top of the board. Eva doubted that she would ever actually see her home or meet her baby, but for some reason, the thought didn't disappoint her. She had changed the picture of the apartment in her head: sturdier bookcases, messier surfaces, a vase of flowers on a high shelf. When the board was finally empty and Sabine had wiped her hands, she turned around to face the room, as beautiful as usual, bright white fingerprints all down the front of her pants.

Over time, Eva's guilt about not returning Jamie's calls had become a simple fact—a thing to live with and, like other ordinary things, to ignore. He called less often, and she thought of him less often. But in the final weeks of the school year, the old habit of wondering about him—where he was, what he was thinking—returned, questions that hovered uneasily in the morning, like the residue of a too-vivid dream, and resurfaced in the afternoon, when she emerged from the library to be accosted by the sun. She checked her phone constantly. The screen was cracked, a cobweb she peered through to confirm that no one was trying to reach her.

Walking past the clusters of people spread out on the grass, all of them laughing, always laughing, Eva staged conversations with him in her head. Guilt turned to grievance. *Where have you been? Where did you go?* It didn't matter that the answers were probably banal. That he'd been at parties and in libraries and maybe he, too, had been in love. She invented new, more dramatic explanations: he had forgotten her, he had abandoned her, he had called her out of duty and then out of pity, and now there would be nothing left.

The school year ended half a dozen times. The last party was never really the last. There was a concert, a picnic, a rave filled with foam machines. The foam started out white and weightless, like snow, but by the time the party was over it was gray—dirty and deflated. Eva saw Eli across the room, suds hanging off his cheek, and for a moment he reminded her of a little boy in a tub, a beard made out of soap, back when the game of being a grown-up only lasted as long as the bath. He leaned drunkenly into the girl next to him.

"Don't look," Lorrie said.

Eli put his arm around the girl.

"Seriously." Lorrie handed Eva a plastic shot glass. "No one's making you look."

Maybe they were fucking. Maybe they weren't. *Fucking* was such a stupid word, a word to make sex sound more glamorous than it ever really was.

Eva stared into the cup. "What are we celebrating?"

Lorrie shrugged. A boy pushed past them wearing his graduation cap and no shirt, his own plastic cup raised in the air.

"Freedom!" he shouted.

"That's ridiculous," Lorrie said. She tossed her head back and swallowed, then dropped the cup on the floor. "It's not freedom—it's just fun."

Early the next morning, Eva dismantled the stack of library books on her desk. Now that she didn't need them anymore—exams over, facts already forgotten—she wondered if they were just another false monument. The books filled two almost unliftable bags. The library wasn't open yet, but there was a man waiting outside on a bench, hunched over, reading a hardcover that was no bigger than his hand. Eva couldn't see the title but she imagined something very old, a translation of an ancient, enigmatic text. Or maybe he didn't even need a translation. She was seized by the desire to learn a new language, preferably a new alphabet. She was already smiling at this thought when the man looked up and she saw that it was the man with the bottle-cap glasses, the man with the pocket of pistachio shells.

"Oh!" Eva dropped her bags on the ground.

The man knew her, but he pretended he didn't. Recognition was an instant, unbidden flash of familiarity—he couldn't have suppressed it if he'd tried. For that moment, his face opened up—softer features, deeper eyes—and then, just as quickly, but not so effortlessly, it closed up. He stared intently at his book and said nothing.

It took Eva a minute to recover. No, not a real minute. She had to admit that it was just a few seconds. The man's book, when he tilted it toward her, looked like English after all. She slid her own books one at a time through the slot of a big metal box marked RETURNS.

She was walking back the way she'd come, the bags weightless over her arm, when her phone rang. She picked it up without thinking, before she had time to wonder why he was calling or whether she would regret responding. Her *hello* was a question, and his was an answer.

Jamie hadn't been in the library or at parties or in any of the other recognizable places she had imagined. He'd been in the wilderness. Nothing extreme, he said. Just a little dose of Thoreau, or something.

Or something. That surprised Eva. It was imprecise, confused. When had Jamie ever been confused?

"What happened?"

He said it was complicated. He would tell her when he saw her in person.

"When will that be?"

"I'm not sure." He sounded distracted. The campus was emptying out; someone might or might not be able to give him a ride.

"A friend?" she asked.

"Sort of."

Eva could feel the cracked phone screen against her ear. For weeks, tiny shards of glass had been falling off, pricking her hand, sometimes her cheek. She held the phone away from her face and put Jamie on speaker. There was an old picture of him that appeared on the screen each time he called—a tall figure standing on a tree stump—but it wasn't how she was picturing him now. She was picturing him in the doorway of her parents' house, his wet hair, his serious face, his evasive replies. She remembered her mom saying, "What's wrong?" She remembered Nick saying, "Something's wrong?" Why not say it herself?

I can tell from the sound of your voice.

But could she tell?

It was the sort of thing you said as reassurance. It meant, *Don't worry, it's just me.* It meant, *I know you.* A profound vow passed off as an everyday comfort—you didn't have to believe every word. Except with Jamie, she did.

Eva tried to remember how many of his calls she had missed. Was it five, or more like ten? Once, while she was showering, her roommate had appeared in the bathroom, obscured by steam, to complain that Eva's phone wouldn't stop ringing. She'd hurried back to the room, the wet, mortifying smacks of her flip-flops following her all the way down the hallway, and found Jamie's name on the screen. "Who is she?" her roommate had wanted to know. Eva had just shrugged, as if she couldn't explain—or as if it weren't worth explaining.

"I'll come and get you," she said to Jamie.

Eva didn't have a car, didn't even know how to drive, but she would have to figure it out. She felt a surge of energy. Lately, the only things she had to figure out were essay prompts, problem sets, the best way to phrase a text message.

Within an hour, she was in the passenger seat of Lorrie's car, a stick-shift Volvo that technically belonged to her uncle, a rich guy in a nearby suburb. Lorrie rolled down the window, turned up the radio, grinned. She loved driving. There was a reason, she said, that so many metaphors involved cars. Take the wheel, hit the road, burn rubber. The joy of it was existential: to get where you wanted to go. And now they were going.

IS THAT YOU?

It took only two hours to reach Jamie, but Eva didn't think it was strange that they had never visited each other. There were smaller distances, after all, that had kept their lives separate. No, not separate—just distinct. But Lorrie didn't understand. She had traveled all over the country to see her friends. She called them all the time, but that wasn't enough—she needed to be able to picture them while they talked, to picture them as they were now, not then. Maine, New Orleans, the middle of Ohio. The libraries, the cafeterias, the fraternities. At one school, the football team lived in a clapboard farmhouse; at another, Greek letters adorned massive brick colonials. There were dorm rooms made of cinder block and dorm rooms with ornate fireplaces, but every mattress was the same scratchy blue vinyl, impervious to year after year of sweat and spills. On these trips, Lorrie had met friends of friends, even friends of friends of friends. One night, she'd had sex with her cousin's roommate's brother.

Next to Lorrie's experience, Eva's inexperience did seem strange. She got carsick. For the last half-hour of the drive, winding along small roads, surrounded by woods, she stuck her head out the window and let the wind roar in her face. When they arrived in front of Jamie's dorm, her hair was tangled and her ears were buzzing.

Eva offered Jamie the front seat, but he got in the back. They didn't stop to see the campus, or even to use the bathroom. They drove south while Lorrie did the talking, and it wasn't until they hit traffic, inching across an old truss bridge, that Eva repeated the question she'd already asked: "What happened?"

Sleek boats glided under the bridge, the steady beat of oars mocking the stop and start of the cars, white wakes zipping and unzipping the surface of the water. Jamie stared out the window, not answering.

"Eva told me you ran away," Lorrie said.

"I didn't say—"

Jamie cut her off: "It's okay."

"What were you running away from?" Lorrie asked, shifting gears.

She was proud of being able to drive a manual. To use a machine, she had told Eva, you should truly understand it. You should learn to speak a vehicle's language. Each sound was a desire, once you knew what to listen for: the mewling plea for a higher gear, the sudden protest of a stalled engine. Eva was wondering if this was really true when Jamie finally answered.

"It only took a few weeks for the most popular kid at school to emerge," he said. "Smart and charming. Attractive. Good with adults, great with peers. I'm sure you know a dozen of him."

Eva thought this might be an accusation, but Lorrie laughed, glancing in the rearview mirror. She seemed intrigued—maybe impressed.

"Every weekend, he'd make ten new friends at some party. At the end of the night, people would go back to their rooms and brag about meeting him. It was like a prize. It meant they were *in*."

The car slowed, but didn't get any quieter. If anything, it seemed to get louder. Up ahead, they could see flashing orange letters: MERGE WITH CAUTION.

"It's a small school, so they'd run into him again within a couple days. They'd make a joke, a reference to something they'd talked about over the weekend, and he'd nod and laugh, and after that, the joke would be an inside joke. They'd tell it every time they saw him, like flashing a special badge. They sometimes wondered why he never made the joke himself, but they didn't really worry about it. He was popular, they were lucky. Why overthink it?"

For the next fifty yards, three lanes turned into one lane. They crept along, neon cones hemming them in on either side. The two unused lanes had been completely torn up, the smooth layer of asphalt stripped away to reveal the rough layer underneath. Then, all at once, the road widened again, and everyone sped up. Eva listened for a momentous humming or an ecstatic revving—some proof of a desire being met—but couldn't hear anything.

"I saw the guy exactly once a week," Jamie went on. "We were in the same small class, and sometimes we sat right next to each other, but we hardly ever spoke. I only ran into him outside of class one time, right before I went to the woods. We were standing at the post office, so I said hi, just to be polite, and right away he looked down at the envelope in my hands. It was something official, with my name typed in all caps. *Hey, James,* he said. He said it as if we'd known each other our whole lives, and he sounded so sincerely happy to see me that I almost let it go. I thought, maybe I should be James.

"Instead, I corrected him. I did it in a casual, friendly way, but the mistake really rattled him. He couldn't recover. He insisted on walking me back to my room, and when we got there, he confessed."

"What did he confess?" Lorrie asked.

"He has face blindness. He has hundreds of friends, or hundreds of people who consider him their friend, but he has no idea who they are."

In the next lane, a car pulled up even with theirs, the same car that had been trapped beside them in traffic for an hour. The driver, who no longer seemed quite like a stranger, glanced at Eva just as she glanced at him. He raised his eyebrows. She laughed, because it was silly but also nice—comforting. Neither Lorrie nor Jamie asked what she was laughing about.

"I stuck around campus for a few more days after that, but it was hard to shake the feeling. Whenever I ran into someone, right before I said hello, I was positive I could see the confusion in their eyes. It only lasted a second, but it turns out a second is enough."

"Enough?"

"Enough to imagine them asking themselves, *Who the hell are you?*"

Eva knew exactly what he meant. The other driver, who just a moment before had seemed so familiar, turned back into an anonymous face, a meaningless coincidence who veered off at the next exit and disappeared forever. Wasn't this what she had been waiting for Jamie to say, to see, all along? The terrible shape of loneliness, the vacant room—empty looks, hollow words—that might turn out to be an entire world?

"So I went to the woods, where I wouldn't see anyone. Not even myself."

But he hadn't said it, hadn't seen it. Not until it was too late. He had told her there were walls between people, and so the walls had appeared. She had sat on her side, chipping away at other people's exteriors and at her own. She had let them inside—literally inside! (The thought of Eli was a bruise, something just under her skin. It hurt to touch, and yet she was also afraid that it would fade.)

Well, now Jamie had understood. It was not a gradual, arduous awakening. Somehow all it took was one look—the blank gaze of a boy for whom everyone was new and unknowable—and suddenly everything was different: no more classes, no more classmates, no more parties, no more jokes. Jamie had understood, and understanding had already changed his life.

IS THAT ME?

The ants reached their peak in the very middle of summer. Eva was renting a room in an apartment in Washington, D.C., where she had a boring internship at an exciting newspaper. It was the kind of summer job that was supposed to turn into another summer job and then another, until it turned into a real job. She was following the right steps. Take enough of them and it would count as a path. The apartment, which she shared with three interns who worked at think tanks, girls who were already friends and were not in search of another, was full of cracks. On the balcony, there was an entire half-inch between the door and the door frame.

The ants marched in as if they had been invited, as if they owned the place. In the bathroom, they formed a polite line along the wall, making unhurried progress toward a bar of soap, everyone taking their turn. In the kitchen, they swarmed a peach, writhing all over it, diving into an obscene split in its skin. Eva's bedroom was mostly safe, but she felt them on her skin all the time. Her own hair on her neck made her shiver. When she closed her eyes, they were everywhere.

She texted Eli one afternoon while she was hiding from the bugs. They hadn't spoken since the spring. The silence had been her rule. He didn't see the point of it: Couldn't they be friends? Couldn't they at least be friendly? It had felt good to be the one to make the rule, until she realized that she would have to be the one to break it.

The first text she sent was a picture of ants floating in poison, a runny white mixture of sugar and Borax that one of her roommates had taught her how to make. It was the sort of gruesome aesthetic Eli appreciated; he was never disgusted by ugly things.

A few minutes went by, and then he laughed at the picture. Or he said that he laughed. (Did she believe him?) Eva hesitated, then sent another text: *How are you?*

He answered with a string of short messages. He never wrote big chunks of text, which gave the impression that he was typing as he was thinking, maybe even typing without thinking. He said he was bored. He was mad at a customer-service representative. He was sort of horny, sort of hungry. He was tired from playing basketball. His shoulder hurt. He stopped typing.

Horny. Eva had never said the word out loud, or even written it down. She looked at the text for a long time. She understood that if she didn't send a response, the conversation would end. He wouldn't say, *And how are you?* Not out of malice, really. He would go eat something from the fridge, he'd ice his shoulder, take a shower. He wouldn't even remember what he'd said.

Eva told herself that it was crazy to be afraid of texting. Texting! She closed her eyes and tried to picture a generic kind of fear: standing on a diving board or waiting to go onstage. All that these scenes required was someone who said *Jump,* someone who said *Now.*

She held her breath, typed a message, sent it without rereading.

It would be nice to touch.

Silence while she counted the seconds. Her palm vibrated.

Mhm

Did that count as jumping? Eva walked from her bedroom to the living room and back to her bedroom—avoiding the kitchen, the ants—to make her body feel useful.

How do you want to be touched?

Just with your mouth

Ok

I'll take my pants off

Eva pictured Eli standing in front of her wearing only a shirt. It was a little ridiculous.

Look up at me

She remembered one of the last good days with him, or one of the first bad days—how to tell the difference? It wasn't warm yet, not really, but to rejoice in the thaw, everyone did everything outside. The patch of grass outside the library, not yet green, filled up with people propping textbooks against their knees. She and Lorrie had been sitting in the center of the main quad, skimming a long Victorian novel. Slowly, a group gathered, as it always did around Lorrie. Eli appeared, though Eva hadn't been the one to invite him. Everyone was lying down except Eli, who was standing up, doing imitations of their professors. He shuffled imaginary notes and stroked his chin. "Guess," he said, so they did. Literature of the Lonely. Game Theory. Modern Apocalyptic Narratives. Reasoning from the Past: Applied History and Decision Making. He paced back and forth, and his audience followed him from their seats on the ground, as if it were a tennis match. They laughed, then laughed harder. Eva could see his pleasure multiplying. She opened her mouth as if to speak, and his eyes flicked in her direction, but only for a second.

Do you want to see?

I do

She understood that this kind of photo was common. She herself had never received one. The angle made his penis look bigger than it really was. His pubic hair was coarse, his thighs pimpled. It was tempting to believe that this mortification was a gesture that meant something—meant more than boredom or anger or ache, more than all the other things that could be turned into desire.

Do you like it?

The effort of reminding herself it meant nothing felt like breaking her own heart. No, she didn't have a better, more original phrase for it.

Of course

Show me

Show you what?

How much you like it

How?

A picture

The heat behind her eyeballs meant she would be crying soon, but she tried to take a few photos anyway. Her shirt pulled up, nipples showing. Pants around her ankles, ass in the mirror. She held the phone between her legs. A pink clam, some sea creature too soft to survive without a shell. Then she deleted all the photos, crying as quietly as she could, as if he might hear.

Are you there?

Use your imagination

Supposedly, this made him laugh. *Ha.* And even then, crying, half naked in the mirror, she felt the satisfaction of having said something clever and good, something he might have said himself. She pulled up her pants, wiped her face. She was out of ideas.

Ok

Ok?

Fuck me

Eva let him do most of the talking—the typing—after that. It didn't take long. The last picture he sent was a white splatter on the hardwood floor, an Oriental rug visible at the edge of the frame.

Hey
Thanks

She turned her phone off without responding, even though she knew there wasn't really any power in this act of restraint. He would not wonder where she had gone. She was still right here, trapped in her own bed by thousands of tiny insects that she could have crushed with the palm of her hand, if only she dared.

She made herself get up and take a walk. The simple, familiar tune of an ice cream truck, like a toy bagpipe, made her smile, so she waited in line with the kids at the corner, towering above them. She ordered rainbow sprinkles, which tasted bad and looked just right, like somebody's idea of childhood. She stood on the grown-up side of the playground fence. Faces covered in chocolate and vanilla, fingers sticky with Italian ice. One kid brandished a cone like a sword, another held it aloft like a torch. A third dropped hers on the ground. The only consolation, of course, was replacement. Eva watched to see if it would work. The girl waited in front of the truck, chocolate and tears all over her face. The man in a white paper hat handed her a new cone, just like the old. Her eyes narrowed—skeptical, aggrieved—and for a moment Eva thought that she might refuse the lie. Then she grabbed the ice cream with both hands, her whole face transformed by the pleasure of forgetfulness.

WHAT'S THE POINT?

Inside his tent, they sat cross-legged at either end of an inflatable sleeping pad. Usually a tent was quiet. Usually a tent was a refuge. No noise, no bugs, no beating sun or lashing wind. But this tent was loud, its thin walls vibrating with sound: cars, pedestrians, a bullhorn above it all.

Jamie had tried retreating into silence and he had tried escaping into the woods and now, nearly three years later, he had gone straight to the noisy, treeless center of things. The tent was in downtown Manhattan, surrounded by other tents. Nylon and tarpaulin flapped proudly, like flags. People chanted in unison; if you bellowed by yourself, someone would bellow back. The point was to make yourself seen, heard, known. There was a difference between camping and encamping.

Jamie had been at the encampment since the beginning—September. There was only one year left of college, but for him it was one year too many. He couldn't do it. No, he had corrected himself:

he *wouldn't* do it. It was important to be accurate. He had vowed to be utterly honest. The school year had arrived (so had the bill), and he had stayed put.

"College is one big performance, if you think about it," Jamie had told Eva. "Every class is a new script to memorize, every party requires a new role to play."

"Maybe," she said warily. "I guess performing can be fun."

"And every time you turn your back on the audience, your grade goes down."

Jamie's mom had moved out to a little house on Long Island, so his dad's place was the only place to be. One evening at the end of August, Eva had stopped by on her way back to school—Lorrie driving again. Technically, dropping out meant failing, but Lorrie said Jamie was brave, and Eva had to agree. It made him seem powerful, even a little frightening: to turn a failure into a success, the bad into the good. They double-parked outside the building, and Eva told Lorrie not to bother coming in. "I'll only be a minute," she said, because already she thought she might want a reason not to stay.

All this time and she had never been inside the penthouse. Later, she wondered whether Jamie would have shown it to her if he hadn't been about to abandon it—to renounce it. That day, he was the only one at home. Following him through the apartment, Eva entertained a ridiculous thought: maybe his dad didn't really exist. There was his bedroom and his study, here was his fan of magazines (all the important ones) and his amber bottles of whiskey (all the expensive ones), but even so, she let herself imagine that it was an elaborate ruse. The props of wealth, the accessories of self-regard—all carefully arranged to create a character, complete with everything except the person inside it, a creation Jamie had invented in order to destroy.

They stood in a sparely furnished living room with a view of the whole city.

"It's beautiful from up here," she said.

The white lights streamed toward them, the red lights streamed away from them.

"It's convenient from up here," Jamie said. "A perfect grid. Miniature, meaningless people, who you'll never have to know."

Jamie turned away from the window in disgust. But the room itself, it seemed, was just as repulsive.

"My dad is dating his interior decorator," he said angrily, sitting down on the coffee table instead of the couch. There was a mangled can of soda on the marble surface, a neglected coaster nearby. "She talks like a yoga teacher, or a therapist—some kind of fake spiritual guide. She says stuff like, *This color is so you.*"

The room was painted and upholstered in many shades of white, except for the throw pillows, which were solid black.

"I told her she should call it interiority decorating, but she didn't get the joke."

Eva laughed, and they could both tell it wasn't a real laugh. She was pretty sure she knew where he was going with this, and she didn't want to follow him. His big ideas weren't what daunted her anymore. At school, she'd gotten used to that kind of intellectual debate—watching it, occasionally participating in it. She could have argued alongside him: against materialism as a creative act, against consumerism as a healing faith. She agreed with his opinions, but she didn't feel them in her gut—she wouldn't have crushed a can in her hand.

"They call this couch minimalist," Jamie said. "Do you want to know how much it costs?"

"Not really."

His face softened. "Sorry. It's just—"

He gestured at the room and fell silent. She could have said, *I know,* but she didn't.

And now she was inside his tent. The protest had a vast and somewhat vague agenda, which Eva had read about in the newspaper. Above all, to dismantle the structure of wealth: a few fat cats lapping at overflowing saucers of milk and everyone else waiting in vain for it to trickle down. The protesters were often criticized for being better at describing this problem than at designing its solution. To Eva, this seemed like a fair critique, but she admired their descriptive powers. She had never been as good as Jamie at grasping the big picture.

The simplest, most immediate message of the movement was that it wasn't moving. When Eva first saw the tents, she was reminded of cows sitting down before the rain, legs tucked delicately beneath them, huddled together under the looming clouds. Skyscrapers looked down on the encampment disapprovingly. Already October had brought winter weather, a dusting of bright white snow against bright blue tarp. In photographs on the news, Eva had even seen people without tents, lying on mattresses with nothing but see-through plastic covering them head to toe. She had thought of suffocation then and she thought of it now, in the cramped, noisy tent. Maybe this was the genius of the protest, that the gesture of their power was also the proof of their helplessness: they weren't going anywhere. They were defiant and they were—had always been—trapped. Panic started its kettle hiss inside Eva's chest.

It must have revealed itself in her face, because Jamie stopped talking and unzipped the side of the tent. "Let's get some air," he said.

Once you were inside the encampment, what had seemed like a densely packed herd revealed itself to be a carefully organized collective. There were streets and street names. There were vats of food, racks of clothes, prayer circles, drum circles. They turned off Jefferson Street onto Trotsky Alley. In theory, it should have been just as beautiful as the grid Eva had observed from the penthouse. And wasn't that the point of coming—to see for herself? When everyone was waving signs in the air, you didn't have to look too hard to understand what it all meant: the young woman with a bandana (DECOLONIZE THE BANKS), the old guy in a Led Zeppelin shirt (FIRE YOUR BOSS), someone's kids scrambling around in hand-knitted hats, feeding the dog that got fed by everyone (MY FOUR-YEAR-OLD KNOWS WHAT FAIR MEANS).

"Do you ever go home?" Eva asked.

A man walking in the opposite direction, who looked more like a professor than a protester, nodded at Jamie, either because they knew each other or because nodding was just what you did around here.

"How would I go home?" Jamie said.

Not why—how. Eva knew that none of the obvious answers (the 5 train, the M103, a cab, a few hours walking) were the right answers, so she said nothing, and that, too, seemed to confirm her wrongness.

She hadn't meant the question as an accusation. She, too, was avoiding home. Lorrie had persuaded her to come to New York for just one night, to sleep on the fold-out couch in her cousin's apartment, and she had said the trip wouldn't count as spontaneous if Eva made a dutiful pilgrimage to see her parents: to use the washer/dryer, to compliment Nick's latest painting, to ask Gail if those were new earrings—to make someone else happy. Lorrie's cousin lived on a treeless street in a neighborhood with more warehouses than houses. She was not happy-go-lucky, but she put her own happiness first. She cut her hair herself and took a little bit of acid every day. Her parents paid half her rent. Eva's own parents seemed far away, so she told herself it wasn't that bad—after all, it didn't feel that bad—not to tell them how nearby she really was.

Jamie stopped short, and Eva's shoulder collided with his shoulder. In front of them, a group of women had started singing. They were old women, with gray, brittle hair, wearing neon safety vests and locking arms.

"*Are you listen-ing? Are you listen-ing? Wash-ing-ton.*"

Eva recognized the tune of the song—a song from when she was young, sitting in a circle on a carpet, trying to match her voice to someone else's. Then the words came back, too: *Are you sleep-ing? Are you sleep-ing?* The women belted their modified lyrics—off key, but they didn't care. They were elderly, eccentric. Eva could tell Lorrie about them and Lorrie would say, *That's hilarious*. It would feel good to make her laugh, as it always did. Lorrie's laugh was loud and liquid—real but not too real, not over the top or out of control, a laugh you'd recognize anywhere but not a laugh that gave her away. And yet already Eva sensed that something would stop her from turning the old women into a joke.

The women made their mouths into perfect "O"s. They had whiskery hairs above their lips, and grooves that turned their mouths into permanent frowns. They didn't care about the tune, because they cared about the words. They had stupid outfits, bad songs, fierce conviction. All Eva had was a joke.

She and Jamie arrived at the statue of the bull. It was surrounded by a metal fence, which had been covered in yet more signs. UNFUCK THE WORLD. CASTRATE THE BULL. Eva had never seen it up close. Its bronze tail was raised in the air like a whip. They were staring up the bull's flared nostrils when a child, three or four years old, appeared behind them and wrapped her arms around Jamie's knees.

"Dad!"

The girl pressed her face into Jamie's pants, as if she were hiding from someone, as if she had only narrowly escaped some unseen menace. When she looked up and realized her mistake, the whole story appeared on her face: shock then shame, shame then anger.

"I know the feeling," Jamie said.

He took a polite step back and let the girl size him up. Silence, a skeptical look, and then—no, not quite a smile, but the door of her face opened up, if only a crack.

Jamie promised to find her dad, but he didn't pat her on the head or take her by the hand, as someone playing the part of the hero might have. He didn't pretend he was anything other than a stranger. Eva could have followed them as they disappeared back into the crowd, but she said goodbye instead.

She didn't want to live in Jamie's tent, but she wanted to want to. To wake up to the sound of singing, to be summoned by the bullhorn's call, to shout until her voice went hoarse.

The girl vanished first. Jamie's head bobbed above all the other heads for a while, and then it, too, was gone. Eva leaned against the fence, a banner flapping noisily above her head: OCCUPY YOUR MIND.

Nick called Eva later that afternoon. He usually texted before he called, for permission: *Is this a good time?* She was at a crowded bar near the canal in Brooklyn, where everyone was playing games. There was a ping-pong table and shuffleboard and something that involved throwing a bean bag into a hole. Lorrie and Eva were sitting off to the side, and Lorrie was making fun of the men—it was almost all men—who wore button-down shirts and leather shoes that were supposed to look like sneakers. Lorrie's cousin had recommended the bar, because you could always find someone to buy you drinks. The men, mostly white guys, were all in their twenties or thirties, but they had middle-aged stomachs and whooped like little kids when they won.

Eva went outside to answer the phone. The street was loud—cars honking, wind whipping at awnings—and she worried that all the city noise would give away where she was.

"Is everything okay?"

"Oh!" he said. "Oh, good. I was just about to hang up."

"What's going on?"

"Nothing's going on."

The door to the bar opened, releasing more noise, so Eva walked down the block.

"I just wanted to hear your voice."

Fear receded and left guilt in its place. She asked him questions so that he wouldn't ask her questions. He told her he'd been working less, painting more—a different style, which had come as a surprise. He hadn't set out to try something new, but now the pace of change was irresistible, one experiment after another. He stayed up late in the studio, like when he was a kid.

"A kid?"

"A student. You know, messing around."

He said it felt like a revelation, but also like regret. "What if I'd experimented sooner?"

Eva didn't know how to respond. Wasn't he supposed to know more about how regret worked than she did? There were things she wanted to undo or redo, but the truth was that she hadn't done much in the first place.

At the corner of the street, a young man sat cross-legged on a piece of cardboard, jangling a paper cup of coins. Nick never gave money to homeless people, because he said there was no way of knowing who really needed it most. For the same reason, Gail always did.

"What do you think about the protesters?" Eva asked, even though she hadn't been planning to.

"Well." He sounded uncertain. Eva pulled the lint off a handful of change from her pocket and dropped the coins into the man's cup. "They don't really know what they want, do they?"

"Bless you," the man on the sidewalk said.

"Does anyone know what they want?" Eva asked.

When Nick didn't answer right away, she regretted the question—

too big, too sincere. He would wonder what she really meant, and then she would have to figure out what she really meant.

"Sure they do," he said eventually. "For example—"

"Maybe it's an experiment. You just said you wished you'd done more experimenting."

"They need a leader. How can you have followers without a leader?"

Eva had wondered this herself, but when Nick said it, she bristled. A smaller, cynical question. It was cold enough to see her breath, but she unzipped her jacket.

"I have to go," she said.

Eva hung up and walked back toward the bar, ignoring the man on the sidewalk, who repeated himself—"Bless you"—as she passed. It was a short block, but by the time she was back at the entrance, where two thick-necked men stood smoking, her anger was already losing its shape, an unearned righteousness that made her feel guilty all over again. For a moment, she thought about calling Nick back. But what would she say? *Sorry* wasn't quite right. Inside, the bar was warm. Men with their hopeful faces, their meaningless triumphs. Lorrie waved her over, pointing at another round of free drinks.

The university occupied one ward of the city. There were thirty wards and thirty aldermen—one student among them each year. Eli announced his campaign during the first weeks of their last year at school. After his photograph appeared on the front page of the student newspaper, a few dozen of his friends—had he always had so many?—appeared around campus wearing T-shirts with the picture printed on the front. Eva walked into the cafeteria and two Eli's stared back at her across the salad bar.

They'd had sex many times in the years since they'd broken up, usually on weekends, when the night got aimless but no one was tired yet. It was embarrassing because it was predictable. Lorrie rolled her eyes; she didn't want to hear about it. Once, Eli had been so drunk that he'd peed in Eva's bed. Occasionally, they were able to convince themselves that inevitability was actually romantic—meant to be. For a few months, they even talked about dating again. If they were falling asleep, his chest against her spine, their legs folded into each other, it seemed like a good idea. Eva hadn't liked spooning when she first tried it—didn't like staring at the back of his head any better than staring at the wall—yet over time she had discovered that this kind of closeness could inspire recklessness: there were some things that were effortless to say when someone's breath was in your hair, when you couldn't look them in the eye.

But in the morning, the dangerous magic of proximity was gone. They were never entangled; they were side by side. Eli would be lying on his back, mouth slack, eyes crusted, one arm flung above his head, as if he was hailing someone in a dream. Not her—that fantasy couldn't quite be retrieved from the dark room, blurred by near-sleep, in which dreams seemed to exist not only inside minds but between them. He'd wake up in pain, his arm all pins and needles, a limb numbed into an object, and Eva would knead sensation back into the flesh. He'd wince. She'd feel nothing.

Eventually, they had agreed to put an end to all that: thinking about dating, pretending to think about dating, fucking. (The word no longer sounded glamorous to her.) She was not his girlfriend and not really his friend, either. Friendly, just as he had once suggested. "It's about time," Lorrie said. The mature thing to do, someone else said, sounding impressed, and, as usual, being impressive was a small satisfaction. Sometimes Eva would hear about people Eli was sleeping with, but it was hard to tell if he had a girlfriend. Once, Lorrie saw him through the window of the nicest restaurant near campus, eating lunch with a brown-haired girl and her parents. Stiff shirts, bloody steaks. An unpleasant ritual, probably, but Eva didn't know the secret language of place settings and wine menus, so she envied it anyway. Later, the brown-haired girl long since discarded, Eva saw Eli kissing someone else on a harshly lit street corner. His eyes were closed, but hers, strangely, were wide open. Not starry-eyed or dreamy—she looked focused, squinting a little, as if determined to see some faraway prize.

Eva tried to be content with nearer prizes, and sometimes she really was. The word *good,* written with a red rollerball pen in the margin of an essay, could calm an afternoon's tempestuous anxieties. Intramural volleyball, with its high fives, its arbitrary camaraderie, its round of celebratory beers, could ease her loneliness for an entire weekend. The school newspaper, where she wrote short articles about administrative decisions, appeared every morning—a routine accomplishment, to be consumed with breakfast, then tossed casually into the trash. Even her dreams became repetitive, disposable, soothing. Eli rarely appeared in them, and Jamie never did. It had been weeks, maybe months, since she'd been lost or naked or drowning, since she'd woken up in a sweat.

In the midst of her contentment, she might receive a text from Eli late at night. *Hey.* A text that could mean something or nothing, ambiguity that could have reduced her to her most basic hopes, her most awful fears. But she was content. She didn't wonder why *good* was not *great*, a beer made her happy not sad, friendship seemed no less valuable than romance. She put her phone under her pillow and fell asleep.

Then one afternoon in Eva's French class, the seat beside her was empty. The next afternoon, too—a whole week in a row. The class was for people with humble ambitions. The goal was not to read great works of literature or master legal terminology; it was simply to speak clearly and fluidly, to be able to say what you meant. Eva and the girl beside her were always paired together for activities and presentations, most of which involved having halting conversations about prosaic subjects, each one designed to utilize certain vocabulary words or grammatical skills: family members, hobbies, what they had done in the past, what they hoped to do in the future. It was an easy class, with few assignments and only one rule: no English allowed. And so as Eva began to watch for the missing girl around campus—she had never seen her anywhere but at the desk to her right—she wasn't sure what she would say if she found her. Would she address her in French?

After a second week of absences, Eva approached the teacher after class.

"Où est-elle allée?"

His response came in English: "Medical leave."

Unlike the teacher's melodic French, these words sounded ugly, almost threatening. He spoke without an accent; he might, it occurred to Eva with a start, have been American. She didn't ask any other questions, because she didn't want to hear any more of that voice, but later, at her computer, she logged into the college directory. She searched *Brigitte* before she thought to search *Bridget.* She found her dorm and knocked on her door.

Bridget's roommate, a short woman with a buzz cut, did not make small talk. She looked exhausted.

"Bridget had a break."

It sounded like a bad translation; for a second Eva wondered if the roommate, unlike the French teacher, was not a native English speaker. But no, she meant a psychotic break. A splintering of reality: Bridget's world detaching from everyone else's. She had stopped sleeping, started hearing voices. She had insisted that the country's biggest banks were terrorist cells. She had peed all over the dorm room. (Something about sterilization.) She said she'd never felt more alive—more like herself. Professors got involved, and then doctors did, too.

Eva and Bridget's roommate stood there awkwardly, their supposedly shared reality between them, and agreed that this was very sad. Eva didn't ask if there was anything she could do, because she knew there wasn't.

"See you around," she said instead.

The roommate gave a short, hoarse laugh. "Probably not."

Outside, Eva followed a manicured path that led to a manicured courtyard. A maintenance worker was washing the dorm windows, one careful stroke at a time, leaving each pane streakless.

A *break*? Yes, she could see the point in breaking something. The urge was sudden and fierce: to kick over a potted plant, to smash one of those panes, at the very least to slam a door. She had spent week after week talking to Bridget, learning how many siblings she had, asking whether she preferred movies or music, agreeing that she, too, would rather be happy than rich. But it was just an exercise, a lesson in foreign words that they would be tested on until they understood.

She didn't do any damage, of course. She held it together. (Did that idiom exist in French?) For an hour, she wandered the campus, making random loops, hoping her feet might guide her—hoping they had a plan of their own. Her legs got tired and her mouth got dry, and when she finally stopped walking it was in front of Eli's door, not her own. Was that chance? Desire? Was it because he, of all people, had seemed closest to breaking through?

They didn't have sex. Eva sat on the bed, and Eli lay on the floor with his knees in the air, because he'd pulled something in his lower back. She wondered if he'd left the door open to prove to his roommates, all boys, that they were just talking.

What he wanted to talk about was the campaign. For the most part, Eva had avoided discussing the race with anyone, except sometimes with Lorrie, who made it all seem funny: Eli's self-seriousness, the repetitive speeches, those stupid T-shirts. But now Eli made it interesting. He told her things she didn't know, things other people probably didn't know, either. He said that he regretted letting his best friend, an aspiring poet, be his campaign manager.

"To him, it's just a game."

"Really?" Eva said. She had always liked the poet.

"It doesn't actually mean anything to him."

"Of course it does," Eva said. "It just doesn't mean the same thing it means to you."

"Now *you* sound like a poet."

Eva wanted to ask what it did mean to him, but she decided not to. Eli's face was very symmetrical, except for his nostrils, which were two slightly different shapes. Looking at him straight on, it was hard to tell, but from above, Eva could see the difference clearly. She smiled down at him.

"Is it obnoxious to say that I want him to believe in me?" Eli asked.

Eva thought about it. "Sort of."

He nodded gravely, running his fingers through his hair until they caught in the curls.

"But I understand," she added.

A few days later, when a reporter at the local newspaper asked Eli for an interview, Eli called Eva first. (He made sure to tell her: "I'm calling you first.") This was his best chance to make an impression on voters, and he said he couldn't trust the poet to help him prepare.

Late one evening, they practiced for the interview in his living room, which was also the dining room. No one else was home. Eva brought practice questions, written out by hand, and Eli wore a dress shirt and a tie, because he said that he needed to get used to the pressure of the knot against his throat. They sat at opposite ends of a table, too large for the room, that had belonged to someone's grandfather—six feet of dark, heavy wood between them. Eva started with softballs: "Tell us a little bit about yourself." "Why politics?" She kept her expression as studiously composed as his. "What's the achievement you're most proud of?"

In his answer, Eli told a story Eva had heard many times before, about a petition he'd helped circulate among the university's cafeteria workers. Officially, they were called dining-hall workers, which Eli said sounded fancier when written in admissions brochures. But they were underpaid and overworked, granted the very minimum amount of paid sick leave, locked out of all the buildings that students passed in and out of unthinkingly. The libraries, the gyms, the ceramics studios, the art gallery lined with lesser masterpieces. The petition had been a success, and Eva, too, was proud of what Eli had done: organizing. All she ever organized were sentences, paragraphs, supposedly big ideas. But listening to him now, with his collar and tie and well-rehearsed story, he didn't sound as admirable as he often did—more than anything, he sounded ambitious. His gaze was focused somewhere just over Eva's shoulder.

Watching him, momentarily distracted from the list of questions in front of her, Eva was reminded of the look that appeared on his face whenever they were having sex, right at the very end. Up until the final moments, he was always attentive, asking her what she wanted, giving her what she wanted, giving her what she hadn't even known she wanted. And then, just before he came—he always asked if he could come—he would briefly vanish. Right on top of her, hips against hips, chest under chest, breath on breath, but his eyes somewhere else completely.

"Next question," Eli said, tapping the table to get her attention. He sat up a little straighter, perching on the edge of his chair.

"Sorry," She looked down at her notes. "Age. Let's talk about your age. As a twenty-one-year-old—"

"Twenty-year-old."

"Oh." Embarrassed to have forgotten, she read the rest without looking up. "Can voters know who you really are if you're barely old enough to know yourself?"

Eli frowned and leaned back in his seat—confused, but only briefly. In a moment, his posture recovered, the grimace disappeared.

"Actually, there are a lot of politicians who know themselves *too* well. Not just the old ones, but especially the old ones. They've had the same opinions, the same proposals for years. They've already decided exactly what they think, so they've stopped asking what their constituents think. Don't get me wrong, I want voters to get to know me. But isn't it more important that I get to know *them*?"

Eva frowned. "So you'll be whoever they want you to be?"

"Well, isn't that the point? Isn't that democracy?" He looked up at the ceiling impatiently, his throat stretching out of his collar. "These questions are too broad."

Eva shuffled the paper in front of her. On the first page, her handwriting was neat and professional, but the more she'd written, the messier it had become. She'd gotten too excited. She could ask him anything!

"You're supposed to be a reporter," he said.

"I am."

She squinted at the words, cursive that wasn't quite cursive—uncrossed t's, r's that could have been v's. Even she couldn't quite read it.

"You're asking about, like, authenticity," he said.

"Voters care about that."

"In politics, *authentic* just means nice—relatable."

The front door to the house opened, and two voices filled the hall: a boy's and a girl's. They hurried up the stairs—laughing, tripping, laughing again. Eva had her back to them, but she could picture it anyway.

"*Authentic* means real," she said.

"Don't get so philosophical."

"What's wrong with philosophy?"

Footsteps right above their heads, a door closing, still more laughing. Eva looked around the room, where everything now seemed like a prop: the baroque furniture and the silk tie had nothing to do with the overdue library books on the floor, the bag of tortilla chips left open and going stale.

Eli's voice had an edge now. "*Real* means laws. It means budgets, benefits, zoning. Schools and teachers and—"

"But if it's all just a performance—"

"Safety. Housing." He took a breath. "Do you know how many homeless people there are in the city?"

Eva had written that number down somewhere—she'd been planning to ask about that number. But now the pages in front of her were all mixed up, the questions all out of order.

"More than five hundred, which is five hundred too many." He had regained his composure. "And by the way, why would performance be a bad thing? Performance is doing your job, getting things done."

He was ambitious, but he was also right. Upstairs, someone moaned and the bed creaked. The sounds were all the usual sounds—it didn't matter who was making them.

"Next question," he said again.

Eva spread all the papers out in front of her and said nothing for a while, uncertain where or how to resume. When she looked up, Eli's expression had changed—his attentive expression.

"What's wrong?" he asked.

When she didn't respond, he got up and came around to her end of the table. Below his dress shirt, he was wearing sweatpants. She could see the outline of his penis. He reached out to touch her shoulder.

"When did you lose your virginity?" she said suddenly.

He pulled his hand back. "What?"

The sound upstairs had become a steady rhythm, which neither of them acknowledged.

"How old were you?"

"Okay, we can stop. Let's stop." Eli loosened his tie. "No more questions." He looked worried.

"No, really," Eva said. She pushed the papers into a stack, the edges into alignment. "I want to know."

Eli was the first person Eva had ever had sex with. She hadn't told him that, even though she knew it was something you were supposed to tell people. She wasn't sure what had held her back. Not embarrassment, really—not pride, not even fear. There hadn't been any blood, as she'd been led to believe there would be. She'd been a little sore, but not a lot. The main effect, as far as she could tell, was that her face had tingled for a long time after, the way it did after swimming laps in a pool, and she kept pressing her hands against her cheeks, as if to make sure they were still there. He'd asked her what she was doing, but she just shook her head; it had everything to do with him and somehow also nothing.

"This was a bad idea," Eli said.

She hadn't told him, but she assumed he'd figured it out—if not that first time, then later, once they'd exchanged stories about being teenagers: kissing, drinking, the time someone knocked on the car window while his pants were down. He had stories about sex, and she didn't.

"When?" she repeated.

He hadn't asked her, and she hadn't told him without being asked. Eli stared at her for another second, then shrugged.

"I was fourteen."

Eva nodded, then got up and went out the back door. On the sidewalk, she passed two girls, barefoot, carrying high heels by their straps. Outside a deli, she wove through a big group that smelled like bacon. A few blocks from home, she realized that she'd forgotten the list of questions on the table, but she didn't turn back. She reached the iron gate to her dorm and unlocked it with a plastic card. She pulled hard, but there was no resistance—the gate swung open automatically.

SHOULD WE GET STARTED?

That fall, Eva had started running, because it was a normal thing to do alone. For weeks, it was unbearable. Each part of her body had been assembled wrong—her chest too small for her lungs, her arches too high for her feet. And why were there so many bones right beneath the surface of her skin? Kneecaps and ankle knobs, the delicate ridge of the shin. She tripped on the sidewalk's overbite, and when she stood up, blood blossomed on her palm in tiny dots, one and then five and then fifty.

But gradually, almost imperceptibly, running became tolerable. Doing something new, even something small, made time slow down, as if it had to stretch to accommodate the novelty, which was a kind of uncertainty: could her legs really carry her that far? And then a little farther still? Even once she could endure running, it wasn't a pleasure, not really. Her heart still thumped in her ears, and the slap of shoes on concrete sounded like a just-barely broken machine—a not-quite-reliable metronome. But for a few minutes now and then, her body became briefly ignorable, and in those moments she understood the other, greater pleasure of the imperfect machine: it could take her places.

She found woods and a reservoir and a baby deer taking a drink. She found a skate park where teenagers in beanies botched tricks and covertly smoked cigarettes, and she wondered if she seemed like one of them—or like an adult. She found a neighborhood of huge houses in soft yellows and elegant blues, where fancy cars gleamed in the driveways and it was always very quiet. The health-food store, the hookah lounge, the church with the turquoise spire, the day care with the seahorse mural—these seemed like private discoveries, because hardly anyone ventured past the borders of campus, or at least no one ventured very far.

Jamie called while Eva was running along the train tracks one morning, the sun newly risen. It was easy to wake up early when she had somewhere to go. Eva's fingertips went numb and turned white in the cold, which had worried her at first, until it pleased her: here was proof that her body could lose feeling, but also gain it, the pink returning to her skin once she was back inside. The Northeast Regional rounded a bend just as she picked up the phone. She could feel the vibrations in the small bones of her ear, where she held the phone and said nothing, waiting for the train to pass. It took a long time, long enough that it began to seem like the train would go on forever. When it was finally gone, just a distant chugging, Jamie said, "I'm at your house."

"My house?"

She pictured her dorm room first, an ugly room with a particle-board desk and a closet that only fit hangers if you wedged them in sideways. Jamie would have had to duck his head to get through the doorway. His feet would have dangled off the end of the bed.

"I mean, your parents' house."

The next image that surfaced in her mind had the warm, low-wattage glow of nostalgia, which couldn't be trusted. Every time she returned home, Eva discovered some detail she had misremembered. The blue hand towels in the bathroom had long since been replaced by the green ones. The fridge door was not the magnet-strewn one of her youth, cluttered with photographs and takeout menus and drawings that had been deemed art, but a new stainless-steel one, blank except for fingerprints. She hadn't really forgotten these new details, of course, but the old ones, though fainter, always felt truer.

"What are you doing there?"

Jamie, too, was his old self in her head. In his tent, she had been startled by his scraggly beard, his muscly forearms; now she turned him back into a teenager with marionette limbs and a pink-pocked face.

"The police came in the middle of the night," he said. "They cleared everyone out and took down all the tents, all the signs. By morning, they'd power-washed every square of sidewalk."

Eva was shivering. "Was it scary?"

"It's all gone," he said, sounding dazed. "As if no one was ever even there."

"Were you afraid?"

She clamped the phone between her cheek and her shoulder, so that she could rub her palms together. She wondered if the rails were still warm—another magic trick of friction. Skin on skin, metal on metal.

"I guess I must have been," Jamie said. "I didn't think about it, though. It was total chaos, this mass of screaming and chanting and batons, but it seemed like I was seeing everything perfectly clearly, clearer than before. Everything was simple. Effortless. I carried this old woman out of the crowd, this old woman named Sharon, and she weighed nothing. Her body seemed so fragile, and mine seemed so strong."

"Adrenaline," Eva said.

"Maybe. But it felt like more than that."

She knew which rails were dangerous and which weren't, but even so she was afraid to touch them. Standing on the splintery wooden ties, she imagined the parallel lines of electricity on either side of her, stretching all the way up and down the coast.

"Are you staying in my room?" she asked.

He'd been in her room before, but not very often. Mostly, he'd been in the kitchen, the yard, the room with the faded couch that needed to be replaced.

"Of course not. Not without asking."

"You don't have to ask."

Was that really true? She might have cared if he'd been there, but she cared, too, that he wasn't—his politeness was too proper, too impersonal. At one crucial point in time, hadn't he been her best friend? Not that they'd ever called each other that.

"I'm in your dad's studio. He just finished something, so now there's a blank canvas set up. Blank, but not white. He says you never paint directly on the canvas, because you have to tone it first. I didn't know that. The one I'm looking at right now is orange—or, like, orange-brown."

"Burnt sienna."

Eva thought she heard the tracks vibrating, so she scrambled down the gravel incline to the path where she'd been running. She had intended to take a long run, all the way to the beach, where it would have been pretty and peaceful this early, but suddenly being there didn't seem so different from imagining being there. She started walking back the way she'd come.

"Where will you go now?" she asked.

"Your parents said I don't have to go anywhere."

They did? Her parents, who got nervous about anything that

involved the police? Nick, who lacked conviction, who liked stability? Gail, who admired strong principles but disapproved of big risks?

"What about *your* parents?"

Jamie said nothing, so she added, "You should call them."

There was no sign of a train yet. Eva felt stupid, cowardly.

"Did I ever tell you that my dad's office is right there, right above the bull? He could have seen us from his desk. Watched us. But I doubt he ever bothered to look."

"Just call."

"Your dad says that when he's done with the painting you won't see any trace of the background color. The orange will be completely covered up."

"Jamie."

Silence.

"Do you have any idea what it's like?" he said at last. "For someone not to care where you are?"

"Of course they care. They're your parents."

"I don't think you do."

After they hung up, Eva put her hands in her armpits to warm them up. She walked all the way back to campus like that, numb fingers between clammy flesh. Feeling came back slowly and agonizingly, as if pain were the easiest sensation to retrieve.

When she was inside and her hands had finally stopped aching, she scrolled through the news, searching for the story that was his story. The facts were simple, the details sparse. Most of the photographs showed dramatic clashes between protesters and police: a man shouting into an officer's impassive face, his own features twisted with anger; a woman kneeling on the pavement, hands yanked behind her back, howling rage. The pictures weren't especially good pictures. At night, the cops were just dark shapes against a dark background. But at the very end of the article there was an image unlike all the others. A man's face filled the entire frame. According to the caption, he had just been pepper-sprayed. His head was tilted slightly back. Brown skin, pink lips, black beard, eyes closed. Someone was cupping the side of his cheek with one hand while pouring milk, as bright and thick as paint, over his eyes. The milk supposedly helped with the pain. It streamed down his cheeks like tears.

Election Day was beautiful and blue. Cloudless. Eli's friends handed out buttons and doughnuts. Eli himself sat on a bench wearing a button—a picture of his face right below his actual face—and drinking coffee, trying to look approachable. Probably succeeding, Eva thought, but she cut across a courtyard to avoid him. The other candidate in the ward, another student, was a girl Eva had never met. She was a year younger than Eva, and she had a column in the school newspaper that was usually smart, often sanctimonious. For the most part, Eva agreed with the columns, but something about them still bothered her.

"What makes her think that the world needs to hear all her opinions?" she asked Lorrie as they walked to the polling station.

"Men get to be self-important all the time," Lorrie said.

"All I'm saying is I can't relate."

"Maybe because you don't believe *your* self is important."

"Correct."

They were in the middle of the street, but Lorrie stopped walking. "Take it back."

Eva laughed and kept moving, but Lorrie grabbed her arm.

"I'm serious. You have to stop it."

"Stop what?"

"Hating yourself."

"There's a car coming."

"Promise me you'll stop."

"You know, most people who seem to hate themselves secretly love themselves," Eva said. "We're all narcissists in the end."

A biker swerved around them.

"Well, stop doing it secretly."

The approaching car honked, and Lorrie ignored it, gripping Eva's arm even tighter.

"Get out of the way," the driver shouted, but just then the light turned red. He pressed on the horn again in pointless frustration.

"See?" Lorrie said.

"See what?"

"Are you going to vote for him?"

They were briefly surrounded by a fresh wave of students crossing the street, and in the midst of it—elbows knocking, bags swinging—Eva freed herself from Lorrie's grasp. She hurried to the opposite corner without looking back.

The polling site was an old church on the edge of the city green, with makeshift voting booths in the basement. Eva filled in every race except Eli's, then stood there looking at his name in print, feeling sorry for herself. The fluorescent lights on the low ceiling buzzed. Then she remembered the people waiting in line behind her and told herself to cut it out. She left the bubble beside his name empty and hurried back upstairs.

From the front door of the church, she could see Lorrie waiting for her outside, her back turned, her hands on her hips. There was something girlish about the posture, but also something motherly. Eva hadn't talked to her mother in weeks. She lingered at the door to the chapel, where light streamed in through tall, unstained windows. Dust floated and sparkled in the empty room.

. . .

Late that afternoon, before the votes had been counted, Eva took a train to New York without telling anyone. A few stops from Grand Central, she remembered the student who'd jumped off the Empire State Building, a suicide note left behind for his roommate to find, so she texted Lorrie something casual and reassuring. *Just taking a trip.* There was no response until she was standing in the atrium, men in dress shoes with beers in paper bags rushing past her to catch their trains home. *Sounds fun.* For a moment, Eva regretted sending the text, wishing instead for the forbidden thrill of making someone worry. She looked up at the emerald ceiling, then back down at the crowd, then up again. She loved this—the rush of strangers ricocheting off each other, spinning out into separate worlds—but she had been told that Grand Central was cinematic, that lost girls were boring, that you could go off to find yourself in the big city, but if you did, no one wanted to hear about it.

Eva went to the concert hall where Lorrie's cousin was a bartender. As she walked from the subway to the bar, it occurred to her that the cousin might not recognize her. They had met just once, late at night, when she had let Eva and Lorrie into her apartment, the one with the coffee-stained futon. Eva had never been to the concert hall. Was it weird that she had remembered what it was called? It wasn't particularly well known. Eva nearly turned around, but she'd come all this way. *Sounds fun.* It was already eight o'clock—the polls were closed now. She leaned her shoulder into the bar door and the noise from inside rushed out.

The concert was in a big space behind the bar, but even the front room was jammed with people. Eva had to wait to buy her ticket. She could see the cousin's bangs through the crowd, the jiggling of her arm when she shook a cocktail. Eva was already preparing her explanation: *You probably don't remember me.* Someone's beer slopped onto the place where her boots had been a second earlier. Lorrie's cousin's eyes flicked back and forth, passing efficiently over her face. Of course she didn't recognize her. Eva was flooded with relief.

Anonymity emboldened her, and a gin and tonic emboldened her some more. For the next hour, while the band finished its set, Eva stared at people openly, daringly: at the man who burped into his elbow, at the woman who nervously twisted her eyebrows, checking her fingertips for the tiny hairs that she'd pulled out. She didn't pretend she wasn't eavesdropping on the person who said, "There's got to be a limit to how much you can love someone in a foreign language." One of the bartenders wove through the crowd holding a broom above his head, and the person's friend responded, "Love *is* a foreign language."

The band wore all white. They weren't famous and they weren't that young, but they were men, so there was still time. Eva liked the songs, even though they all sounded pretty much the same. While they played, she constructed various fantasies about the drummer, who kept his eyes shut most of the time. There was a certain romance in imagining his eyes open and up close. She only had cash for one more drink, so she waited, watching people sway and bob in various approximations of release, leaning against a wall that was damp with someone else's sweat. But when the show was over, the drummer disappeared, and it was the guitarist who asked what she was drinking. She'd been holding onto her cup—chewed ice, chewed lime—in preparation for exactly this question, but when she looked down at the bar it was gone.

"Nothing," she said, bewildered.

"Oh, totally," the man said apologetically, as if he'd made a mistake. He ordered two seltzers.

There was a moment in which she could have explained the misunderstanding, and then the moment passed. Eva sipped the seltzer and tried to look appreciative. The man explained that most bands got drunk before they performed.

"But it fucks with my rhythm."

He was long-haired and broad-shouldered, and Eva wasn't sure if she found him attractive, so she asked herself whether someone else would have found him attractive. The guitarist was looking at her expectantly.

"Sorry," she said. There was an empty cup in her hand again. "What did you say?"

Did she want to get out of here?

His apartment made no sense. It was hardly furnished—a chair, no couch, a table lamp on the floor—but all the shelves were cluttered. On the kitchen counter: an electric coffee grinder, a hand coffee grinder, a panini press, a blender, a wok, a tiny pan the size of one fried egg. She wished, with a desperation that unnerved her, to be drunk. She wished, even, to pretend to be drunk.

His tongue felt like a tentacle, probing. He kept asking, "Is this okay?" Eventually, she found herself repeating it in her head, like a mantra: *This is okay.*

Eva barely slept. The first time she woke up, the guitar next to the bed looked like an animal. She sat upright, naked, with no idea where she was. Then she remembered and went looking for her phone, which had run out of battery in the pocket of her jeans. When it came back to life, she learned that Eli had won the race. *Good for him.* She made herself say it out loud.

"Good for him."

In the morning, she left before breakfast—there was only one chair, only the one-egg pan—and on the train back to school she fell instantly asleep. She dreamed that she was on a stage, and when she looked down at the notes in her hand, she realized that she had written a speech when actually she was supposed to sing a song. Her parents were in the audience, wearing shirts with her face on them. They were embracing, so that half of the face on one shirt pressed into half of the face on the other shirt—not quite symmetrically, but almost. They rocked back and forth, looking up at her, waiting for her to begin.

WHAT'S IT LIKE?

On a Sunday morning, Eva stayed in bed and scrolled through the missed-connections website. She had assumed it didn't even exist anymore, its quaint, shot-in-the-dark approach to destiny eclipsed by algorithms that promised not only to determine your fate but to optimize it. Yet here it was. Or here they were—the missed and the missing.

We locked eyes in the elevator. You pressed floor five.

We stopped at a red light. Your bike, my car. You turned left.

Where did you go?

Eva herself wasn't looking for anyone, and she doubted anyone was looking for her. It had been three months since she'd moved to Washington, D.C.—four months since she'd graduated—and these days the only strangers she made eye contact with were babies. Holding a child's attention over the hard plastic seats on the bus or over someone's shoulder at the grocery store could turn her whole day around, briefly stilling the fears that gathered strength as she faded further into what was called the real world, a world where her black sweater and gray slacks and white phone were as unmemorable—as unreal—as everyone else's. But in the speechless, amazed eyes of a baby, she felt briefly distinct. A baby could tell if you were good or bad. Adults pretended to have these same powers of discernment, but after years of judging and being judged, they no longer knew how to simply look.

We traded dollar bills in the laundromat. Mine was too crinkled for the machine.

You paid for my coffee. No milk, no sugar, one ice cube.

The authors of these posts were called users, as everyone on the Internet was. They described the people they were looking for in precise and tender detail—red hair was auburn or chestnut, moles were beauty marks, smiles flashed and sparkled—but rarely described themselves. Maybe it was too risky, in that sea of strangers, to try to conjure their own image out of someone else's memory: *Remember me?* Maybe they knew that what people really wanted had nothing to do with the other users—what they really wanted was the swoon of recognition when someone shows you to yourself.

The site probably didn't work. There were surely more unhappy endings to these stories than happy ones. But the genius of it was in giving you only beginnings, and this was another way in which Eva accepted she was like everyone else: she, too, wanted a fresh start.

There were reasons to hope. Her summer jobs at the newspaper had turned into an actual job, just as she had planned. The apartment where she lived was a little bigger, a little nicer than the last one she'd shared. She stayed alert for other signs of progress. At the office, everyone labeled their lunches in the fridge (DON'T EAT), but on Fridays there were doughnuts, and then all her co-workers—glazed fingertips, palming crumbs into their mouths—seemed more approachable. At the corner store, the cashier wore big, padded headphones and nodded blankly when she asked for the tampons behind the counter, but when she asked louder, he gave her a thumbs-up and pulled all the options off the shelf (lite, regular, ultra), as if there was nothing to be embarrassed about. Of course there wasn't. On days like that, on good days, Eva knew better than to believe the corny stuff they'd said at graduation, but some part of her did anyway: the horizon was big, the future was hers.

There were less good days. No free breakfast, no acts of grace. She slumped at her desk and didn't proofread her emails to her boss. Her neck hurt—her wrists, too. She probably had a vitamin D deficiency. Googling, she learned that 91 percent of office workers did. Sometimes she held the elevator for her neighbor, and sometimes she jabbed at the button again and again, willing the doors to close while she was still alone. It was an old, slow elevator, and every time she rode it, she worried about getting stuck.

On one of the less good days, a Friday night without plans, Eva lost several hours to the Internet. A little before midnight, her roommate knocked on the door. Eva erased her browsing history—it wasn't embarrassing, but she was glad to see it disappear—and closed her computer.

"Come in," she said, trying to sound upbeat.

Molly was always upbeat. She was almost thirty, but to Eva she seemed more like a teenager. She was obsessed with trends—what was in, what was out. She saved up to buy tickets to big stadium concerts and told Eva that the thing she missed most about home was the mall. It was only after months of living together—every morning Molly offered to make Eva a smoothie, and every morning Eva declined—that Eva learned anything else about what home meant. Molly had grown up in South Carolina, where her dad was the pastor at a megachurch, a kind of local celebrity. Then, one Christmas, hundreds of files of child pornography were discovered on his computer. Molly had been the one to discover them. After her dad went to prison, the rest of Molly's family, her mom and her brothers, had moved to a different small town. She talked about them every now and then, but rarely about the place, or the people, that they'd left behind. She hadn't been to church in years. Once, Eva asked if she missed anything besides the mall, but Molly just smiled her same sunny smile: no, that was pretty much it.

"Let's do your moon point," she said that Friday, perched on the edge of Eva's bed.

Molly did everything she could to stay healthy—balanced. She couldn't afford acupuncture, but she read websites about tension release and ordered tiny vials of essential oils. The moon point, she explained, was in between the index finger and the thumb, where the flesh felt soft and hard at once, like a raw chicken breast. According to a blog, it was one of the most important points for pain relief.

"Dental pain, especially."

"Okay," Eva said, putting her hand in Molly's lap.

"Maybe you grind your teeth."

"I don't."

"Clench, at least."

"Sure," Eva said. "Maybe."

Molly warned her that it might feel like something was opening, like something was being unlocked. This sounded pleasant, like the satisfying pop of a car trunk, the release of heat when it yawns all the way open. Molly pressed down and looked at Eva hopefully.

"Cool," Eva said, uncertainly.

Molly let go. "That's enough for now."

Once Eva was alone, she vowed not to go back online, because she didn't want to be misled. On the Internet, the world was built out of links, and searches always led to results. When her laptop's battery ran out of charge—when it died—it could still come back to life.

. . .

Jamie had not moved out of her parents' house. At a certain point, not moving out meant the same thing as moving in, but no one ever put it that way. Not to Eva, at least. Maybe they had all sat down and discussed it. A candid, careful conversation. Or maybe it had just happened, the result of some force—habit or inertia, desire or fate—that seemed bigger and stronger than they were. Eva assumed he slept in her bedroom, because there was nowhere else for him to sleep. Now he had been there for an entire year.

Eva called her parents on the weekends, and sometimes they mentioned Jamie and sometimes they didn't. Her dad said that he was working at an after-school program nearby.

"Arts and crafts, that kind of thing," Nick said. "He's always had a good eye."

"He has?"

Later, her mom said that he'd found a job at a computer-repair shop in the neighborhood.

"What about the after-school thing?" Eva wanted to know.

"He has a knack for technology," Gail said.

"Why does he even need a job? He's rich."

Which was how Eva found out that Jamie refused to speak to his parents and refused to accept their money. *No,* she heard Nick correcting in the background—they refused to give it.

"Are *you* giving him money?"

Nick picked up the other phone, and then Eva could hear him clearly.

"He wouldn't accept it," he said.

Wouldn't or hadn't? She didn't ask, because she wasn't sure if she wanted to know.

"That's not the kind of redistribution he believes in," Gail explained. She was standing close enough to Nick that Eva could hear her voice through both phones—her teacher voice. In this case, Eva considered pointing out, wasn't she the student?

"Do you?" she asked. "Believe in it, I mean."

"I'm interested in it."

But Gail was interested in everything. She wasn't, as far as Eva could tell, attached to anything.

"Jamie can be very persuasive," Nick said. "You know, some people say persuasion is an art. And he does have a certain—"

"Artistic sensibility. You've told me."

When Eva hung up, she wanted to complain to someone. Molly was in the kitchen, unloading groceries and mouthing lyrics to a song Eva couldn't hear. Molly's groceries never made any sense: meat and fake meat, whole milk and yogurt made from nuts. She said everything was worth trying. If she liked the label, she bought it.

"Oh no," she said when she saw Eva. She took her earbuds out.

"What?"

"You look like you're about to cry."

"I do?"

Eva looked around, as if for a mirror, but there was just a blurry reflection in the microwave door. Molly probably thought crying was cathartic, and she was probably right. Eva didn't say she missed her parents, because Molly had a better reason to miss hers. They hugged, and Molly reminded Eva about vitamin D supplements. Also sunshine.

Jamie made a trip to D.C. at the beginning of winter, the city's least interesting season. Snow, if it ever arrived, was pretty and feeble and dissolved on impact, unable to make a lasting mark. The city's residents, steadily losing interest on the other side of their fogged-up windows, were deprived of the drama of being buried, the calm of being covered, the satisfaction of digging yourself out. It was changeless and uninspired.

Jamie didn't tell her he was coming until he was on his way. That wasn't so unusual—he had never arrived announced—but what had once seemed like boyish spontaneity now made her a little uneasy.

Molly, sitting on the kitchen counter, legs dangling, wanted to know what Jamie was like.

"What is he like?" Eva repeated.

Molly looked up from her phone, where she was scrolling through swimsuits. Swimsuits were always on sale in the winter.

"You know, his personality." She glanced down and clicked on a striped bikini. "Or his interests. What is he into?"

Eva bristled. A dumb question. No one could be mashed up into a lot of traits and a few hobbies. Except, of course, it was a question she herself asked all the time, a desire so basic it should have had a name, like hunger or thirst: the desire to get to the essence of things. What *was* Jamie into? Art? Politics? Enlightenment? Software? And what was he out of? He seemed to be continually changing, and yet any minute now he would appear at the door as he always did—entirely, unmistakably himself.

They went to the Natural History Museum, because museums were free. Eva invited Molly, not expecting her to say yes (she was only being polite) and Molly agreed enthusiastically. While the three of them wandered through the Hall of Mammals, Eva tried to get Jamie to talk about his life.

"So—why computers?"

Jamie stopped beneath a pedestal where a tiger was posed on its hind legs, its massive paws reaching toward a gazelle's velvety neck. Many of the taxidermy animals in the museum were more than a hundred years old, but they looked not only new but eerily undead. The tiger was more frightening than you might think.

"It's just a job," Jamie said.

"But how did you learn? Aren't there lots of different codes?"

"Different languages," Molly corrected, which surprised Eva. Since when did she know anything about computers?

"I've been thinking about vocations," Jamie said. "Not looking for them or anything, but thinking about them."

It was tempting to imagine that the tiger had died in exactly this pose, frozen in the same scene they were now witnessing a century later. Eva knew that wasn't how it worked, but she didn't like imagining the taxidermist as he manipulated the creature's limbs, lifting one paw and then the other, like guiding a child into a fresh pair of clothes.

"I looked it up, actually," Jamie continued, moving to the next display. "Vocation is from *vocare*. To call. Profession is from *profiteri*. To declare publicly."

"Okay." Eva didn't remember any Latin. "A call and a response."

"That's a Christian thing," Molly said eagerly. "Like, called to serve."

In front of them, several flying squirrels were displayed in midair. A caption explained that the squirrels didn't actually have wings—what looked like flight was just a leap of faith.

"No one talks about servants anymore," Jamie said. "But everyone talks about callings. Work is our religion now."

Eva glanced at Molly, wondering how she would react.

"Maybe it was inevitable," Jamie went on. "I mean, we already worship money."

"But—" Molly stopped, her mouth slightly open.

Now Jamie was looking at her, too.

"Never mind," Molly said.

Jamie shrugged, but he kept watching her, no longer paying attention to the squirrels. Eva could tell that he was curious—but about what? It made her briefly, unbearably furious: not to know how to ask.

"Let's go," she said impatiently.

Eva took them upstairs to the minerals and gems. These were always her favorite exhibits, dimly lit displays that made people lower their voices. The gems themselves were striking yet simple—boring, even—but she liked to wander from one glass case to another with no paintings to interpret, no wall text to squint at, no particular information to absorb.

Eva worried that Jamie wouldn't share this pleasure. He might dislike precious stones for the same reason he disliked money, might tell her that what she thought was wonder was really just value. Her phone buzzed in her pocket.

It was an email from her boss. He was traveling in Europe. There was a pile of papers on his desk. Could she possibly? He was sorry to impose. He acknowledged it was a Saturday.

Eva felt a flash of pride when she told Jamie and Molly that she had a work emergency. She said her boss was in Europe, and she didn't say that he was on vacation. She didn't go so far as to say that she had been called, but the lesser, cruder fact was still true: she had been asked.

The task took longer than she expected. She had never been on the other side of her boss's desk. It was a mess. Not one pile of papers but many, sheets pushed into haystacks, marked up with a pen that smudged. There were mugs with coffee hardened at the bottom and a picture frame with the picture slipping out of view. Spotting a notepad covered in doodles, Eva instinctively averted her eyes; it wasn't important, but still, it seemed private. In the end, once she had found what she needed, Eva did look at the drawings—loops and spirals, his own name in bubble letters—as a kind of reward for not doing any of the more invasive things she would have liked to: open his drawers, flip through his notebooks, listen to the voicemail blinking red on his phone. She didn't look at the documents he'd requested, either, but that was for her sake, not his. She hoped they were important. She couldn't risk giving up the hope.

When Eva finally made her way back to the museum, Jamie and Molly were sitting on the front steps. Jamie had two soft pretzels, one in each hand, and he was chewing intently, big crystals of salt showering onto his lap. Eva knew right away that something had shifted between the two of them, but she didn't know how she knew. Their torsos were half turned toward each other, like the twin shells of a clam. Had something changed in Molly's face?

On the bus home, no one said much. Eva asked if they had liked the gems, and Molly seemed distracted, as if she had to work to retrieve the memory. Yes, they were nice. Maybe, Eva thought, whatever had happened with Jamie was romantic. Maybe they had grazed hands in a ruby-lit room or in the sharp glare of diamonds on a velvet cushion. Maybe Molly had leaned in to see the intricate internal structure of beryl (Eva's favorite, an emerald that seemed to contain many replicas of itself), and her hair had brushed Jamie's cheek. These possibilities, instead of threatening Eva, reassured her. Ordinary romance, after all, was not unknowable. It was a story that only ever ended in two, unoriginal ways.

Jamie asked to stay for dinner. Molly was the one who cooked, so she was the one who said yes. He didn't ask if he could help, he just helped. He showed her a trick for peeling garlic cloves and another for cutting onions: stick out your tongue. They laughed together, pink tongues pointing in the air, and maybe that was romance, too—silly and innocent. Eva laughed with them.

When they had finished eating, Eva asked Jamie about her parents. "How are they doing? Are they all right?"

Jamie smiled.

"What's funny?"

"It's just—they ask me the same thing about you."

What could he tell them? He rarely called her anymore. He didn't know the names of her friends or the title of her job. He might have been surprised to learn that she could run twelve miles, that she was reading a lot of poetry—writing some, too—that she had a recurring nightmare in which she was the star of a play whose script she had never read.

What *did* he tell them? Eva gathered the empty plates, streaked red with pasta sauce, and stacked them like a fortress in front of her.

"Your dad seems—I don't know. Older, but not older in the usual sense. Older like you can tell he's lived more life. Like he's more alive."

"More energetic?"

"The other day he said, *You know, grown-ups keep growing up, too*."

Molly pushed her chair back and took the stack of plates from Eva. "Not all grown-ups."

She said it in her usual upbeat voice, almost as if it were a joke. Eva watched her at the sink, rinsing each plate and then each fork and then each knife. All afternoon, the expression on her face had been abstract, but now it was solid again. Long strands of spaghetti slipped down the drain. She had probably told Jamie everything—about her dad, about her discovery, the before, the after. She scrubbed the dishes, and they disappeared into foam. Jamie got up and helped Molly clean. That was usually Eva's job, but she stayed where she was, marveling at their graceful choreography in the small kitchen, never bumping into each other or reaching across each other. They weren't friends, exactly. They had only known each other for an afternoon and they might never see each other again. What had happened wasn't romance—she could see that now. It was trust.

ARE YOU WITH US?

In the spring, Nick told Eva that Jamie's computer job, like all the other jobs, had ended. Now he spent most days at the church.

"What church?"

"He hasn't told you about the church?"

There were thousands of churches in Brooklyn, brick spires all over the skyline, some of them centuries old. But this church wasn't one of the historic ones; it was new, trendy. A labor organizer Jamie knew—one of the guys from the tents, as Nick put it—had helped start it, then hired Jamie as the tech-support guy. It was the kind of church with PowerPoint presentations. The job itself didn't seem very demanding, but lately Jamie was spending more and more time there. On Sundays, he slipped out before anyone else in the house was awake.

Eva had a lot of questions. Who led the church? Who belonged to it? What did it stand for? Nick didn't have many answers.

"Stand for?" he said. "I don't think that's how it works. A church isn't a cause."

"Isn't it?"

"Well," he admitted. "I don't know."

"But you haven't asked."

"I have not asked."

Eva thought of all the things that she, too, had never spoken aloud. It pissed her off: Nick's ignorance, her cowardice, Jamie's—Jamie's what? You couldn't be pissed off at someone for going to church.

Since he moved in with her parents, Eva had taken comfort in picturing Jamie on his back, staring at the same ceiling she had stared at for years. When she was young, she'd pretended that the ceiling was the sky and the cracks were constellations. But actual constellations were notoriously difficult to recognize: one person saw a goat and another saw a triangle; what someone called a belt could be reduced to a shaky line of dots. Why had she assumed—worse than that, why had she hoped—that she and Jamie would try to see the same thing?

After she and Nick hung up, Eva moved around the apartment anxiously, aimlessly. She rearranged things on shelves, picked up dishes in the sink as if to wash them, then put them back down, intention already slipping away from her. Finally, to escape Molly's sympathetic looks, she went outside.

For weeks, the city had been at its prettiest. Tourists came just to see the flowers, and the flowers obliged. They emerged in sequence, one raucous color after another, vying for the grandest entrance to the party. Ethereal cherries—hard, recalcitrant buds that suddenly burst into clouds of pale pink—were bested by ostentatious azaleas, in fuchsia, coral, scarlet; not even the white was demure, its shock of blossoms like a gaudy wedding dress. Magnolias, all eroticism, were followed by dogwoods, all elegance.

But like any party, it was ugly when it was over. Petals had wilted and been trampled all over the ground. Eva trampled them some more. A night of rain had made even the most persistent flowers hang their heads. Taking note of the muddy ruin, Eva vowed not to forget it—to steel herself next year, when the trees would once again tempt her, when the tourists with their clunky cameras and narrow lenses would let themselves be tempted.

In May, Eva forgot about Mother's Day. She sent a card late: a red carnation on the front. Gail insisted that she didn't care about the holiday—she resisted all forms of sentimentality, or at least all displays of it—but after the card arrived, she asked if Eva would come home.

"I want to see you, that's all."

Guiltily, Eva wondered how to say no. She had made time for her parents—invited them to D.C., gone on a rare family vacation—but she was avoiding New York.

"Where will I stay?" she asked.

"What do you mean?"

"My bedroom."

"Oh," Gail said. "We'll figure it out." After a second, she added, "It's so beautiful here."

Eva took the Metro to the Amtrak to the subway. On trains, she never did anything but look out the window. Planes offered a more dramatic perspective, but bird's-eye views lacked specificity. What she really wanted was to see into someone's backyard—the fence rattling, the kids waving as the train hurtled by. A whole trip could pass like that, following passengers in her mind: off the platform to the parking lot, then all the way back to their driveways, where they might be greeted by dogs and families, or where they might press their foreheads against steering wheels in the suburban posture of despair. And so by the time Eva was making her own way down the platform in New York, she was able to think of her journey as a story that didn't quite belong to her, that might have emerged, limitless with potential, from some stranger's imagination.

Farther north, it was as if the season had reversed itself. Leaves were just beginning to unfurl, and the most hopeful pedestrians shed their coats and shivered in anticipation. Even Eva, who knew what came next—squashed flowers, squelching ground—could not deny the sense of possibility. When, at last, she turned onto her parents' street, there was an enormous inflated Easter Bunny, as tall as Eva, at the bottom of someone's stoop, one ear sticking up, the other flopping down. It must have been there for weeks. She walked a little faster, wanting someone to laugh about it with.

But the house was quiet when she got there. It was small enough that she would have heard right away if someone was home. Upstairs, she inspected her room from the threshold of the door, looking for what had changed. It was like one of those kids' puzzles: how many differences between these pictures can you find? None, it turned out. The room looked just as it always had. Maybe this meant that Jamie had left everything exactly as he'd found it, but instead Eva pictured him carefully restoring order before she arrived, undoing all the changes he'd made, erasing all the ways that he had made the space his own. Now it possessed a secret, alternate life; what she saw before her seemed like merely a flimsy set.

She ran her hand along the bookshelf, and when she got to the window, she saw that they were home after all—all three of them sitting cross-legged in the yard. Jamie's tent was there, too, the same one Eva had been inside at the protest, but it looked bigger now, all on its own. From up above, Eva could see the shiny top of Nick's bald head and the part in Jamie's hair, which was long again, the longest she'd ever seen it. Her mom's hair was different—dyed a dirty blond that was probably supposed to mask the gray. Her fake color was almost exactly the same as Jamie's real color.

Because Eva didn't look like her parents in any meaningful way, she had always envied family resemblances: a jumble of redheads piled in a station wagon, matching eyes peering out of a professional portrait. Eva had the same muddy brown eyes as her dad, but so did a lot of people. The mole on her right foot was the mirror image of the mole on her mom's left foot, but no one ever saw that.

Suddenly Jamie looked up at her, and then her parents were looking, too. Eva's first instinct was to step back from the window. On the train, speeding anonymously past one house after another, she could see without being seen. Now she had no choice: they waved and she waved back.

They did normal family stuff. Took a picnic to the park, went to the movies, argued about something in the newspaper. Jamie disappeared for hours at a time, and Eva wasn't sure if this was politeness—not wanting to intrude—or privacy. Her parents never asked him where he'd been.

He really did sleep in the tent. On Saturday before it got dark, Eva and Jamie sat in the yard, alone for the first time since she'd arrived, facing each other in matching mildewed lawn chairs. The fly was off the tent, and she could see his sleeping bag unfurled inside. He said the forecast was good enough that he might even sleep under the stars, not that there would be any stars to see. Sleeping outside, he'd realized how rare real darkness was in the city. They both looked up at the sky—watered-down blue, dissolving clouds—and while their heads were tilted back, he invited her to church the next morning.

Eva looked down but he was still looking up. She refused to take this for granted. "What church?"

"I haven't told you about the church?"

"No," she said, more fiercely than she intended. A squirrel perched on the fence behind Jamie was staring at her. She stared back. "You haven't told me anything."

Jamie shrugged, as if it wasn't a big deal, and this seemed unlike him—unlike, at least, the way Eva remembered him. Hadn't he understood, better than anyone, the proper weight of things? The squirrel's eyes were all pupils, glassy black beads that never blinked.

"It's not what you think," Jamie said.

"How do you know what I think?"

"It's a church, but it's more like a prayer group. Or even like a reading group."

Eva didn't reply.

"You like reading," he said.

This was true, but Eva was annoyed that he had pointed it out. The squirrel stopped staring and scurried down the fence, disappearing behind Jamie's tent with a flourish of its tail.

"I'll come," she said.

They biked across town early the next morning. Eva hadn't been on a bike in years, and it was scarier than she remembered. A man scampered into the street, ignoring a red light, and Eva had to swerve to avoid him.

"What the fuck," she shouted. Jamie, riding ahead of her, twisted his head around in surprise. At the next light, he took hold of her handlebars.

"You can't do that," he said.

"Do what?"

The light turned green, and she shook his hand off her bike, pedaling past him through the intersection—wobblier than she would have hoped.

The church was in a big open space above a fried-chicken restaurant. Sun streamed through unwashed windows, and the room smelled like grease. Long ago, it had been a doctor's office, then a yoga studio, now this.

"One kind of healing after another," a man named Kenny said, smiling wryly.

Kenny seemed to be the one in charge. There were twenty or

thirty people in the room. No pews, just folding chairs and a few inconvenient pillars. At the front of the room, a projector screen had been set up, along with an electric keyboard and a microphone stand. A couple of the people in the chairs were old—a gray-haired woman wizened like a bird, a man in orthopedic shoes—but mostly they were young, wearing T-shirts, checking their phones. Someone jiggled a baby on her knee. More than half of the audience was white, the rest mostly Latino. There was a pair of Black men, the older one wearing a suit, looking unimpressed by the casual crowd. Kenny, who greeted everyone in English and then in Spanish, couldn't have been older than forty.

Jamie made sure the projector and the piano were plugged in, then took a seat beside Eva in the back row, near the outlet. They all stood up to sing. Just one song, and Eva wasn't sure she could have endured another—the synthy chords and awful lyrics, something about God having your back, holding your hand. A few people in the crowd stretched out their arms, as if this were more than a metaphor.

Kenny was the keyboardist and also the pastor. He wore a button-down shirt and unripped jeans, a small gold hoop in his ear.

"He went to the same college as you," Jamie whispered to Eva. "But he was a heroin addict before that."

Kenny didn't use the microphone. His singing voice had blended indistinguishably with everyone else's, but his speaking voice was deep and not always smooth, scratching, occasionally breaking, without any trace of embarrassment. Eva had expected a more conventional sort of charisma. She was not naïve enough to have imagined Bible thumping or rapturous fits; still, she had assumed some sort of performance was required. But Kenny was not a salesman, not a showman, not even an especially energetic host. He was the kind of host who set conversation in motion, then sat back, passing dishes and refilling glasses, and only later, when you found yourself beside him at the kitchen sink, when all the talk had slowed to an awkward spin, turned out to know enough to keep the dialogue going all by himself.

"I keep thinking about the gospel of Mark," Kenny said. "My favorite gospel."

It sounded more like an offhand remark than the opening of a sermon. Favorites were everyday preferences: white or wheat, Colgate or Crest—not Mark or Luke.

"If you read a book as many times as I've read the Bible, you're allowed to like some parts more than others," Kenny said. Several people laughed, and Eva stiffened at the possibility: had he known what she was thinking?

He liked Mark best, Kenny went on, because Mark showed Jesus's many selves; he showed the pain of multiplicity—of being both man and God, beloved and despised, alive and destined to die.

"When Mark recounts Jesus's parables," Kenny said, "the point isn't just to show the depth of all that Jesus understood. The point is also to see the agony of being *mis*understood.

"We've all felt that agony, so why shouldn't Jesus have felt it, too? We think of him as a teacher, but how many teachers are perfect? Jesus was opaque and stubborn and confusing. In fact, a lot of the time he sounds less like a patient teacher and more like an impatient student. You know the type—the student who knows more than all the other students, who wants them to learn faster and think bigger, who doesn't understand why they can't see what he sees."

This way of talking about religious figures was disconcerting, as if they were all just regular guys. Jesus. Mark. Kenny. It didn't seem so different from what nonbelievers insisted—that the legendary be made ordinary, that the man who walked on water be seen as a pedestrian like any other.

"If Jesus was impatient for everyone else to understand, you might wonder why he didn't make himself more easily understood. Why he spoke in elaborate metaphors and mysterious prophecies, why he was always being so—well, being so weird.

"There are Christians who think that all the cryptic stuff, the weird stuff, is a kind of test. A way to find out which believers get it. It's an idea you see across a lot of religions—that God, whoever he is, is always testing us. But that's such a sad, small kind of faith, don't you think? A faith for the few, for the best, the brightest, the good-grade getters. How many people here got bad grades?"

All over the room, hands went up. Jamie raised his without hesitating, and Eva, her fingers laced in her lap, felt ashamed. Even once Jamie lowered his arm, she was afraid to look at him.

"What if the whole point is that belief is hard to get? What if the truth is that Jesus himself was sometimes confused—sometimes terrified—by just how powerful faith could be?"

On the screen behind Kenny, a paragraph of text appeared: the parable of the bleeding woman. Kenny asked for a volunteer to read aloud, and a man in the front row raised his hand. Eva could only see the back of the man's head, the sheen of hair gelled into place, and when he spoke, his voice was not commanding, barely loud enough to hear. (If she spoke like that, Eva thought, she would know better than to speak in front of a group.)

According to the parable, the bleeding woman had been hemorrhaging for twelve years, a steady ebb of life that no doctor could stop. She sought out Jesus as a last resort: she'd heard about his miracles, and needed one for herself. When she found him, he was in a crowd with his back to her, surrounded by other miracle-seekers. She reached out to touch his cloak, and in an instant, for the first time in over a decade, the blood stopped. Without saying a single word—not who she was or what she needed—she had been healed.

The man with the gelled hair saw too late where the story was headed and tried to add a final note of triumph, but his timid voice just lilted strangely.

"Keep going," Kenny said encouragingly, clicking ahead to the next PowerPoint slide, where only one sentence appeared. "This is the most important part."

The man cleared his throat.

"Immediately aware that power had gone forth from him, Jesus turned about in the crowd and said, *Who touched my clothes?*"

Kenny stepped back in front of the screen.

"Power had gone forth from him," he repeated. "Jesus didn't release the power—it escaped him. So he did what any of us would have done: he whirled around to see who had taken it.

"Can you imagine," Kenny asked the room, "having that much power? A power that can transform people, and yet a power that you can't completely control?"

Eva could see that the gelled-hair man was nodding, and he wasn't the only one. She watched Kenny scan the rows of bobbing heads and approving looks, and for a moment their eyes met. She looked away.

"The thing is, you do have that power," Kenny said, while Eva stared furiously at her hands. "You don't have to be a god to wonder at the force of your effect on someone else. Maybe even to fear it."

In other parables, Kenny explained, Jesus was not quite so surprised by his miracles. A blind man is made to see. A paralyzed man stands up and walks.

"Most people think that's his most impressive stuff. We call that kind of talent a gift. But this parable tells us about another kind of gift, one that's there for the taking, that you don't have to ask for and that you definitely don't have to earn. The gift is grace, and all you have to do is reach out and try to touch it."

Kenny took a long drink from a plastic water bottle, stopping only when the bottle had crumpled in his hand. "So. Why don't you? Why don't you just reach out?"

Outside, a door below them must have opened: there were shouts and kitchen sounds and a bag of glass bottles tossed onto the ground. The smell of French fries, which Eva had managed to forget, now seemed impossible to ignore.

Kenny repeated himself. "Why don't you just reach out?"

He said it seriously but gently, the way you might coax the truth out of a child. In the instant before Jamie spoke, Eva knew that he would be the one to speak:

"Because then what?"

In the rows ahead of them, people twisted in their seats to look at him, their faces visible for the first time—open, eager faces.

"Because when you reach out," Jamie continued, "you can't be sure what will reach back."

Kenny nodded, letting these words fill the room, as if they were a special truth that needed time to be absorbed. There was no denying that he was watching Eva now, and this time she didn't let herself break his gaze. There was moisture on the back of her neck and between and under her breasts.

"It might turn out to be nothing," Kenny said. "A piece of fabric between our fingers, as ordinary as the clothes on your own back, or else it might turn out to be everything."

Now Eva was really sweating. All these open faces, and wasn't openness what she had wanted? To be let in? A room of strangers stared at Jamie in wonder, as if he'd said exactly what they'd been thinking. The old, birdlike woman smiled sagely. The baby clapped his palms in delight: *Again!*

No, not again. Eva leaned forward in her chair, her shirt pulling away from the plastic, leaving a damp shape on her back. When Kenny clicked to the next slide, she stood up and walked out of the room. In the concrete stairwell, she started to run, her footsteps loud and fast, echoing her, mocking her. *What are you so afraid of?*

She had thought that Jamie wanted to show her something. She had thought—had let herself think—that the something was him. It wasn't until she was out on the street, unlocking her bike, that she realized she'd left her helmet under her folding chair. Jamie would bring it home, of course—he didn't forget things like that. She'd have to thank him. But she wouldn't mean it, she decided, kicking off the curb and pushing out into traffic, her hair blowing wildly across her face.

The sun was setting when Eva got back to D.C. Not a breathtaking sunset, no streaks of gold or purple—just a pink haze and a fingernail moon dangling above her. Molly wasn't home, but they texted each other more or less identical pictures of the sky. Eva poured herself a glass of water, charged her phone, and unpacked her bags right away. This was important. If she left the bags where they were, in the middle of the rug in the middle of her room, they would stay there. Over the course of the next several days, she might unzip them to remove essential items—glasses, underwear, the pair of socks she preferred to all her other pairs of socks—but the bags would get heavier, more solid, more unassailable.

When she was finished unpacking, she sat on the edge of her bed and listened to a mindfulness app that Molly had recommended. Molly said that after you'd been in transit it was important to get grounded. This was either a stupid phrase or the perfect phrase. Eva slid off the bed so that she was sitting on the floor. For seven minutes, the voice from the app instructed her to observe where her thoughts and feelings arose in the body. Everything, she learned, arose in the body. She listened attentively to the voice, but she wasn't entirely convinced. Most of the time, her anxiety seemed more like something that surrounded her than something that emerged from within her. If she was observing herself from above, as she often felt she was, it might have been mist, enveloping her head, making it almost impossible to see her own face.

She closed the app and went back to her routine. Once she'd showered—a methodical progression through the many bottles lined up on the edge of the tub—she wrote out a grocery list. It would have been easy enough to memorize, but she wanted the pleasure of crossing things off. On the bus to the store, she googled complicated recipes that she would never actually make, that called for mysterious equipment she didn't own: zesters, immersion blenders. Immersion sounded nice.

The store was terribly organized, but Eva had studied it carefully and could move efficiently from one necessity to another. She was rounding the corner where the cereal aisle turned into the cleaning-product aisle when she saw Eli, a red shopping basket hanging from his arm, empty except for a package of twin toothbrushes. He was staring listlessly at a shelf of olive oil, but he turned when he saw her. For a few seconds, they just stared at each other.

"You look like you're about to accuse me of something," he said at last.

"Do you live here?"

"I hope that's not a crime."

"How did I not know that?" Eva asked.

He shrugged. The toothbrushes slid from one end of the basket to the other.

"Did you know *I* lived here?" she said.

He didn't answer, because at the same time, an old woman, small and hunched over, reached out and touched his elbow.

"You're tall," she said, in a throaty voice.

He laughed. "I'm not."

"Taller than me! Reach that bottle for me, will you?" She pointed to a row of red-wine vinegars.

"Of course."

Eli stretched his arm toward the highest shelf, his shirt rising up to reveal the soft, hairless skin of his hip. He touched the woman's hand as he passed her the bottle, and Eva thought she saw her blush.

When Eli asked if Eva wanted to cook dinner together, the question did not seem difficult or dangerous. Maybe he *had* been avoiding her, but did it matter? Maybe this was just another thing to cross off the list, or maybe it was the thing she hadn't known she wanted.

They went to her apartment. It was late, Molly's door already closed. Eva showed Eli how to caramelize onions—"patience"—and he told her that mayonnaise was the secret to the perfect grilled cheese. The bread turned golden. The cheese sizzled when it melted onto the pan. She made salad dressing, lemon juice stinging her fingers where she'd bitten the nails too short, and tossed the leaves until they glistened. There was salt scattered carelessly all over the countertop, but you could only see it in a certain light. They ate side by side, chewing loudly, their lips and hands shiny with grease. The salad shone, too. Eva felt the pleasure all through her body—the taste in her mouth, the warmth in her throat, something like gratitude all the way down in her gut. It was almost enough. But more was better, and this was another conviction her body told her, or gave her: that she could take even more, that she could feel even better.

They washed their hands, but they didn't wash the dishes. They left them in the sink. Eli touched her hips and then her face. He tasted like garlic, which was how she knew that she did, too. Eva took him to her room, where the empty suitcase lay open in the middle of the floor. It had been a long time since she'd had sex, and though she always told herself that didn't matter, the truth was that it did. She had forgotten the feeling, and now she remembered. She was aware, therefore, that this moment was about to be a memory, too. His breath in her ear, his mouth on her stomach, the strange and thrilling fact that he had touched parts of her that she never had. A memory that would become a possibility: if he could only go deeper, get closer, he might tell her something that she didn't already know.

HOW COULD YOU?

Many people worship a silent God. For them, hearing his voice is a mark of special favor—the kind of thing that only happens to prophets. But if God is really that far away, it's only because we're keeping him there. It may not be easy to accept that God isn't listening to your prayers, but it's actually much harder to accept that he is. To accept that when you ask, he'll answer. For one thing, people will think you're crazy. Believing in God is okay, but talking to God? That's for people in cults, for the guy on the corner warning about the end of the world.

What I want to tell you today is that it's for everyone. You can have a conversation with Jesus—an ongoing, ordinary conversation. You can talk to him about your boss or your breakup or not being able to pay the rent. Does that sound too boring for God? I assure you it's not. Faith is as mundane as it is profound. It's something you have to do every day.

There was a video camera at the back of the church. Probably Jamie, in charge of all the tech stuff, had been the one to put it there. Every week, you could watch the sermons online in real time. Eva never watched the whole thing, because that would have felt, in some sense, like a defeat—like letting him win. (Who was *he*? Jamie? Kenny? Jesus? She didn't know.) But it became a kind of ritual to listen to Kenny's voice for a few minutes when she woke up on Sundays. She wore headphones or turned the volume as low as possible, because she didn't want Molly to hear. (What would Molly think? Molly, who hadn't been to church in years; Molly, who listened to the same pop song from the nineties to get herself out of bed every morning.) As soon as the video loaded on her phone, Eva looked for the back of Jamie's head in the audience. Each week, the crowd got bigger, and each week it took a little longer for Eva to find him.

She still didn't like the sermons, exactly. They could upset her, like the one in which Kenny insisted that Jesus's love was unconditional. Part of Eva understood why you'd want to be loved like that—maybe she wanted it, too. But another part of her objected. Didn't everyone need conditions? Couldn't everyone be pushed to the limit? She tried to imagine an unbreakable heart. She turned the video off. She chose a playlist and unplugged her headphones, turning the volume up high.

"Hey, that's *my* song," Molly called from the other side of the door.

But whenever Eva decided that she'd never watch another Sunday service, her curiosity would gradually return, like a fragile air bubble rising through the depths of some gentle body of water. She couldn't imagine where it was coming from. She told herself that eventually it would reach the surface—and then maybe it would pop.

Eli had a not quite entry-level job on Capitol Hill. He'd skipped at least one rung of the ladder—Eva wasn't exactly sure how. When she googled the senator he worked for, someone she hadn't heard of but probably should have, the man looked more or less as she expected. White hair, jowly. There were enormous bags under his eyes, which his glasses, worn at the tip of his nose while reading at a lectern, did little to obscure.

Eva had agreed to be friends with Eli. She knew that if he'd asked, this time she would also have agreed to be his girlfriend, but he hadn't. To his credit, he'd told her some things that were nice to hear. For instance, when they had finished having sex, he'd held her left breast in his right hand, the way you might hold a piece of fruit to judge its weight or ripeness, and said that it was the perfect size for a breast. Later, when the lights were off and she was telling him about Molly—choosing all the right details, remembering all the best stories—he laughed appreciatively.

"You're good at that," he said.

"At what?"

"At people, I guess. Describing them." He paused to think, and it still excited her—the possibility that he was thinking about her. "Capturing them."

So what if thinking and saying nice things didn't add up to being in love with her? Eva needed friends, too. Lorrie, who for years had seemed like her closest friend—the friend who helped her get close to other friends—had moved back to Los Angeles, where she was busy trying to become a filmmaker. Lately, they only talked while Lorrie was stuck in traffic. The next time she called, Eva told her about running into Eli, but not about sleeping with him, because Lorrie would have disapproved. She encouraged Eva to use dating apps. At the very least, she said, it was an anthropological experience. She'd met a rare-books dealer, a sculptor who was also a weed trimmer, a famous actress's estranged son, a fruitarian. Eva conceded that these dates sounded interesting, but she wasn't brave enough to actually meet people like that; it was enough to hear about them, while cars three thousand miles away honked in the background. Eva tried to describe the missed-connections website, but Lorrie didn't see the allure. There were pictures on the apps, she said—you needed pictures.

That Eli's job sounded boring helped Eva accept the boundaries of their relationship; Congress did not impress her. Even someone like him, she thought, was probably taking coffee orders and writing memos and watching C-SPAN for hours on end. In the newspaper, she read about an elevator at the Capitol that only elected officials were allowed to ride, and after that, she liked to picture Eli crowded into the other elevator—the one for everyone else. Blue and gray suits sardined in a little box, all of them craning their necks to see which button had been pressed, blindly hoping that they would stop at the right place.

But that fall there was a political race that everyone was talking about—a special election. Suddenly Congress didn't seem as boring as Eva wanted to believe it was. The leader in the race was a young woman from New York. Not even thirty (but almost), she was new to politics. Her previous job had been as a nanny for people with luxury condos and strollers that cost as much as used cars. In interviews, she was careful not to mock these people—they were voters, too—but she didn't pretend that the job had been easy or pleasant. At the playgrounds in fancy neighborhoods, the kids were all white and the nannies were all brown. They unwrapped snacks that cost as much as their hourly rate. The parents always gestured at the kitchen cabinets, the fridge, the fruit bowl overflowing on the countertop. Help yourself.

This, the candidate said, was what generosity had come to mean: giving when the giving was easy, when you'd hardly notice that what you'd given was gone. And charity was a nice hobby if you believed in self-sufficiency. You could feel good—virtuous, heroic—about even the smallest gift, because you didn't *owe* anyone anything. Listen again and there was impatience lurking beneath that magnanimous gesture, that polite phrase: *Help yourself.* Those were the words of someone who made a habit of giving but a religion of taking.

The candidate admitted that takers often came out on top. They got rich, got respect, got rewards that could be measured and many more that couldn't be. But what if all that changed? She admitted that it wouldn't be easy. What they said about change was true: you really did have to make it. But she was ready to be creative. She wasn't doing it out of the goodness of her heart—she was doing it because it made sense. There would come a time, she said, when helping yourself wouldn't be enough, or wouldn't even be possible, and then everyone would have to do something new, something simpler, something better: help each other.

It sounded good. It even sounded right. Eva read as many articles about the candidate as she could find. She understood why other people thought she was inspiring, which wasn't quite the same thing as being inspired herself. The more she read, the more she longed to find the candidate's flaws. Characters, Eva had been taught, were always better when they were flawed.

But the candidate was a rising star; it would have been too soon to predict her waning powers. The articles noted mainly how young and brilliant and charismatic she was, and Eva—who had not felt brilliant since the final grade on her final exam, who now understood how convenient and absurd it was to sum someone up with a single letter, A to F—decided to be skeptical. She texted Eli: *Are anyone's political ambitions pure?* He didn't respond right away, which she assumed meant that he was busy at work, which made her embarrassed that she wasn't.

Eva's official title at the newspaper was Researcher. She had doubted, at first, that she had the right qualifications for the job, but it turned out that researching mostly meant googling. She worked for the investigative team, which at any given time was conducting several secret projects. In general, Eva wasn't important enough to be let in on the secrets. She was given specific, inscrutable tasks—procuring documents, tracking down email addresses. She made a spreadsheet of every livestock veterinarian in Wisconsin. She wrote memos about pharmaceutical companies and defense contractors, and called the same talent agency in Hollywood dozens of times, where the same woman—she sounded as young and nervous as Eva did—kept forwarding her to a voicemail box that was full. Someday, when the articles were finally published, Eva might figure out the hidden purpose of her tasks, but most of the team's investigations simmered for months or years. Many would eventually be abandoned altogether.

After texting Eli, Eva put her phone in a desk drawer, where she wouldn't be able to see it light up with incoming messages. She checked her email, even though the inbox was already open in another window—her fingers seemed to do this automatically. When she saw a new message in bold, she got excited, until she remembered that it was an email she had sent to herself, a link to a video clip that she was saving to watch, from the candidate's recent appearance on a late-night TV show. Eva couldn't find her headphones, so she made sure the sound on her computer was turned off, then clicked. The segment began with footage from some of the candidate's recent rallies, the camera panning to show the size and intensity of the crowd. Everyone's mouths were moving, and even though Eva couldn't hear them, she could see that they were moving in unison. Then the B-roll ended and the candidate walked onstage in a pantsuit, all black and somehow more fashionable than most politicians' pantsuits—maybe it was the way the legs tapered around her ankles. Her hair looked professional, but her smile looked normal.

Eva watched the candidate and the talk-show host for ten full minutes, their muted conversation transformed into a volley of raised eyebrows and furrowed eyebrows, pursed lips and exposed teeth, shoulders turning in and turning away, laughter and more laughter. They both glanced at the audience from time to time. Eva could tell that the host knew when to engage the viewers, to remind them that they were part of the conversation. The candidate didn't seem quite as well practiced. When she looked at the crowd, she was looking *for* something—a reaction, a sign. She needed something from them, and Eva, in spite of all her skepticism, found herself wanting to give whatever that something was.

Right before the clip ended, the camera turned to the studio audience, where everyone was clapping politely, no doubt as they had been instructed to. Then the video started all over again, and Eva closed the window, returning to her empty inbox. Usually, this depressed her, but now she felt energized. She opened the newspaper's website and read three articles in quick succession. Afterward, she felt more knowledgeable than before. She scrolled through the rest of the headlines, following links back and forth from the homepage, reading news from one city and then another, one continent and then another, marveling at the extent of this web—truly worldwide.

Every day, a little before one o'clock, two other researchers came by on their way to lunch. Usually, Eva waited impatiently for them, taking small bites from the sandwich she'd brought in a Ziploc bag, even though she was never very hungry. That afternoon, she told them to go ahead without her, and staying put made her feel briefly powerful: her own company was enough. There was a stapled packet of pages on her desk, a legal brief, that she'd already read but had barely understood. She read it again, this time making check marks here and there in the margins.

She remembered her sandwich before she remembered her phone. They were both in the top drawer of her desk. Maybe she would take her lunch outside. The phone, when she retrieved it, showed a breaking news alert and a low-battery warning and one message from Eli.

Her question had been sincere: *Are anyone's political ambitions really pure*? She couldn't tell if his response was, too: *Who wants to be pure?*

If you think about it, Christianity is one of the earliest grassroots movements, and Jesus is the ultimate community organizer. Just look around. See what he started?

And yet today, when religion gets political, it usually gets ugly. Evangelicals are known not as followers of Jesus but as followers of a political party. Tell me, can a voting bloc ever be a real community? Is Christianity really defined by all these issues that it's against? What can we say, instead, about what Christianity is for?

These questions are both easy and hard. Easy because I'm holding a book that contains all the answers. Hard because if we not only listen to them but live by them, we will have to change the world. We will have to fight poverty and stop wars and confront racism and get guns off our streets. We will have to organize and demonstrate. We might have to go to jail. We certainly will have to do a whole lot more than pray. Because here's the thing. To change the world, you will have to first change yourself.

That Sunday, the church was almost completely full. There were only a couple empty chairs at the back, the ones closest to the camera, which made it seem to Eva as if she were sitting in them herself. A few rows ahead of her, a man was stretched out across three chairs, covered in several layers of jackets, evidently fast asleep. Eva thought he was probably homeless. For several weeks now, Kenny had made a point of mentioning that the church's collection would be evenly divided, with half going to its operational budget—small but essential—and half going to unhoused friends of the church. They were called friends because no one was ever called a member. A church was only a real church, Kenny said, if anyone could come—if anyone could belong.

Eva thought Kenny looked straight at the camera when he said this, but she might have been imagining it.

Eva closed her laptop before the sermon was over. It wasn't even noon yet. The day stretched out ahead of her, bright and boring. She took a long walk without a destination. At sidewalk tables, people leaned back in their chairs to take pictures of fluted drinks and eggs slathered in thick white sauce. Gross, but her mouth watered anyway. She checked her email every couple of blocks, in case someone from the office had tried to reach her. Her bosses worked all weekend and late at night, but these days they never seemed to need her.

In a neighborhood with garages and pretty lawns, she reached a park where all the leaves had been raked into tidy piles. At a picnic table, a children's birthday party was in full swing. The cake had already been cut and plastic plates of half-eaten slices were abandoned on the ground. Attention had shifted to a piñata, a yellow-and-pink unicorn dangling from a tree branch. The kids, six or seven years old, clamored underneath it in a tight knot, while the parents surrounded them in a circle, just enough space between all the adults to make casual conversation difficult. The moms and dads wore strangely somber expressions, as if the game were a rite of passage. The kids, corralled into a semi-orderly line, took turns swinging blindly at the piñata with a plastic Wiffle-ball bat, missing again and again. While Eva watched, the rules of the game were incrementally altered. The unicorn was lowered, then lowered again. The blindfold was removed, then trampled under someone's shoes. Just when it seemed the whole thing would have to be abandoned, one of the parents broke out of the circle and, without consulting anyone, without saying a word, ripped the piñata in two. Candy showered to the ground. For a moment, none of the kids moved, dumbfounded by this violent breach of contract. Then they all unfroze at once, scrambling to claim as many pieces as they could.

It was only once the spell had been broken that Eva noticed the girl on the other side of the ring of parents. She had not taken any swings with the bat, had not even joined the line. She was walking around the picnic table in an abstracted way that, if she had been just slightly older, would have seemed erratic, might even have been a cause for alarm. Her hand trailed inquisitively over the surface of the wooden bench, her sneaker investigated an overturned plate, revealing a flattened, garishly colored piece of cake. When the girl crouched down to take a closer look, Eva saw that her lips were moving soundlessly.

Nostalgia ambushed Eva with sudden, piercing specificity. It wasn't the shape of a memory that returned to her—not an occasion, or even an event—but the texture: the way dirt had felt, brushed off her palms; the way words had felt, murmured under her breath; the way everything around her, the air itself, had felt better, more important, more electric, because she had renamed it, because she was transforming it, because she was filling it with a story that no silly birthday party or ordinary afternoon could provide.

Eva's parents had referred to these transformations as make-believe. Even as a child, she had been stung by the term. Make-believe was for kids who played with dolls and sipped theatrically from empty teacups. Eva took offense if anyone asked about her imaginary friends. She had no use for apparitions like that—companions who pathetically followed you wherever you went, scapegoats who appeared whenever you needed them to. Her own imagination was not about filling a lack (of real friends, for example). She wouldn't have been able to explain it then, but over time she began to feel that these fantasies revealed something like—well, like the truth. She knew it sounded strange. She knew that she wasn't any of the things she had imagined being: an orphan, a nun, an alpine explorer wandering in the mountains, a pop star dazzling in front of a crowd, an empress, the president. But her fictions expanded reality, and that was the realest thing about the world, the hardest part to grasp: it existed beyond you.

One of the adults, a woman who had been filming the piñata's demolition with her phone, noticed the girl and with her free hand tried to pull her into the circle. The girl resisted. The woman, gesturing at the other kids, said something Eva couldn't hear but could easily imagine. *Look at everyone else. See how much fun they're having?* A cajoling voice that barely hid a scolding voice. *Why can't you see what we see? Why can't you do what we do*? For a moment, the girl weighed her options, glancing briefly at the piece of cake, now twice abandoned, and then she gave in, letting herself be pulled into the game, toward all the supposed prizes.

Eva kept on walking, but the image of the girl returned to her throughout the day. At some point, Eva had stopped playing make-believe, though she couldn't remember exactly when. She hadn't let it go on too long, hadn't caused anyone to worry, hadn't been called weird or spacey or "in her own world." She was technically a grown-up now, and grown-ups were the ones who, in the midst of scary books or movies or games that got out of hand, were supposed to reassure children that it was all "just pretend."

But why *just*?

Was there anything more powerful, more frightening, more likely to turn your whole life upside down?

Eli's apartment was small but beautiful, because he lived in it with his older sister's girlfriend, Coco, who had better taste and more money than he did. She was probably the same age as Molly, but she seemed much older. She had art on the walls, owned a spice grinder, only smoked weed in the bath—to decompress. (The sturdiness of her long-distance relationship was another sign of maturity.) One Friday night, she hosted a party to listen to all of Beethoven's symphonies. By the time the ninth one began, Eli and Eva were the only ones left. Eli hadn't invited her to spend the night, but Eva, hoping he might, made herself useful in the kitchen, returning crackers to their boxes, wrapping whittled pieces of cheese in plastic. While she cleaned, Eli told Coco that even though the special election was weeks away, Congress was already being upended by the candidate. (This was still how Eva thought of her, as if there were no other contenders in the race.)

Eli said that his boss, the jowly senator, had hardly paid attention to the candidate at first. She wasn't from his state, or even a particularly contested district. He was certain that she would never be a senator, just a representative. She seemed energetic but naïve, likely to sink just as quickly as she had bobbed to the surface—he'd seen it happen before. But as the candidate's odds of winning increased, the senator's public remarks about her grew warmer, while his feelings in private became angrier. Sometimes his anger simmered, sometimes it roiled.

"This is all confidential, by the way," Eli said.

Coco laughed. "Who would I tell? Who would care?"

Eli ignored her. Eva splattered the dregs from abandoned wineglasses into the sink. There was probably half a bottle's worth in all, dribbling down the drain—a not-that-cheap bottle, either. She ran the tap and the water turned purple, then pink, then clear.

"In terms of strategy, I get it," Eli continued. "He feels threatened."

"Well, too bad. Politics is change." Coco was sprawled on the couch. She made sprawling look elegant.

"Who said that?" Eva asked.

"It's not a famous quote. It's just a fact."

"Maybe so," Eli said, "but when change comes, no one wants to be the one left behind."

"So what, you're a conservative now?" Coco smiled at Eva, as if this were a joke they shared, so Eva quickly smiled back.

"I'm just saying I see where he's coming from," Eli said.

Coco mimicked him in a stilted voice: "I see where he's coming from."

"Fuck you."

They weren't really fighting. At least, Eva was pretty sure they weren't. It was the same way Eli fought with his sisters or with Lorrie or with any of his other friends. They took for granted that they agreed on most or all of the fundamental things—they never actually named those things—and so they argued the way other people exercised: heart rates climbing, neck muscles clenching, pushing themselves a little harder or faster, and then, with a clatter of dumbbells falling to the ground, going back to regular life. It wasn't quite a game—they cared about what they were talking about—but in the end it was still just practice.

Surveying the dirty-rimmed glasses and the bowl of discarded olives, olive meat still clinging to the pits, Eva felt inadequate. Maybe she should read the op-ed page, or join a gym. But she laughed at the thought. She hated the sanctimony of people who were sure they knew best, and she especially hated treadmills. She would have liked locker rooms, where everyone's bodies and belongings and strange rituals were on display, but you weren't supposed to look at any of that; people made a show of not looking. Eva turned the faucet back on full blast, so that water sprayed her shirt and drowned out the rest of Eli and Coco's conversation. When she had washed and dried all the glasses and arranged them facedown on the counter, Coco came over, as if only just noticing what Eva was doing.

"You shouldn't have," she said.

It was the kind of thing people said to be polite, but Coco sounded disappointed, as if she might have really meant it. *Should* she have? Eva looked at Eli for some sort of clue, but Eli was looking at his phone. It was only when she announced she was leaving that he put the phone away. He seemed taken aback, and that was a small triumph: so he had wanted her to stay after all. Eva was briefly tempted to change her mind, but it was too late for that.

At the door, Eli kissed her goodbye. Usually, they only kissed as preamble—if the kissing would lead to more than kissing. Pointless kissing was a rare, pure pleasure—something you could give yourself up to. You didn't have to wonder when to do the next thing (unbuckle a buckle, pull a shirt over a head), because there was no next thing. Lips forgot their clumsiness, tongues performed their full symphony, a hand explored the many ways to hold a face. This kind of romance was a delicate art, determined by the smallest changes in pressure, the precise tilt of the head. Your eyes were closed the whole time.

One evening after work, instead of going home, Eva wandered down to the National Mall. She'd never seen the monuments after dark. In daylight, the massive stones and larger-than-life statues were too ostentatious, but at night, she discovered, they were luminous, a little otherworldly. They were huge slabs of rock mysteriously planted in the ground. The Washington Monument pointed straight up at the moon. She texted Eli—*Meet me downtown?*—because she wanted him to see how strange and unsolid it could all become. The museums empty, the memorials ghostly, a lone hot-dog wrapper skittering across the ground.

Just beyond the reflecting pool, she lay on her back and looked up at the sky, starless but still vast—still miraculous. She wasn't always so susceptible to beauty. Most of the time, *miraculous* was not a word she would allow herself to use. Her willingness seemed like a sign, proof that she was ready for something—anything—to happen.

She heard Eli before she saw him, and smiled to herself. Then she heard a second voice. Two heads appeared upside down above her, his and hers, ugly from below. Eva scrambled to her feet. It was only once she was standing up, a chill all down her spine, that she realized how cold the ground had been.

The woman was named Reshma. She was small, narrow-shouldered and thin-waisted, but she had sharp edges that made her seem imposing: steeply angled hair, collarbones clearly visible beneath her skin, a pointy nose, pointy black boots.

"We saw a fox," Eli said. "Right out in the open."

"Like an omen," Reshma said.

"A good one?" Eva asked.

Reshma laughed. "It looked sickly. It had patchy fur. Hungry eyes."

They walked around the Washington Monument and crossed the street, where two long sandy paths on either side of the Mall led all the way to the Capitol steps. There were shuttered concession stands and a darkened carousel, glinting every now and then as the headlights of passing cars illuminated a horse's gold mane or a chariot's gilded door.

Eli explained that Reshma was the chief of staff for the candidate.

"Wow," Eva said.

She thought Reshma might deflect questions about the job—that was the modest thing to do—but she didn't. She referred to the candidate by her first name. *Jess.* They had known each other in college. Then Jess had become a nanny and Reshma had gone to work on political campaigns, losing one election after another. Her colleagues told her to get used to defeat, but Reshma couldn't—or wouldn't. She decided it was time to rethink her approach.

"Time for a new generation of leaders."

When Reshma said this, it somehow didn't sound like a cliché. She said she'd known right away to call Jess. They hadn't seen each other in years, but there was something about Jess's presence that Reshma still remembered.

"What was it?" Eva asked.

A pack of teenagers passed them, boys who knocked against each other as they walked, shoulders against shoulders, a fist against an arm. When they reached the carousel, one of them stopped and rattled the fence.

"It's the difference between capturing and captivating an audience. With Jess, you never feel like you're being held hostage."

Eli nodded vigorously.

"But what about her politics?" Eva said.

"Oh, they were good enough."

The boy gripping the fence shouted ahead to the others, but got no response. He gave the fence another shake, waited one second, two seconds, then let go and ran to catch up, his too-big boots clomping as he went.

"So she's just the face of the movement?" Eva asked.

Reshma and Eli exchanged a look, which Eva couldn't read.

"I wouldn't say *that*."

Now they, too, had reached the carousel's locked gate. From where they stood, the horses were just dark shapes. Eva thought she could still hear the boys in the distance—a lot of voices mixed together and one that stood out—but maybe she was imagining it. She gripped the top of the fence and hoisted herself up. Her fingers stung, but she held on, swung one leg over, then the other.

"What are you doing?" Reshma said.

"Don't be crazy," Eli said.

She didn't answer them. She sort of hated them. Up close, she could see the horses clearly. Everything was smaller than she remembered, because she was bigger. She had to bend over to see the horses' flared nostrils; their legs were twigs, their hooves the size of her palm. When she sat down, the tiny saddle vanished beneath her.

The seat dug uncomfortably into her tailbone, so Eva stood up, balancing on the horse's rump, then climbed hand-over-hand up the metal pole that passed through the center of its body. At the top of the pole, she dangled like that, high enough that she felt the old joy of the ride. When she closed her eyes, she could almost feel the carousel spinning.

Then she opened them and a flashlight was sweeping back and forth across the Mall. She told herself not to panic, which didn't make her not panic. While she adjusted her grip on the metal bar above her, her fingers aching even more now, she saw Eli grab Reshma's arm—or was it her hand? They ran away like that, fading into the dark.

Eva counted to three and then she let go. While she fell, her entire body surged into her head. Then she was on the ground, her feet burning with the impact of her fall, and the flashlight was gone.

The mission isn't to convince you of anything. If there was a simple way I could, we wouldn't be here every week. You'd just believe what I told you and then move on with your life.

A good Christian is not free of doubt. The choice to face your doubt is a choice you have to make over and over again. Whether to speak to Jesus, to listen to Jesus, to listen for Jesus. To hear him in the voices around you and the voice within you. To accept that this voice will not always tell you what you want to hear.

What do we need to hear? Some people turn to faith for comfort, but real faith will reveal uncomfortable truths. I want you to understand that faith is not the opposite of doubt. Faith is not the opposite of fear.

The fear of not knowing the answer. No, even before that: the fear of asking the question.

The fear of changing and also the fear of not changing.

The fear that you've never really existed in anyone else's head.

The fear of your own head.

Eva rolled over and went back to sleep.

. . .

At the very beginning of her campaign, Jess had predicted that she would have to contend with racism and misogyny from her critics, and of course she had not been wrong.

Her most overt attackers, wielding slurs and memes and an animated video of a gang rape, circulated in places most people preferred not to look, and so could easily ignore. Other, subtler opponents, who insisted that they were merely posing questions, not launching attacks, surfaced on certain high-decibel TV channels or lurked in generally well-written magazines. They said their questions were simple, by which they meant innocent. They wondered if Jess had enough experience. They called her by her first name, not her last name. They urged voters to consider whether she could hold her own. And they wanted to get to the bottom of the question of race. As everyone knew by then, Jess's father was an immigrant from Colombia and her mother was a white woman from the part of Pennsylvania that's more like Ohio. These facts were repeated many times, in slightly different contexts, with slightly different phrasing, to support very different conclusions. Jess confirmed the facts, ignored the conclusions. In one early interview, she had discussed the history of the term "person of color" (it was French) and offered a few thoughts on both its value and its limitations. But this had led to many more questions and many more attacks, so she had not mentioned it again.

As the election neared and Jess's popularity grew, her opponents searched even more frantically through the contents of her past, desperate to find something to smear her with. Her past, however, was short and uneventful. She'd been drunk and stoned before, but so what? By gamely producing these skeletons from her closet, she turned them into a pile of plastic bones. She had never harassed or abused anyone—she had never even been anyone's boss.

In the last week of the campaign, an old, homemade music video of Jess went viral. It was supposed to be humiliating: a silly dance, filmed late at night in a dorm room with an unsteady hand. A few of her most strenuous critics insisted that the video was damning proof, but of what, they couldn't seem to agree. Unseriousness? Stupidity? Youth? Within a few days, there was a new video of Jess watching the old video, laughing—giggling, really—her hand pressed against her heart, as if the person dancing was a loved one she hadn't seen in a long time, singing and waving from some faraway place. That video received hundreds of thousands of likes.

On the night of the special election, Eva, Eli, and Coco hung a sheet on the wall and hooked up the projector. A red-and-blue map appeared on the sheet. There was a bottle of champagne in the fridge, but Eva didn't know who'd bought it. The other staffers from Eli's office had gathered at a bar downtown to watch the returns, even though it wasn't their boss who stood to win or lose. They claimed they were interested in the larger issues.

"The balance of power, et cetera," Eli said.

"Shouldn't you be at the bar, too?" Eva asked.

He just shrugged and went to the kitchen for another beer.

Coco muted the TV until the newscasters started talking about the race. They called the candidate Jessica, which had seemed normal to Eva until she heard Reshma call her Jess. Now Eva imagined her as two different people: Jessica was someone who made speeches and went on late-night TV and visited the local deli for a photo op with an Italian sub; Jess was someone who had to scrub mayonnaise off her pantsuit, who had to watch recordings of her interviews and try not to cringe, who had to worry about not only what her victory would mean for the country but what it would mean for her sleep schedule, her exercise schedule, her biological clock. Both versions of her were probably inventions. Maybe she was someone else entirely—someone at once unrelatable and unadmirable. Maybe she didn't like babies, or maybe she was naturally thin. She might have been one of those people who only needed four hours of sleep.

Her face—Jessica's, not Jess's—flashed on the wall, and Coco turned the volume up. Eli emerged from the kitchen as soon as he heard her name. He was wearing a windbreaker, one shoe on, the other unlaced in his hand.

"Where are you going?" Coco asked.

"Nowhere yet."

He perched on the edge of a chair, as if ready to stand up at any moment, and put the other shoe on while staring at the TV, his hands blindly tying a lopsided bow. It was a professional-looking shoe—brown leather with an unscuffed sole. He had his work phone in one pocket, his own phone in the other. One of them, Eva didn't know which, started ringing, and all three of them looked at the sound emerging from his pants. When he answered the phone, Coco turned the volume on the TV down again, low enough that Eva could hear Reshma's voice clearly.

"We did it."

"They called it?" Eli said. "They haven't called it here."

She kept repeating herself: "We did it, we did it."

"Turn up the TV."

But Coco just stared at Eli, looking confused.

"Jesus Christ, will you turn it up?"

Coco threw the remote at him and it bounced off his chest, clattering under the table. Bending over to retrieve it, he, too, began to repeat the words. *We did it.* Softly, maybe not even loud enough for Reshma to hear. *We did it.* He turned up the volume just as the news anchor was announcing her victory.

"I'll be right there," Eli said, loudly this time. He put the phone away and double-checked his shoelaces.

"Since when do you work for her?" Coco said.

"Since tomorrow."

"What about your boss?" Eva asked, trying to make her voice as casual as she could.

He looked at her for a moment—a depthless, distracted look—then left without answering.

After that, Eva and Coco got drunk. The champagne first—sickeningly sweet. Foam slid down the bottle's glass neck and Coco put her mouth right over the top. They burped, abandoned it for tequila. On TV, three people sat behind a table talking: two men in blue who occasionally turned to ask a woman in red for her opinion. They kept asking what direction the country was going in—where it, or they, were headed.

"Do you think he'll be famous someday?" Eva said abruptly.

"Probably." Coco splashed another drink in each glass. "There's a quality certain people have. It's like—Well, I don't know what it's like." She swallowed, grimaced. "Do you know what I mean?"

"Maybe." Eva had been sitting on the couch, but now she was sitting on the rug.

"Actually, it might not be anything about *him*." Beside her, Coco slid a little farther onto the ground and leaned her head on Eva's shoulder. "It might be something about us."

From this angle, Eva could see a few pimples on her hairline. Maybe she wasn't so old, so unapproachable. Eva reached out and traced a zigzag from one pimple to the next, which made Coco laugh—a nice, real laugh. She sat up so their faces were level. They kissed. Coco kept laughing while kissing, which somehow, along with the drinking, kept Eva from worrying, or from thinking very much at all.

She must have fallen asleep on the floor, because she woke up on the floor. Her shirt was half on, one arm in its armhole, the other not. Coco was curled in a chair, breathing loudly through her mouth.

When Eva stood up—it wasn't that easy to stand up—she started toward the front door, then stopped at Eli's bedroom. His unmade bed, the sheets twisted like a rope, the blanket trailing on the floor. She couldn't remember which side of the bed was his side, so she lay down in the middle and fell asleep again, the TV talking to itself in the other room.

In the morning, Eli hadn't come home, which was both relieving and devastating. Her jeans were inside out on the floor. She was cold, but she couldn't bring herself to retrieve the pants, or even the blanket. She imagined leaving the room—fleeing, even—but it was like watching someone else: her body did not follow her mind. Dead legs, heavy head. She would puke later, presumably.

If she ran her thumb over her lower lip, she could still remember how it had felt to kiss him. How mysterious your mouth could seem when it was being explored by someone else. But then it was over, and she had kissed someone else, and maybe he had, too. Romance had turned back into a coarse, unsurprising force. Whatever they were doing with each other was not a difficult puzzle or an interesting riddle. He had only wanted her to stay when she had decided to leave. He would never love her enough, because she already loved him too much. He would never truly wrong her, and she would never be quite right.

Is that a new answering machine message? You sound different. But I hate it when people say, "You don't sound like yourself." That's not what I mean. You can't sound "like" yourself. You are yourself.

Oh, fuck. It's Jamie. Did I not say that?

The other day I overheard a woman making a phone call, and when the other person picked up, she said, "Hey, it's me." At first, I thought, that's so presumptuous. And then I thought, no, that's perfect.

What do you think?

I guess it could be both.

Ten seconds of silence, then twenty. She almost hung up.

Is there a time limit for these? Well, that would be okay. If it cuts me off, if it's already cut me off. I'll be glad to have kept talking, even if you never hear it. You might not listen in the first place. That hadn't occurred to me. But I have a feeling you will.

Has it been a happy birthday, Eva? That's what I was calling about. I hope so.

I really hope so.

Jamie called in the middle of the afternoon. Eva's birthday fell on a Friday, so she'd taken the day off work, for no real reason—she didn't have any plans until the evening. She didn't silence the call, just let it ring inside the pocket of her sweatshirt, vibrating against her stomach. She thought she'd gained some weight recently, though she wasn't sure, because she didn't own a scale. She didn't want to be the kind of woman who weighed herself. (Was there really any difference between being a woman who weighed herself and being a woman who wanted to?)

Eva didn't listen to the voicemail right away. She made coffee, then realized she would have preferred tea, but she had already taken a sip, and somehow the bitter taste prevented her from changing course. She drank half the cup and poured the other half into the kitchen sink. She listened to another one of Molly's apps, this one for yoga. Each episode advertised its gentleness. The voice in the app instructed her to stand in mountain pose, tall and solid. *Okay*. She straightened her spine. *Easy*. Although sometimes she felt too solid—too dense.

Other times, she felt like she was floating. She got lost thinking about this contradiction, and when she remembered to listen to the voice again, it was explaining child's pose.

No, not that. She exited the app, then deleted it. She clicked through to the window where Jamie's name appeared in urgent red. She pressed play, and then he was there. Here. His voice filling up the room and entering her body. "I have a feeling," he said. She cupped her hand over her ear, as if listening to the ocean. She worried about him. Did she miss him? Did she wish that he'd come back, or did she wish that she'd move on? It was just a feeling.

WHY IS THAT?

Her parents were beside themselves. Jamie was moving out. Her mom called her and then her dad called her, and by the end of each call all three of them were on the line.

"But why?" Gail asked.

"Was it something we said?" Nick asked.

"We said he could stay."

"Should stay."

Eva didn't answer right away.

"Honey?"

"I'm here," she said.

"And?"

It was 9 p.m., but Eva was still at the office. For weeks, she and her boss had been investigating a small story that he thought might be a bigger story: a high-rise apartment that had gone down in flames. Everyone agreed it was a tragedy, but he said it might also be a crime. Eva had read through pages and pages of building codes and made long lists of rules and violations. It was a whole new language:

403.13 smokeproof exit enclosures. 403.14 seismic considerations. Then, that morning, her boss had announced they were at a dead end. The landlord was a bad guy, but badness wasn't enough. Her boss's boss was losing patience: some stories, he said, really were as small as they seemed.

"Maybe he needs space," Eva told her parents.

"Space where?" Gail asked. "We don't know where he's going. He just keeps saying he'll figure it out. Whatever that means."

"He says we have to have faith in him," Nick said.

At that hour, the office was empty except for a haggard-looking reporter who never seemed to go home. He'd been sent to several war zones and drank Diet Coke at all hours. In his company, Eva felt tired and important—felt able to decide, with a burst of thrilling conviction, that she would not abandon the story. Smallness seemed like a challenge now. Her boss's doubt made it easier to believe: there was still more to find.

"He's always been elusive," Gail said.

"But now he's being evasive," Nick said.

"All this talk of faith."

"We'd prefer some facts."

Down the hall, the war reporter yanked a mangled piece of paper out of the printer. Eva looked back at her computer, where she was typing up yet another information request about the fire. Everyone else complained about this kind of bureaucracy, but she enjoyed the formality of it—a letter on letterhead, sent in the actual mail. As long as you knew what you were looking for, all you had to do was ask. It was the rest of reporting that frightened her, not the polite requests but the tough questions. She found an envelope in her desk. She was out of stamps. The war reporter pressed his forehead against the printer in despair.

"Eva?"

"Hello?"

Eva had heard that on one of his trips to Baghdad, the reporter was almost blown to bits. Stumbling through the rubble of the city, he'd kicked over a concrete block and found a bomb underneath.

"I have to go," she said.

A sigh on the other end of the line—she wasn't sure whose.

"Everyone always has to go."

They were only a few months into the new year, but already Eva's sense of time was scrambled. A week of sun ended with snow. The ice-cream truck drove prematurely down her street, its jingle mournful and confused. In January, Molly had stopped eating all mammals, then all meat, then everything animal, including honey. She lost weight. In February, just weeks after being sworn in, Jess had proposed a landmark piece of legislation. Eli, whose new title was Communications Director, had moved out of Coco's apartment and his sister had moved in—the happy couple reunited at last. He'd gone to live with a couple of boys who were starting their own business, in an apartment a few blocks away from Eva's. Sometimes, Eva complained to Molly about seeing Eli too much: getting coffee, doing laundry, pacing back and forth on the sidewalk with his phone pressed against his ear, talking urgently or nodding urgently. Then she would go a whole week without running into him, and she would complain about not seeing him enough.

Eli and Reshma were always together—they worked all the time—and then, at some point, they were *together*. Eli never told Eva this directly. He acted like she'd always known—and maybe she had. Now when Eva saw him, she usually saw Reshma, too. She watched them walk to the subway in the morning with matching coffees, matching phones, matching urgency. One evening, she saw Reshma alone in the laundromat, pulling clothes out of the dryer, unpeeling his sock from her shirt.

Everything was happening to other people, and now it was snowing again. Climate change, the experts said. Eva had apocalyptic dreams. Every night, the world ended in a new way: a flood, a drought, a sheet of ice that trapped her, flames that chased her. The flames woke her up and she threw open the window, then shrank back in confusion from the cold.

Molly said Eva was reading too much about the fire, and she was probably right. While she waited for new information, Eva returned to old information. She read the same fire-department report again and again, scrolled through photos she'd already seen many times. An article in a local newspaper had released time-stamped images of the blaze at fifteen-minute intervals. It had started in the middle of the night: the building had been completely dark until—a streak of light—it began to glow from within. Staring at the photos one night when she couldn't fall asleep, her phone propped up on her stomach, Eva wondered about the people on the other side of the camera. Who was taking the pictures?

A sight like that would have summoned people to their windows—an audience. Eva imagined them turning on their lights and then instantly turning them back off. It would have felt wrong to watch with the lights on. She thought about them standing there, dark rooms behind them, unaware of how many other people were standing above and below and across from them, everyone watching, everyone waiting. How far did heat from a fire like that travel? Would their windows have been warm to the touch?

There was an entire profession, Eva learned, devoted to figuring out why fires happened. The field was called origin-and-cause investigation: where the first spark came from, how it caught. It was a complicated science—chemistry, electrical engineering, gas chromatography—but it was also an art. You had to have an eye for detail. You had to study the patterns on the wall, to know why certain burns looked like puddles and others looked like the letter "V," to understand what made glass crack like a spiderweb and what made it shatter all at once. Fire investigators compared themselves to detectives or archeologists. "The fire tells the story," one of them said in an article Eva read several times. "I am just the interpreter."

But she didn't have enough information to interpret. She waited for a response to her letter, and it didn't arrive. She drew a floor plan of the building and stared at it. One night, she dreamed about a tsunami, and when the wave receded, she was the only one still clinging to the shore. Even in the dream, she wished she'd let go. A few nights later, she woke up from a nightmare about a volcano—lava squelching between her toes like mud—and discovered she'd bled onto her sheets. That one she could laugh about. She trudged through slush to buy more tampons.

Stop feeling sorry for yourself, Lorrie texted. *Come to California.*

When Eva's information request went unfulfilled for the second week in a row, she bought a plane ticket.

The greenness in Los Angeles was overwhelming. Lorrie lived on a hill—a mountain, they called it—looking out over the city, with winding roads and tree-lined streets, where all the yards looked a little wild. Eva had known to expect palms, their giraffe necks and shaggy trunks, which seemed to thrive even in parking lots, but here were tall pines and ancient-seeming sycamores, cacti and rosebushes, shrubs laden with hard red berries. She knew that in a few months it would all be yellow and dry, and in a few more months the fires would arrive, turning the sky heavy and orange, but all that was hard to believe. Lorrie went to work and Eva walked up and down the streets, sweating through too-thick socks. Trees heavy with leaves, air heavy with fragrance. The branches seemed to bend under the weight of all their greenery, as if they might be about to snap.

In the evenings, Lorrie made stir-fries and salads. Her roommates scattered herbs from the local farm stand over everything—more green. The smog made the sunset better than ever. While they ate at a table with pieces of cardboard wedged under the legs, Lorrie told them about the man she had recently started dating. Five or six dates, including one that had lasted thirty-six hours.

"You know, the stage of a relationship when you start asking each other security questions," Lorrie said.

"Security questions?" Her roommate tossed the salad with tongs.

"Those questions you answer to retrieve your password. Like, favorite pet, mother's maiden name, make and model of your first car. That's where we're at. I know he's a cat person, not a dog person. I know he always orders butter pecan."

What she didn't know was where he worked. He was the personal assistant for someone important—someone famous—and he was legally forbidden to tell her who.

"An actor?" one of the roommates said.

"Or, like, a CEO?" another wondered.

Lorrie shrugged. "Could you live with that?" she asked.

"At some point he'd tell you, right?"

"Or maybe you'd have to marry him to find out."

"He says it's not a big deal." Lorrie brandished her fork like a baton while she talked. "He says it's his job, not his life."

But she wasn't sure if this was really true. One weekend, he'd flown to Hawaii to hand-deliver a crucial document that his boss had forgotten at home, then turned around and flown back without ever leaving the airport. (These details, apparently, were safe to disclose. Lots of famous people went to Hawaii.)

"Are there any clues?" Eva asked.

There were often dog hairs on the man's sweater, but he didn't own a dog, so Lorrie assumed they belonged to the celebrity's dog. Short and white. As evidence went, it wasn't very revealing.

"It probably wouldn't be that hard to figure out," Lorrie said, "but I'm not sure if I'd even want to."

"I would," the first roommate said, leaning forward eagerly, the ends of her hair dangling in her salad.

"Because what would happen if I did?" Lorrie asked.

Sometimes on a date with the man, she'd leave the room—to go to the bathroom, maybe, or to order another drink at the bar—and when she came back, he would be lost in his phone, typing something very quickly with his thumbs. It would take him a second to realize she'd returned, and from the surprise on his face when he looked up, she could tell that he had been somewhere else entirely, that he had briefly vanished.

One of the roommates wanted to start googling the man right away. The second, talking through mouthfuls, didn't see the point in dating him at all. The third, a woman named Simone, with hair dyed black from a bottle, disagreed with both. She said that Lorrie's predicament represented the ideal state of a relationship.

"Everyone should have a secret world," she explained. "People think a secret has to be a threat, but that gets it all backward. Privacy is good for stability. Ignorance can make a relationship happier, healthier."

"That's a pretty convenient excuse," Eva said. She hoped Lorrie would turn to look at her, but she was staring intently at Simone.

"No," Simone said patiently, in a voice that made Eva feel like a small child. "Even people in love need somewhere to hide."

"Especially people in love," Lorrie said, nodding emphatically.

"Pass the wine." The first roommate pointed at the green bottle sweating in front of Eva's plate.

Eva handed over the bottle without taking her eyes off Lorrie. "You can love him even if you don't know him?" she asked.

There were four people in the house and four cars on the street. That was how it worked in California. Eva could have borrowed one of them, except that she still didn't know how to drive. She was used to this being a novelty, occasionally an embarrassment, but now it seemed simply like a trap. A whole city was waiting, and she was stuck in one place. On the last day of her trip, she lay on her back in the small grassy yard behind the house, staring at the orange of her eyelids, wishing she were on the highway. The windows rolled down, the wind numbing her face. She laughed at her own cliché.

Whenever she didn't have anything else to think about, Eva returned to the same fantasy. She is eighteen. She is in love with Eli and he is in love with her. Her hair is longer than it has ever actually been. She is eighteen and she is opening a door or walking into a party or picking up her phone—it can happen in any number of mundane ways. What she discovers in the fantasy is that Eli has been having sex with someone else. Maybe she comes upon them in the act. (This was the most indulgent version of the fantasy. So what?) The woman isn't anyone in particular. Whoever she is, she has very small breasts or very big breasts, because Eva, in the fantasy as in life, has very average breasts. The two bodies separate when they're caught, like bugs when you flick on the light. Or maybe Eva never sees the woman's body, maybe she only hears her voice, because the woman calls her to confess. Or maybe not even that—maybe someone else is the one to tell her: *There's something you should know.* This sort of revelation was supposed to be mortifying, degrading. She knew that. And yet, for Eva, the fantasy was a release. If the evidence is unearthed on a phone, she throws the phone across the room. If the truth is revealed in a sticky-floored bar or a cinder-blocked room, she slams a door, topples a lamp, kicks a bed frame. (Why are men the only ones allowed to punch walls?) If it happens outside, she screams until her throat burns. All these were sounds she'd only ever made in her head: shattering, banging, crashing, whatever raw noise was waiting inside her lungs. All that uproar and then, of course, silence. That was the real fantasy. What would have—could have—happened next? What if all that time, all that future, had been set free?

The back door slid open noisily. Simone stood at the threshold, her head tilted slightly toward one shoulder. She looked like one of those old photos where color has been added by hand: against the pure black of her hair and the stark white of her face, all the other shades of her face—the tint of pink on her lips, the ring of green in her eyes—seemed not quite believable.

"We're going to the beach," she said.

We turned out to mean just the two of them. Lorrie called while they were driving (the windows were not rolled down, the A/C was blasting) and sounded surprised to find them together, maybe even a little wounded. She said she would come meet them later.

Simone drove them all the way out to a spot in Malibu, where a rickety set of stairs led down to the ocean. The stairs probably belonged to somebody.

"Whatever," Simone said.

As they descended to the beach, they saw that the sand was strewn with pale, cylindrical objects. Or were they creatures? They weren't moving, but up close, they looked like semitranslucent slugs, about as big as your biggest finger, their bodies ridged with rows of hard bumps. Simone picked one up. With her other hand, she scrolled on her phone. *Sea pickles.*

"What looks like one animal is in fact a colony of animals," she read aloud. "A single organism is only the size of a grain of rice."

Simone held out the pickle, which was actually many pickles. Eva opened up her hand. It was slimy, a little cold.

"Don't worry," Simone said, flinging out her towel and stripping down to her bathing suit, the same black as her hair. "It's dead."

From inside the pocket of her discarded pants, she produced a palm-sized notebook and a pen, and started to write, her hair curtaining the page.

Eva spread out her own towel. "Can I ask?"

"Ask what?" Simone said from behind the curtain.

"What you're writing."

She swept the hair away from her face and looked sideways at Eva. "It's funny. Most people don't ask."

Eva looked out at the ocean. She didn't really like the beach, where everything was infinite. The never-ending waves, the always-receding horizon, more grains of sand than you could count.

"Maybe you're not the easiest person to ask," she said.

That made Simone laugh. "I guess I should tell you, then, since you've been so brave." She put the cap on her pen, which was a fancy pen. "I'm writing a book. Not in here of course"—she waved the little notebook—"but you never know when you'll find new material."

She narrowed her eyes as she smiled, which made the smile steely and unreadable.

"There you are!" Lorrie appeared at the top of the steps. She clattered toward them in her sandals, hard plastic slapping hard wood.

What counted as material? Was it the strangeness of all the creatures? The vastness of the view? Was it something that Eva had said? Or was it something that Simone hadn't—a thought that was hers alone?

"What the fuck is all this?" Lorrie said, disgusted.

All those thoughts. Murky, swimming things—one organism that multiplied into hundreds. Simone was closing her notebook, slipping it back into her pocket. Lorrie was tiptoeing through the sand, as if the creatures were something that might explode. She leapt onto Simone's towel and shuddered.

"Beaches are supposed to be paradises," she said. "But leave it to you to find one that's hell."

Simone looked pleased.

The three of them didn't have as much to say as they had at the beginning of Eva's trip, when Eva had asked a lot of questions and Lorrie had done a lot of talking. Simone was always content to listen. Eva buried her feet in the sand, patting the surface until it was smooth. Eventually, maybe only to fill the silence, Lorrie asked her what she was working on at the newspaper.

Eva hadn't thought about the fire for days, but now the images returned to her all at once, accusing her. What else had she been thinking about? What else could be as important? Her feet were cool and a little damp.

"What's wrong?" Lorrie said.

She could try to explain it, but all the details were boring. *Smokeproof exit enclosures.* She didn't even know what the details meant. They meant something to her, of course, but that part was even more unknowable. *Seismic considerations.* She wiggled her toes and the sand cracked.

"A bunch of different things," Eva said.

"A bunch of different things are wrong?"

"No, I'm working on a bunch of different things."

There was an awkward pause. Simone lifted her head off her towel and briefly met Eva's gaze.

"This guy I work with almost died," Eva said after a few seconds. "He was in Baghdad. There were bombs everywhere. Improvised explosive devices. People hid them in boxes or soda cans or even in roadkill."

"Roadkill?" Lorrie asked.

"Like, inside animal carcasses."

"Wow."

"He was walking through a bombed-out building and he accidentally kicked over a piece of rubble and there was a bomb right there, inches from his foot."

Lorrie gasped. Simone glared at her.

"But it didn't explode," Simone said.

"No," Eva admitted. "It didn't explode."

They were silent.

"His interpreter really did die, though," Eva added. "After the reporter left. The rest of his family—the interpreter's family, I mean—had fled the city after the invasion, but they wanted to come back to see their old neighborhood. To see what was left. The interpreter tried to dissuade them, because he knew just how little was left, but they insisted, and eventually he agreed. The whole street was in ruins. As soon as they opened their front door, the house blew up."

"Who did it?" Lorrie asked.

"He was more than just an interpreter, actually. They call it a fixer. A local journalist, or sometimes just a local—someone who takes you around, who knows everything you won't."

"They probably can't figure out who did it," Simone said.

"Yeah," Eva agreed. "There's no way to be sure."

Simone put her head back on the towel and her forearm over her eyes. Eva wondered if she would write the story in her notebook later—if it counted as material. Her face, at least the part of it that was visible, seemed serene.

Eva left them on their towels and wandered along the shore alone, until she rounded a bend and was out of sight. There were mansions high up above the dunes and big PRIVATE PROPERTY signs staked into the sand. She thought she saw someone outside a bungalow nestled into the cliff, but it was just a wet suit dangling off the porch. She stepped on the pickles because Lorrie had avoided them—she stepped on them to prove that she could. When she had walked as far as she dared, she stopped and filled her hands with creatures. Strange and slick, but not actually moving. She stood at the ragged edge of the water, where the tide tried to tug the sand out to sea, and threw them one by one as far as she could, until her hands were empty again. Then she turned and hurried away, before the waves could spit them back.

"Where were you?" Nick said.

"Where *were* you?" Gail said.

Eva explained while she unpacked her suitcase.

"California?" They sounded shocked.

She waited for them to ask other questions. There were stories she was excited to tell: the celebrity's assistant, the sea pickles. Driving back from the beach, Lorrie had told her about a monastery in her neighborhood called the Self-Realization Fellowship, which sounded like rehab, or a yoga studio—someplace for people with problems and money and spandex—but was actually for monks. They walked around in gold robes. Eva hadn't seen them for herself, but she wished she had—that would have been an especially good story.

"We called Jamie, but he hasn't called back."

"Can we call him again?"

At the bottom of Eva's suitcase there was a thin layer of sand. She thought she might tell her parents about the monks anyway—might describe them as if she'd seen them.

"Just wait," she said.

"We left a voicemail."

"We aren't sure if he checks his voicemail."

Eva carried the bag to the kitchen and carefully tipped it into the trash. Lorrie said the monks walked around the neighborhood—she herself saw them all the time. Once, she'd spotted a few of them driving on the freeway.

"I should really learn to drive," Eva said, because she didn't want to talk about Jamie.

Her parents said nothing, because they did.

"Good thinking," her dad said eventually.

"It gets harder as you get older," her mom admitted. Gail had a license but rarely drove, never parked.

Eva turned the suitcase all the way upside down. She couldn't see any more sand, but she could hear the grains landing in the trash.

"Maybe *you* could call him," Gail said.

Eva sighed. "Fine."

They said goodbye before she'd told any of her stories—the real ones or the invented ones.

The office, when Eva returned, seemed even busier than she remembered. Everyone was chasing stories. On her way to the bathroom, Eva passed a man hunched over his desk, phone pressed against his cheek. "We wouldn't reveal you as the source," she heard him say.

Every story had to be traced back to someone, someplace. Was that what Jamie was really after? The beginning of it all, the ultimate source? The origin and cause?

Then again, lots of people seemed to want religion so that they could find out how the story ended. The apocalypse, Eva had to admit, was an impressive finale, but the afterlife was a letdown—an interminable epilogue. What were you supposed to *do* for eternity? When she went back to her desk, the man with the unnamable source had closed his door.

There were phones with cords in every cubicle, but no one really used them. A few women, old enough that they had been called secretaries before they were called assistants, still recited crisp scripts into these phones. Eva had never answered hers, had certainly never asked anyone to *please hold.* The machine blinked red with messages she didn't bother to check. She called Jamie on her cell phone.

"Hello?"

She could tell from the tone of his voice that he didn't know who was calling. For a moment, she could have been anyone: a telemarketer, a stranger, a robot without a body. *Wrong number,* she could have said. She almost hung up.

"It's Eva."

And then, of course, his voice transformed. (But who, for that instant, had he imagined she was? Who had he hoped she was?) He explained that he'd lost his phone.

"It was worse than I expected. Just a thing, I thought. Replaceable. But then I bought a new phone and realized I didn't remember a single person's number. I couldn't reach anyone."

Eva considered how many numbers she knew by heart. Two, maybe three. Her parents were still her emergency contacts.

"So what did you do?"

"What could I do? I had to wait for people to call me."

"Did they?"

"Some did, some didn't. When they do—well, it's a weird feeling. It's as if I've been waiting and waiting for them, and suddenly there they are. I mean, most of the time I haven't been waiting. It'll be someone I haven't thought about for months, maybe years. It's a good feeling, but I'm not exactly sure what it is. Is it the feeling of finding them, or the feeling of being found?"

Eva smiled. She hadn't been literally lost in a long time. With her phone, there was always a map in her pocket. But of course she could still remember the fear: looking up and realizing, as if waking up in someone else's dream, that she had no idea where she was.

"It's a religious feeling," Jamie continued. "People talk about finding God, but it's really the reverse. *He* finds *you*."

Eva stopped smiling. Did every conversation have to come back to God?

"So all the nonbelievers—he's just still looking for them?" she asked.

"Not exactly."

"A God who's always losing track of people doesn't exactly inspire confidence."

Jamie laughed, and it bothered her: not being able to get under his skin.

"Of course he can see you," he said. "That's not the problem."

Eva waited.

"He can see you—he just can't get through to you."

Jamie had sounded happy, and now he sounded sad. It was easy to argue with him as long as he was being sanctimonious, but it wasn't an argument anymore. It was a burden that Eva didn't want: his judgment, his disappointment, her failure.

"Since when have I been the one who's hard to get through to?" she asked.

"What does that mean?"

"You're always chasing something, always looking for someone to take you in. A movement, a church. My parents. You say you're porous—too porous. But have you ever actually *let* someone in?"

Eva wasn't sure if she should continue, but Jamie said nothing. He was calm and patient, ready to hear her out.

"It's like that tent," she went on. "You'll set it up wherever you want. Not just in the woods—in the middle of the street, in someone else's backyard. I don't know where you're living right now, but I bet it's not yours."

"Is that why you called? To ask where I am?" There were footsteps in the background. Eva had assumed that he was alone. "Do you really want to know?"

For so long, she had wanted to know everything. To know what happened at his fancy school or in his fancy apartment building—all that see-through glass. To know his parents, his brother, the teacher in tweed. To know what he'd been learning week after week at college, until the boy with face blindness, with prosopagnosia (yes, she'd looked it up), had made him understand it all at once. To know what he wanted from the crowd, the collective, the congregation, the community—all those words that meant one person wasn't enough.

She ignored Jamie's question.

"Why is that?" Eva said. It was her turn for questions. "Why do you always want to be where you don't really belong?"

In the silence that followed, she heard more footsteps—approaching, receding. Maybe her anger had surprised him. It had surprised her, too. Like the scratch of a match against match paper, and then a whole dark room revealed.

A hand reached over the top of Eva's cubicle and dropped an envelope onto her desk. She craned her neck to see whom the hand belonged to, but whoever it was had already disappeared.

"Thank you," she said to no one.

"For what?" Jamie asked.

"I wasn't talking to you." She picked up the envelope, anticipation crackling in her chest. "I'm on deadline. I have this story—it might be big."

"You're writing it?"

Hearing the curiosity in his voice—pure, real curiosity—Eva's anger shrank as quickly as it had flared. And what did she feel now?

Relief? Or was it regret? For a moment, the envelope didn't seem to have anything to do with her: the letter, her hands holding the letter, the fire, the story behind the fire. Then she returned to herself. Whose hands could they be except hers?

"I have to finish the story."

They hung up and Eva tore open the envelope. *This is in response to your request.* She grinned and turned the page.

But there was only one more page. In bold letters across the top: REDACTED. The rest of the text had been crossed out with a series of thick black lines, so that only the most pointless words were left exposed. *Moreover. However.* Anything that meant nothing. *Hereafter.* She squinted and put her face right up against the paper, but it was impossible to see what was underneath the ink. In the last sentence, there was just one word that she could read. *Finally.*

WHAT DO YOU MEAN?

Molly insisted on Halloween decorations, because Halloween wasn't allowed when she was a kid. Not for Christians, her dad had pronounced. Back then, she hadn't really cared; she didn't like candy that much anyway, and she was easily frightened, so haunted houses were no great loss. Now, she told Eva, she understood the greater loss: the chance to pretend you were someone else. A fleeting chance, admittedly—costumes that got thrown out, face paint that got washed off—but that, too, was profound. She had been raised to fear changes in her character, to believe that there were certain errors you could never wash off.

Molly decorated too early, so that by the time Halloween arrived, the fake cobwebs above the door were soggy with rain and the jack-o'-lanterns' toothy smiles had softened and curled in on themselves, like the gummy smiles of old people. She and Eva sat on the stoop with a plastic bucket of candy, but there weren't as many trick-or-treaters as they'd hoped. Their neighbor, who had forgotten about the holiday, started handing out loose change, then dollar bills, and all the kids flocked to his door, ignoring theirs. Eva and Molly went inside early, Eva looking for signs of Molly's disappointment. But she seemed happy, her eyes clouded with nostalgia for other people's childhoods. Maybe you couldn't call that nostalgia—maybe that was just longing.

Somehow the candies were all vegan: chewy, neon, sweet, sour, everything shaped like different-sized pills. They sat at the table in the kitchen, unwrapping them one by one, until there was no longer a rush of sugar, just the constant ache of excess, like a wound in their mouths that they kept on widening.

"We'll be sorry tomorrow," Eva said.

Molly shrugged. "But not now. Don't be sorry now."

Eva stretched a piece of banana taffy into a long yellow strand. As a child, she had loved Halloween with an intensity that could be hard to bear. With so many costumes to choose from, she changed her mind constantly, right up until the very last minute.

"You don't have to be religious," she told Molly, "to wish you were a better version of yourself."

The next morning, Eva brushed her teeth twice, trying to scrub away the mossy residue of sugar. She pictured the candy in her stomach, a formless, chewed-up wad, drained of all its artificial color. It was at times like these that she understood the urge to make yourself throw up—to see what was inside of you. But in the end, she was too afraid: the heaving chest, the acid mouth, control escaping through your throat.

She was walking down the street, thinking about vomit, when Eli called her name. He jogged to catch up with her, his backpack jostling back and forth. She smiled without meaning to. (In general, she was careful not to seem too happy to see him.) While they walked to the Metro, he explained that Jess and his former boss—the old, jowly senator—were locked in a private disagreement that seemed at risk of becoming a public one. Eli's mouth twitched in agitation. So far, Jess had avoided the senator, just as Eli had advised. "Stay in your own chamber," he'd said, and she'd laughed. "You're saying a woman's place is in the House?" It was a joke, but he'd touched a nerve: she didn't like being told to mind her own business. Politics, Jess said, was the business of caring about other people's business. The fight with the senator had started out with a specific dispute—a draft bill about childcare subsidies—but its source had long since been forgotten. Now they were arguing about everything.

"Or, you know, nothing," Eli said impatiently.

Jess thought it was productive. They were finally getting to the heart of the matter: what was government *for*? The senator, meanwhile, said their differences were about strategy, not ideology. He kept insisting that they stood for the same things, but he'd been around long enough to know that the person with the strongest beliefs was not necessarily the person with the strongest ideas. He told Jess that she was going to have to learn how to package her principles.

"Sounds condescending." Eva frowned. "Like he's saying Dad knows best."

"Yeah, it didn't go over well."

They rode the long escalator down to the subway platform. All the tunnels in the city were deep underground, because the city was swampy—soft, unstable earth. The stations felt like caverns, dimly lit and cold.

"The thing is," Eli said, "he has a point. You can't just go around saying exactly what you believe."

The train barreled into the station. Somewhere above them, a tinny voice announced its arrival.

"But isn't that the reason you like Jess? That she tells the truth?"

"Truth." Eli said it with pretend gravity, as if her questions were weighing him down. It was not the first time Eva had felt accused. "Lighten up," he used to tell her, back when they were dating. She'd tried—to drop it, to let it go. But what if you missed the things you'd given up?

"I'm serious," she insisted. "How many politicians really tell the truth? It's not a crazy question. I'm not asking you to be a philosopher."

"Do you think that would really solve our problems?" In the middle of the tunnel, the train lurched to a stop, and Eva almost fell onto Eli, then stumbled into a stranger instead. "The reason I like Jess is that she has plans. Green jobs, affordable housing. Have you heard about ghost guns? She's the only one talking about them—"

"What I meant—"

"Look." He was exasperated now. "Honesty doesn't *do* anything."

They emerged from the tunnel. His stop. Eva's thoughts escaped through the doors, and then he did, too. It wasn't until the train had pulled away from the platform that she realized she'd missed her own stop, the one before his. She switched trains at the next station and headed back through the familiar dark.

Eli invited her to a party Jess was hosting. Nothing official, he assured her. The opposite, in fact: Jess had said that all she wanted was to throw a party like her old parties. No strategists, no lobbyists, no celebrities, certainly no reporters. Only regular people, she insisted. Eva wasn't sure whether she should be offended. Was *regular* just another word for boring? She didn't think of herself as a reporter, but it would have been nice if Eli did.

The party started in the afternoon. For the first time since being elected, Jess was taking an entire Saturday off. Eva didn't have any other plans, but she kept inventing reasons to delay leaving the house.

Eventually, it got dark. Molly came home from a bad date and put on sweatpants. Eva texted Eli. *Sorry. I lost track of time.* She was changing out of her jeans when he texted back: *We're still here.* Her pants around her ankles. *See you soon,* he wrote.

Jess lived less than a mile away. She answered the door herself. The same woman Eva had seen all over the Internet, but smaller and wearing socks.

"I'm Jess," she said, even though she didn't need to say it.

She leaned forward, and before Eva understood what was happening, they were hugging. Eva, in her puffy jacket and boots with a heel, felt too big, too tall. Maybe she looked surprised.

"Sorry." Jess laughed. "I've never been a hugger. I don't even like huggers. But I'm so tired of shaking hands."

Eva slipped off her boots. Without her coat, she had a brief, unexpected urge to hug Jess again, but of course she didn't. There were only half a dozen people in the living room, half-drunk beer bottles on bookshelves and windowsills, a glistening metal bowl empty except for unpopped popcorn kernels. It was obvious that Eva was way too late. Eli, sitting at one end of a gray couch with a glass of red wine, smiled but didn't stand up.

"This is Eva."

Jess was the one who said it, and Eva felt a surge of gratitude to her for saying it. Since Eli kept smiling and remained silent, Eva added, "Eli's friend." Everyone nodded. Reshma emerged from the kitchen with a tray of Oreos.

"The theme is regular people and regular food," she explained, placing the tray on an ottoman.

Eva accepted a can of beer, even though she had recently resolved to drink only out of desire, not desperation—at the very least, to start and end the night with a tall glass of water, sipped slowly and mindfully. She was pretty sure she didn't have a drinking problem, but she didn't like the haze of hangovers, the way they made her whole life seem vague. She gulped the beer gratefully.

In the days leading up to the party, Eva had read the news about Jess diligently, going back into the archives: twenty or thirty articles that all contained her name, plus a few more that didn't—for context. By the time she had finished reading, she felt well informed. She felt good. But now no one was talking about politics. They were playing Truth or Dare.

"Dare," said a man sitting on the floor, grinning. He had a patchy orange beard and long legs folded underneath him.

"Take your shirt off," said a woman on the couch.

"Boring!" A man with long braids leaned forward in his chair. "Take your shirt off and—"

"Stand in the middle of the street."

"Stand in the middle of the street and shout, *Fuck the man*."

Everyone looked at Jess, and Jess looked at Eli. She was perched on the armrest of a mustard-colored chair, drinking water from a jar.

"As your director of communications . . ." Eli said in a nasal, bureaucratic-sounding voice that made people laugh. Jess was the last to stop laughing, which would have embarrassed Eva, but Jess didn't seem to mind.

"Yeah," Eli continued, talking normally again. "Maybe not the best idea."

There were tamer dares after that. The man with braids sang a punk anthem in falsetto. A woman in a boxy dress shirt sucked on a bouillon cube for sixty seconds, her face puckering from the salt. A short guy with huge arm muscles put his toe in his mouth. No one picked Truth.

Eli tried to skip his turn—mostly, Eva suspected, so that the others would insist.

"Dare," he said eventually. "But make it good."

It was Jess's idea.

"Close your eyes," she said, and he obeyed.

When Jess gave instructions, her voice changed. Calm and firm, quieter but somehow stronger. Eva recognized it: her public voice—her Jessica voice. She told everyone else to stand up and find a new seat. She herself stood on the mustard chair while choreographing, staring down at the tops of their heads.

"No talking," she said sternly, when the short man whispered something. "Don't give yourself away."

Eli's job, Jess explained, was to identify them all, one face at a time, without ever opening his eyes. His fingertips would be his only guide. From her new spot near a crowded bookshelf, Eva watched Eli react. With his eyes closed, he looked defenseless—possibly even nervous.

It was easy at first. The red-haired man was obvious because of his beard, and when the woman in the dress shirt bit Eli's finger playfully, he guessed her right away. Another woman had a hoop through one nostril. While Eli stroked the clean-shaven cheeks of the next man—big nose, high forehead, chapped lips—Eva imagined his fingers on her own face, pressing, inquiring. She felt a little excited and a little afraid.

Next, the clean-shaven man guided Eli to the couch, where Reshma was sitting cross-legged on the middle cushion. Eli ran his index finger down her nose and checked her upper lip for stubble. He traced one eyebrow, then the other. He cupped Reshma's whole face in his hands and Eva saw a ripple of satisfaction across his own. He was serious, confident.

"Jess."

When he opened his eyes, he laughed, but no one else did.

Had he touched Jess like that—the way you cradle something fragile or precious, the way you hold it up to the light?

Once, when Eva and Eli were having sex, long after they'd broken up, she'd asked him to choke her. Gently. He'd stopped what he was doing (thrusting, murmuring, something normal). *Really?* The question made her hesitate. Maybe she wanted it or maybe she'd just heard about people wanting it. In the end, she said never mind.

Reshma stared at Eli, then took his hands off her face and reached around him for another cookie.

"Your turn, Jess," she said.

"Do I have to?" Jess's voice was louder again, not quite as steady.

"Your turn," Reshma repeated.

Jess sat back in the chair, which now dwarfed her, the high back of it looming above her, the yellow bright against her dark clothes: black turtleneck, black denim, black socks. These changes in scale—she had seemed small standing in the doorway, then tall standing on the chair, and now seemed even smaller than before—made Eva watch her more closely. The black socks were actually navy.

"Okay," Jess said, uncertainly. "Truth."

Reshma made a sound that could have been a laugh or a cough. A few guests turned to look at her, but she ignored them, separating two halves of a cookie and carefully scraping the icing off with her front teeth.

"Evie, ask one," said the red-haired man.

Eva didn't correct him. She looked at the alphabetized bookshelves so that she didn't have to look at Jess. Everyone was waiting. She scanned the shelf for an author who was out of order and couldn't find one. *Jump.*

"Who have you abandoned?"

"What?"

"Like, someone you've left behind along the way." She traced the cracked spine of a book with her finger. "There must be someone, right?"

When Eva turned to face the room, everyone was looking at her. Eli's eyes were narrowed and accusatory; the woman with the nose ring might have been about to cry. Panic gripped Eva's chest, then squeezed. What did they know that she didn't? Someone's bracelets jangled, and she flinched.

Jess seemed taken aback, but as the question hung in the air, her surprise shifted into something else. She wasn't angry—more like intrigued. A tilt of the head. A slight, wry smile.

"Oh God," Reshma said.

She was the only one not staring at Eva, because she was staring at her phone. She held the screen up, unable to speak, her other hand covering her mouth. This seemed to Eva like a performance of shock, but maybe only because she hadn't seen very much actual shock: a good performance, after all, was always based on something real. And here it was—reality. Jess had already grabbed Reshma's phone, and other devices quickly emerged from back pockets or between couch cushions. There had been a shooting at a high school in New York. Kids were dead. No one knew exactly how many, but it was a lot. Jess left the room and Eli followed her. Reshma sat frozen for another second; then, as if a switch had been flipped, her hand dropped from her mouth, her gaze returned to the room, and she, too, was hurrying away from the incriminating scene—the *regular* scene, all their trivial props and effortful pleasures, which they could now see had merely been setting the stage for ordinary, awful disaster.

WHERE DID YOU GO?

Seventeen kids plus three adults. The shooter among the dead—among the kids. It happened in Queens, in a neighborhood called Utopia, at a school right next to a cemetery. These details were quickly made symbolic; people didn't believe in signs until, suddenly, they did.

Eva's parents called her a few hours after the news broke, just to be sure she was all right. For a second, impatience flickered through her chest: of course she was—she was hundreds of miles from the scene of the crime. Then it vanished.

"I'm all right."

It was the kind of event that prompted people to check in. Lorrie texted. Molly called her mom, which she only did on holidays. The next day, Eva's bosses were somber, solicitous. Even Eli said something: *Sorry about the party.*

It would have been easy to check on Jamie. That Sunday morning, Eva lay in bed with her laptop on her chest. She hadn't watched Kenny's sermons in a while. He might say something consoling. She might see the back of Jamie's head. If she rewound the video to the very first frame, she might also see the blur of his thumb over the lens.

"He's all right."

She said it out loud and put the laptop away. She listened to her eyelashes against the pillowcase, amplified in the empty room until they were as loud as the beating of giant wings.

"We're all right."

Her voice strained with the effort of belief.

In the days that followed, there were fewer cries of grief, more calls to action. Sorrow was a spontaneous sound; you didn't know what your sadness sounded like until you heard it for yourself. But outrage had a script—the kind that Eli probably wrote. Arguments were rehearsed, performed, applauded. There were eulogies that sounded like campaign speeches. Eva felt the loss of the sense of loss. She scrolled through photographs of smiling teenagers, all of them now dead, trying to picture herself at the same age, then picturing Jamie instead—a clearer image. That was the Jamie she'd known best.

She bought the newspaper in print so that she could cut out the obituaries and save them in a folder somewhere. She bought a banana, too, the way she used to, but it wasn't ripe enough—starchy and bitter when she took a bite. The obituaries were long, though the lives had been short. A lot of space was devoted to describing the teenagers' dreams: the people they had hoped to become. Brian wanted to play at Carnegie Hall and Yadira wanted to go skydiving. Xiang wanted to join the army and Austin wanted to cure cystic fibrosis, because his little brother had it. Admirable dreams, but Eva knew they wouldn't have come true, even if no one had died. Brian would have quit the violin, Xiang would have dropped out of basic training. That wasn't the sad part. The dreams would have changed, and the dreamers would have, too. Eva imagined Yadira flying at ten thousand feet in the air and deciding not to jump. She imagined Austin's brother dying of something no one expected—a car accident, a bottle of pills. Then what?

That was the sad part.

She took a cheap bus home for the weekend, because she thought home might be comforting. The bus broke down twice. The second time, all the passengers filed out onto the side of the highway so that it could be towed away, and for a few minutes, before a new bus came to pick them up, they waited there in the cold, watching the cars stream past. Eva had been sleepy for most of the bus ride—out of it. Now she was in it. Too in it. When you were driving on the highway, it was possible to believe in the illusion that all the cars were moving at a slow, stately pace, but if you were standing beside the highway, the reality of speed could not be ignored. The cars were bullets whizzing past her face. The danger was right there, roaring in her ears, blowing her hair in every direction. Nothing prevented the cars from swerving into the people, or the people from running into the cars. They were a group of total strangers, with nothing in common except their final destination. Eva could see it clearly: someone breaking free of their informal ranks, sprinting across one dotted line and then another, lines that were nothing but promises that everyone would stay in their place. Eva sat down, because she was afraid to stand up, afraid that she might be the one to run. And why not? It could happen to anyone. Dizzy, she put her head between her knees. It was only when another passenger—another stranger—tapped her on the shoulder that Eva realized the new bus had arrived. By some unspoken agreement, everyone took the same seats on the new bus as they had on the old bus. Back on the road, the cars seemed slow again, but she knew that the bus would get there too fast, that there was no stopping whatever terrible thing she now felt certain was coming.

OR ARE YOU AGAINST US?

Whenever she visited her parents, Eva acted like a child. Old habits and discarded poses came right back to her, like the lyrics of a song she thought she'd forgotten, then surprised herself by remembering every word, as long as someone else started singing first. Usually, she was embarrassed by her regression, but this time, she found herself looking forward to the familiarity.

The house was loud when she arrived. Upstairs, Bob Dylan wheezed into his harmonica. Downstairs, the radio was talking to no one. In the front hall, where Eva waited at an unseen threshold, the two soundtracks became one: raspy poetry, the traffic report, the chorus, an ad for Lasik surgery, the bridge. Nick opened the door to his studio, and the house got even louder.

"*How does it fee-eel?*" he sang, stretching the vowels absurdly. He looked tan, even though it was almost winter. He was holding a pair of scissors.

"Can you turn it down?"

"*To be on your own.*" He crooned at the scissors as if they were a microphone.

In the kitchen, a chipper advertisement abruptly gave way to a somber newscast. "In Utopia—"

"I said, can you turn it off?"

"—mourners gathered."

"*A complete unkno-own.*"

Eva went into the kitchen and unplugged the radio.

"Okay, okay," Nick called after her. "Sorry."

The song continued for another few seconds—he let the chorus finish—and then there was silence. He appeared behind her in the kitchen doorway. Not as tan in this light.

"Do you want to put your bag down?"

She hadn't noticed she was still carrying it—her coat, too. An image came to her: a man weaving a child's arms through the straps of a backpack. Was the image a memory, or just an idea? She let the bag slide off her shoulder. She unzipped her coat but left it on.

"What are the scissors for?"

He was getting into collage. For years, he explained, he'd dismissed it as a craft, not an art, but now he was beginning to understand its beauty.

"I've been so superficial," he said. "I mean, literally. The surface is the painter's great passion."

Collage had texture, dimension. He liked playing around with all the bits of colors, almost like a puzzle. It didn't matter—or it mattered less than he'd thought—if they didn't quite fit together.

Gail came through the front door, weighed down with grocery bags. She hugged Eva and hurried to put things in the freezer. Eva tried to help unpack, but discovered she no longer knew where everything belonged; opening a cupboard where cereal boxes had once been stacked, she found a row of vinegars—more types than she knew existed, sediment clouding at the base of the bottles. There was a new blender on the countertop, the same kind that Molly used for smoothies, and coffee gurgling in a fancy machine that Eva had never seen before. When everything had been put away, Gail poured them each a cup.

"We don't drink regular milk anymore," she said.

"Regular?"

"We like almond milk. Or oat. There's macadamia milk, but it's expensive."

Nick took his coffee upstairs. The music resumed, softer but still audible. *You're invisible now, you've got no secrets to conceal.* Holding her mug with both hands, Gail explained that, with Nick spending long hours in his studio, she was trying to get out more.

"Out where?" Eva asked.

The almond milk separated in the coffee, white flecks floating at the surface. Gail took a noisy sip. She'd joined the block association. She went to public sessions of the city council and signed up to volunteer at polling stations.

"Wow."

"It's not activism," Gail added quickly. "I'm just getting involved."

At the middle school where she taught, she'd started a civic-engagement club. Her students wrote one letter a month, to a public person of their choice. It could be anyone. There were letters to the surgeon general, the points leader of the NBA, the president's dog.

"We want them to find their voice."

Eva had never lost her voice, but it happened to Gail exactly once a year. After the first week of school—five days of too much talking—she came home hoarse, and by the next morning, she could barely make a sound. It was practically a routine, but Eva had never gotten used to it. If Gail's voice had simply faded, like the gentle turning of a dial, Eva might not have minded. Instead, it transformed: gravelly and strange, then gone altogether. She was a different person, clutching her throat and smiling silently through conversations. She was less of a person.

"To find their voice," Gail repeated, "and then to raise it."

This sounded like something on a motivational poster, or from one of those books that made changing your life seem as easy as assembling a desk chair. Eva had never known her parents to read that kind of book. She stirred her coffee vigorously, until the almond milk disappeared and the drink was a single, uniform color.

"You're sure you don't want to take off your coat?"

As soon as Eva stopped stirring, the white flecks reappeared.

The day after Eva arrived, Gail announced that she was going to a rally for gun control, and at the last minute, Eva went with her. The crowd gathered in a park at the base of the Brooklyn Bridge. Everyone was wearing orange. So was her mom, though Eva hadn't understood why until she saw her blend effortlessly into the crowd. It wouldn't have made a difference if Gail had told her—Eva didn't own anything orange—but she was annoyed anyway. When the group began moving across the bridge, she fell a few steps behind Gail and then a few more, until she could barely see her.

There were more women marching than men. According to their signs, a lot of them were moms. The wind ripped at their posters and swallowed up their syllables, but they seemed undeterred. Ahead of Eva, a woman with a thick braid down her back was holding two children by the hand, swinging their arms in time with the crowd's chanting. The children had braids, too.

Eva could picture herself as a mom, but she couldn't picture her kids. Their faces were like faces in dreams—blank or blurry, even though you somehow knew who was who. Eva couldn't see any of the faces in front of her, either, and this was briefly terrifying: all the backs of heads, all the backs of signs, everything unreadable. Eva missed a beat and fell out of sync with the chant. For a few seconds, she could hear herself above the crowd. An ugly, jarring sound, but she couldn't tell which was worse—her own voice or everyone else's. She shouted a little louder, and one of the braided girls spun around, glaring at her. Eva noticed that she had pale eyes and a lot of freckles, but the girl turned away again, her hair landing with a thump between her shoulder blades, before Eva could notice anything else.

On the other side of the bridge, people were gathered in a stone plaza facing a makeshift stage. By the time Eva got there, the governor, wearing an orange T-shirt stretched tightly over a blue dress shirt, was already halfway through his speech. The T-shirt said MOMS DEMAND ACTION. Eva googled to see if the governor had any kids. He did: pretty daughters with fake smiles, adults by now, though the Internet produced pictures of them at every age. The governor was making lofty, familiar promises. The air was brisk, but his face was red with effort, and dark half-moons appeared under his arms. A ponytailed woman standing beside Eva hoisted a sign in the air: DON'T LOOK AWAY. Eva's attention wandered, and eventually so did she, weaving her way through the crowd, looking for the fastest way out. When she had pushed through the last row of people, she texted Gail to tell her that she was leaving. The text took forever to send. Eva stopped and watched the screen for a while, as if she, too, were stuck. *Not delivered.*

"Fuck."

A woman with a baby strapped to her chest glanced at her disapprovingly. Eva gave up and put her phone in her pocket. When she looked up again—away from crowd, not into it—she was looking at Jamie.

No, not Jamie. A second later, her mistake was ridiculous. The man in front of her was tall and thin like Jamie, but he was old. His hair wasn't blond, it was gray. Eva couldn't see the man's face, because his head was bowed, but now that she was looking closely, she could see that he had a beard. Not a scruffy, fashionable one—a long, slightly unkempt one. His wiry body, reappraised in light of his mangy beard, looked even wirier. It looked a little wild.

The man's shape-shifting unsteadied her, and in her confusion, it took Eva a moment to realize that he was praying—chin against chest, fingers interlaced. There was a semicircle of about fifteen people surrounding him, set slightly apart from the crowd, at the very edge of the plaza, where trash cans were jammed full of signs that protesters discarded as they left. Everyone in the group had the exact same posture. Hunched over, they all looked as old as the man, even though some of them were young. They seemed meek—vulnerable. Many held hands, and one or two knelt on the cold stone.

Watching the prayer circle, Eva grew less and less aware of her surroundings, the noise of the crowd behind her blending into a single, irrelevant soundtrack. She was lost in thought—or was it the absence of thought?—when a man collided with her shoulder, knocking her briefly off balance.

"Sorry," he said, though he didn't sound it. He hurried past her toward the crowd, followed by a second man, who avoided Eva's eyes. Both men were tall and muscular—the kind of muscles you get at the gym. They were each carrying a sign with the same message written on the front and back. All caps, bright red:

~~**THOUGHTS**~~

~~**PRAYERS**~~

ACTION

Eva glanced back at the worshippers, to see if they'd noticed the signs, but of course they hadn't—their eyes were closed.

"No. More. Bull. Shit!" one of the men shouted toward the stage.

"No. More. Bull. Shit!" the other one repeated.

With each syllable, they jabbed their signs in the air, their muscles flexing and unflexing. Gradually, the people around them joined in—hesitantly, at first, voices wavering, then stronger and louder, their uncertain rhythms brought into confident alignment.

"No. More. Bull. Shit!"

"No. More. Bull. Shit!"

Eva had willingly chanted these same words on the bridge; not even the moms, it seemed, took issue with profanity. But now the sound of the men's voices seemed to implicate her—in what, exactly, she wasn't sure. Looking around at the crowd, at the sweating governor and screaming men, at the mothers and daughters, she wondered how much they really had in common. Maybe it was a lot: opinions or values, a sense of duty, a moment of passion. Or maybe it was just the commonest thing of all—the fear that they, too, were going to die.

Her phone vibrated. *Where are you?* She couldn't read the tone of Gail's text. Was she worried? Annoyed? Just curious? Right before Eva turned away, the man with the wiry body and the mangy beard stood up straight and opened his eyes. His gaze landed on her, so briefly that afterward she wasn't sure if it really had. If he saw or heard the men in the crowd, he didn't show it. He had already turned away, murmuring something to those close enough to hear, his lips moving, but just barely.

Jess was standing onstage when Eva returned to the crowd to look for Gail. The sight of her was disorienting. What was she doing here? But of course she was here: her home, her voters.

Her speech had just ended and she was standing patiently, a little awkwardly, as the applause rose and fell and rose again. When the cheering finally died down and she walked offstage, she spotted Eva right away. She waved enthusiastically. Eva, remembering the last thing she'd said to Jess—"Who have you abandoned?"—waved back cautiously. Jess ducked under the rope that separated the speakers from the crowd. She was wearing her usual black pantsuit, but her knitted hat was the same as everyone's knitted hat.

Eva admitted she'd missed the speech, and started to apologize, but Jess just nodded.

"I'm sure you've heard one like it."

Eva was taken aback. "Doesn't that bother you?"

"What do you mean?"

A new speaker was onstage—a kid squinting nervously, holding the microphone too far from his mouth. Eva couldn't hear him over the cheering and clapping.

"Everyone repeating everyone else," she said.

"And then repeating themselves?"

"Yeah." Eva looked back at the crowd. Ahead of her, a teenage girl wore an orange scarf wrapped all the way up to her nostrils. "How can you know what they really think?"

"You can't," Jess said. "But does it matter?"

At first, Eva thought the girl was yet another person praying; her palms were pressed together in front of her heart. But no, the palms were moving. She was just warming her hands.

"Is repetition such a bad thing?" Jess continued. "I mean, don't you like the way it feels—when one person calls out, and the whole crowd responds?"

The girl took a step forward and her scarf unraveled, revealing her mouth.

"Isn't that what everyone wants?" Jess asked.

"A response?"

Just then a woman appeared beside them and touched Jess's arm. She was old—she had gray in her hair and wrinkles around her eyes—but something illuminated her eyes that felt new. Energy, maybe. Or passion? Whatever it was, there were tears, too. She was crying steadily.

"My godson," she said. "He—" Her voice caught. She swallowed, then tried again. "My godson. It was a long time ago."

She was pulling on Jess's sleeve now. Jess waited, a long but not uncomfortable silence. Finally, the woman pursed her lips and shook her head. Her eyes tried to say whatever she couldn't. Jess put her hand on the woman's hand.

"I can only imagine."

IS THAT ALL?

When Jamie's life fell apart, Eva was watching TV. The season finale of Molly's favorite show, in which fifty contestants each tried to find love over the course of a lot of speed-dating. The catch was that they never saw the other contestants' faces. This was supposed to reveal something profound about the nature of love—about beauty, too. Was it really, as was so often claimed, on the inside?

That night, a man and a woman who had already agreed to get married were going to see each other for the first time. Several years earlier, without any warning, the left half of the woman's face had been permanently paralyzed. She had never regained control of the muscles. Her mouth drooped, her left eyebrow was frozen in place. Every smile was a half-smile. She had not told the man any of this, because it was against the rules: you weren't allowed to describe your appearance, to set expectations high or low. In an interview—what Molly explained to Eva was called a confessional—the woman admitted that she was hoping the man, too, had some secret flaw. (That was how she referred to it: her flaw.) She said she almost expected him to.

What else, she wondered, would explain why they had connected so instantaneously, so completely?

It happened around the same time that the woman began speaking—confessing—to the camera. Of course, Eva only pieced this together afterward. There was so much to piece together.

Jamie answered every question he was asked. (Kenny refused to say anything at all. Not to the doctors, not to the police, not to his ex-wife—the only person they could figure out to call.) They told Jamie to start at the beginning, and he nodded. He didn't seem to notice that he was crying, that he had not stopped crying since he'd woken up in the hospital, the right side of his body covered in bandages, his left wrist handcuffed to the side of the bed.

Eva, who in the days that followed found it difficult to get out of her own bed, often thought about those handcuffs. She hadn't seen them herself, but her parents had. Jamie had called them instead of his own parents. Later, they told her that he occasionally seemed to forget that the handcuffs were there, lifting his arm to reach for something or toward someone, then looking down in surprise, reality returning with a sudden pull at his wrist.

Maybe the beginning—or the beginning of the end, which was probably what they meant—could be traced back to January. The grim part of the month, when people no longer acknowledged the newness of the new year. Everywhere signs of good cheer were being taken down or taken back: Christmas trees chewed up into wood chips, colorful lights unwound, no one wishing each other a happy this or a merry that.

But Kenny loved that time of year. Any Christian could do Christmas, he told the church. There was nothing wrong with the holidays, but what about the ordinary days? If no one told you it was time to stop and celebrate, if there wasn't all that literal song and dance, could you *make* the time? Could you find a reason to rejoice?

The answer seemed to be yes: every Sunday, there were more and more people in the room. Pretty soon, the church (that is, the community) was no longer fitting into the church (that is, the building). Kenny refused to turn anyone away. People crowded into the stairwell, listening to his sermons, or, fine, sometimes sleeping through them. Half the people at the church had homes and the other half didn't. Some of the haves wanted to give things directly to the have-nots: herbal tea, low-sodium broths, gluten-free cookies. After the service, while Jamie was folding up all the folding chairs, he often found the cookies wrapped discreetly inside napkins, uneaten. Meaning well, he tried to explain to those who arrived with Tupperware full of whole grains, was not the same as doing good. For that, there were official church funds, which Kenny had put him in charge of. Kenny had been putting him in charge of more and more things. Jamie handed out supplies to anyone who asked, and even to those who didn't: socks, sliced bread, hand warmers, subway cards. An elderly man thanked him, and Jamie just said, "Of course."

At the fried-chicken place below the church, people started complaining. The crowd. The smell of the crowd. One week, the restaurant owner appeared in the doorway in his apron and shouted. The next week, he slurred. After that, Kenny and Jamie agreed that they couldn't stick around much longer. A church could be anywhere—they didn't need spires or altars, didn't even need pews—but it had to be safe. Kenny preached on the many meanings of the word *sanctuary.* They broke the lease. They looked for a cheap place and found out there was no such thing. For a while, they gathered in parks, stamping their feet in the cold, but the coffee never stayed hot, their numbers started dwindling again, and Kenny developed a cough he couldn't shake.

Then a woman who was brand-new to the church, a painter from Denver, told them about the warehouse where she'd been living. It was on a desolate block in Bushwick, next to an abandoned lot filled with rusting construction equipment, where plastic bags snagged on toothy machinery and whipped in the wind. The units were meant to be artists' studios—one empty room, with one huge window—but for months now, she'd been spending every night on the floor in a sleeping bag. At the end of the hall, there was a bathroom with no mirrors, where she washed up in paint-splattered sinks. None of this was allowed—there were zoning laws, some fine print in her lease—but the guy who owned the warehouse lived in Rhode Island, and no one in the building had ever actually met him. He'd inherited the warehouse from his parents or his grandparents; way back when, his family had actually put it to use warehousing stuff. But the guy didn't like thinking about his inheritance—he preferred thinking he was independent, even a little bit punk—so he rented the space to a bunch of artists and told them he wouldn't bother them if they didn't bother him. In the mornings, the painter could see the sun rise over a hilly cemetery to the east, its crypts glowing orange.

Kenny rented the biggest studio, on the top floor. The lease was in Jamie's name, because Kenny had bad credit and Jamie had good credit. When he was just a kid, his parents had set up his bank accounts and paid the bills. His good fortune wasn't fair—the luck of the draw, he said—so he was happy to help. In the Bible, Kenny explained, God decreed that every fifty years, all debts should be forgiven. It was called a jubilee. Kenny said real Christians understood that joy was light and debt was heavy, that there were certain burdens you couldn't believe your way out of, that true jubilation would never be simply a matter of the heart.

At the studio, they held services as usual. They never pretended to make any art. The building turned out to be mostly vacant, and Jamie liked to wander the halls, peering into rooms. Some of them were locked and some of them weren't. The windows were so big that even the weak winter light filled up the space. The glass was thick and old, cracked in some places, yellow panes here and there that looked like aging teeth. There were a few artists on the first floor, but their rooms were spare—no paint, no plaster. Everything they made, they made on screens.

On Sundays, when everyone except the painter had gone, Jamie found himself wanting to linger. The building was hollow, the rooms were cold, the street was rustling with trash, but he sensed something in it. A possibility, maybe. Something luminous—no, numinous. He stayed until it got dark, then biked back to Gail and Nick's house, a small beam of light from his handlebars guiding the way.

The warehouse itself didn't seem to mean much to Kenny. He arrived at the building on Sunday mornings and left on Sunday afternoons. Jamie never forgot that Kenny had another life: a day job, an apartment, a roommate with a cat. Kenny didn't like talking about it. He didn't call it his fake life, but that was how it seemed. Jamie wanted his life to be all one thing.

He moved into the studio—the church—as soon as he could feel spring at hand. He didn't ask Kenny, he just did it. He didn't tell Eva's parents where he was going. The insulation was shit and the concrete floor was cold, but that was okay with him. He lost his phone as soon as he arrived, and that was okay, too. There was no shower, but so what? It was a kind of art, or at least a kind of creativity: making do.

A thin partition separated his room from the painter's room, and through it they came to share a certain intimacy: coughing, humming, a pencil scratching, something that sounded like jumping jacks. They both kept their doors unlocked and wide open, but they rarely spoke. In the mornings, while Jamie stood in front of his window, he pictured her standing in front of hers, their faces turned toward the same early light.

And then, with a suddenness that seemed like vengeance, a cold snap. Crocuses were buried under snow. Every form of eagerness was punished: the first green spears of daffodils, the expectant purple buds of cherry trees. Branches and flowers were coated in a delicate shell of ice, as if they were being preserved, except that they were being destroyed.

On the first cold night, the painter appeared in the doorway with an extra space heater, and when Jamie protested, all she said was "Don't be stupid." The heater didn't work well. He finally fell asleep with his hands in his armpits, his toes aching. On the second night, she appeared again and showed him how to zip their sleeping bags together. She told him to take off his clothes, and this time he knew not to object. Warmer that way. Tolerable that way.

He woke up with her breasts pressing into his shoulder blades. They dressed inside the sleeping bag. They could feel their nakedness but they couldn't see it. They stood silently in front of the same window. He felt desire, but not for her.

For whom?

For what?

He didn't know, of course. Wanting was not knowing, not knowing was believing.

On the telephone wire outside, a row of birds was shouting at the sky.

That morning was a Sunday morning. When the room was packed full of people, it was warm—almost hot. That made Jamie laugh. Hours earlier, he'd been convinced he would freeze to death, and now he was sweating, his shoulder against someone else's shoulder, his thigh against someone else's thigh—it didn't matter whose.

And so when the snow started falling in the middle of the sermon, it seemed to Jamie like a sign. He had never received one before, or if he had, he'd never noticed it, never trusted it. The message was simple. Not a revelation, just a fact: it's cold out there but it's warm in here. The sign said, *Stay here.* Everyone in the room had been looking for something—some had longed for church, others had dreamed of a home—but now they could stop looking.

Jamie bent his head. The sleet against the windows was gentle music. He had never learned how to pray, because Kenny said there was nothing to teach.

Thanks, he said.

Every night that week, two men who had nowhere else to go slept in the church—the room. Jamie wanted to show the men he trusted them, so each evening he left them alone, twisting the lock on the doorknob and leaving them with the key, then following the painter to her studio. On the last night—he didn't know it was the last night—her space heater hissed and the partition between the rooms vibrated in the wind. That their bodies fit together had nothing to do with them. Bodies were just pieces. He could tell when she was asleep by the way her rib cage moved beneath his arm, slow and steady. His own breath fell into the same rhythm. His chest was another room that could grow and shrink, that he couldn't see inside.

That was the beginning, and then there was the end.

Everything was dark, until everything was awesomely, blazingly light.

When?

They all had notebooks. They all wore watches. But he had no idea. It was only many hours later that he had thought to check the time, and then it meant nothing to him. You don't measure before and after in hours.

Then what?

They turned to a new page in their notebooks. Again he looked dumbfounded. They repeated their questions. Surely he could do this much. He nodded. (Still crying.) He tried his best.

The sound, the heat. The way smoke stuffs your mouth. The way it stuffs every open space in your body, like lots and lots of cloth, until you're all filled up. All closed up. The wall between the rooms is a wall of fire. For an instant, he could swear that beneath the rippling curtain of flames there are faces staring back at him. Huge faces, larger-than-life faces. They stay completely still, their expressions unperturbed by the fire that licks and gnaws them, and then they are gone. The room is orange and red, until it is suddenly black. Not dark—black. A color that is a thing, consuming everything it can, too thick and deep and real to push through. Then he's in the hall, where the air is a little better, a little clearer. He gulps. He coughs. He crouches very close to the ground. He doesn't think about being naked, because his skin isn't skin, it's heat. When he reaches out his hand to look for the door to the next room, the hand vanishes in the smoke. It goes someplace where he is not. His fingers are closing around the metal knob. It's locked, of course. He's the one who locked it. Then his fingers are burning, and then—or maybe all this is happening at exactly the same time—he's howling. He should be letting go. You're supposed to let go without thinking about letting go. But he keeps burning and yelling and holding on.

Later, they told him how it happened, which wasn't the same as why it happened. The space heaters were plugged in for too long, the plugs were frayed, and all those tubes of oil paint were an accident waiting to happen. The painter jumped out the window, then ran as far as she could on two broken ankles. Not very far, but far enough. (Where was she now? Was her wrist locked to her bed? He had a lot of questions, but it wasn't his turn to ask them. He might never get a turn.) They told him that he had been dragged unconscious out of the building. In a few places, his clothes had melted into his skin.

What they didn't tell him was that one man was dead and the other was dying. No, they kept that from him. They still had more questions.

He stopped crying. He closed his eyes, and it was only then, staring at his eyelids, which were at once a solid surface and a never-ending void, that he realized what all those faces had been. Her paintings. They might have been people she studied or people she remembered or people she invented as she went along.

The woman with the half-frozen face had put on makeup and a sexy red dress. She stood on one side of a thick curtain, waiting to be revealed. The camera showed her from several angles. Her good side, her bad side. She was wringing her hands, so the camera zoomed in: red nails to match the red dress.

"I can't watch," Eva said.

"Shh," Molly said.

What they knew and the woman did not was that the man was very handsome. Conventionally, symmetrically handsome. Whatever his flaws were, they weren't visible. The camera showed him, too. He waited patiently, jaw squared, hands clasped behind his back.

The woman had told the camera that she didn't want to find the perfect man. She would never be able to trust him—to trust that he really loved her. The curtain lifted very slowly. You couldn't see who was lifting it. Fancy shoes, slender ankles. The woman let her hands drop to her sides. The man's belt buckle glinted. Eva saw his waist, her breasts, his shoulders, her collarbones, and then, before either face could appear, she grabbed the remote. The screen went black.

Molly let out one single wail. She kept staring at the TV, but she didn't try to turn it back on. After a moment, she took a deep breath and regained her composure.

"Well," she said. "Now we'll never know."

CAN I ASK YOU SOMETHING?

Eva's boss, a stocky, serious man whose half-gray hair seemed to testify not just to age but to experience, took her out to lunch and asked her where she saw herself in five years. She considered giving the right answer, telling him about all the projects, all the passions that she wanted to pursue. Then their sandwiches arrived and she told him the truth instead. Her friend (possibly her best friend, or possibly her ex-best-friend) had been in jail for 155 days, waiting for a trial that might send him to prison for thousands more. She hadn't seen him, hadn't even spoken to him. She didn't want to think about five years from now. All she could think about—constantly, obsessively—was five years ago.

Her boss didn't stop eating his sandwich while Eva talked, but she could tell that he was listening carefully. Reporters were good at that. You couldn't decide what you were listening for in advance. You had to keep your mind wide open. You had to know it when you heard it.

He wiped mustard from the edge of his mouth and told her that there was an opening for an editor at the Wellness section. He could recommend her for the job.

"You're very conscientious," he said.

Eva wasn't sure if this was a promotion. Editor sounded better than Researcher, but she never read the Wellness section—it wasn't serious. There were articles about insomnia and Botox and the causes of bloating. Occasionally, they reported on the latest brain-imaging studies, as long as the results weren't too complicated or too ambiguous.

"You're very thorough," Eva's boss added.

"Thorough," she repeated. "I'd rather be—"

Her boss's mouth was full but he cut her off with a wave of his napkin, swallowing in a hurry.

"You'd rather be what? Brilliant? A genius?"

"I guess."

Eva put a potato chip in her mouth and it crunched loudly.

"I'm not your boss because I'm a genius." There was something between his teeth. He saw her see it and quickly closed his mouth. When he opened it, the teeth were clean. "I'm your boss because I work hard."

Eva wrapped up her food—she'd barely touched the sandwich—and agreed to think it over. When they parted ways, he gave her a meaningful, parental look.

"It might do you good."

Since the fire, Eva had avoided returning to New York for as long as she could. "Come home," her parents kept saying, and she kept not going. But in August, the weather forced her hand. The air hummed with heat and cicadas, whose beady red eyes and menacing drone made the humidity seem like a plague. Eva's office, blasting with air-conditioning, was another extreme: her fingertips went numb while she typed.

In Brooklyn, it was warm but not hot. She arrived just before the sun went down and sat in the backyard by herself, covered in bug spray, watching mosquitoes hover around her ankles without ever landing, repelled by some invisible force. She sat there until it got dark, fireflies flashing their secret code back and forth across the lawn.

Her parents wouldn't stop saying how happy they were to see her. "Your favorite," they said when dinner was served, and Eva looked at her plate in surprise: this? The food tasted abstract after that, as if she weren't really the one chewing it. On a Saturday morning, she slept past noon and emerged from her bedroom a sullen teenager, angry at the hours that she'd wasted. Downstairs, Nick was eating lunch and Gail was lacing up her shoes.

"Where are you going?" Eva asked.

"Visiting hours."

"Visiting who?"

Gail finished tying her shoes but stayed bent over, not looking at Eva.

"Jamie," she said, as if this were obvious, and maybe it should have been. "We go every weekend. We take turns, me and your dad."

"Why didn't you tell me?"

Gail straightened up. "I didn't think you'd want to know."

Eva could have said that she was wrong, but she was right. They had asked her to come home and she hadn't. They had asked her to send him a letter and she hadn't.

Letters, they had explained, were the only way to reach someone in jail. You couldn't call him out of the blue—he had to call you. First you put your number in the mail, and then you waited by the phone, which might or might not ring. They had done the right thing, and Eva had done nothing but count the days. She made a tally for each one, blue ink on white paper, a row of bars that stretched all the way across one page and then onto another. Her parents said there were pencils in jail, but no pens. No spiral binding, either—too dangerous. Erasers were in high demand, short supply. Her dad told her Jamie's joke: "Everyone here is trying to undo things." He would have told her more, but Eva closed her eyes. *Stop*. She pictured the blue tallies instead of picturing Jamie. *I can't.*

When Gail was gone, Eva and Nick pretended they were absorbed in various tasks in the kitchen, but they kept getting in each other's way. He was standing in front of the drawer she needed to open. He washed the bowl she was still using. She plugged in the kettle after he plugged in the toaster, and the fuse blew. Eva abandoned breakfast and went out into the yard again. The grass needed to be mowed. The black walnut stump no longer made her sad. A vine had climbed halfway to the top of the fence, then given up.

Eva had also given up. She knew she should feel guilty about it, and a lot of the time, she did. Others seemed to agree: Gail had shamed her, Nick had not absolved her. But if it had been merely guilt, she would have known what to do. She kicked a tuft of grass, or maybe it was a tuft of weeds—the yard was mostly weeds. There were old bulbs in the flower beds that had stopped blooming and never been dug up.

Had the fire really been an accident? Was he really—that word her parents kept using—*innocent*? Jamie hadn't meant for anyone to die, and yet he'd believed that everything would be fine. He'd had an idea, and he'd called it a sign. He'd had a feeling and he'd called it faith.

Eva stood on top of the tree stump. She'd counted the rings once, but couldn't remember the number anymore. Years ago, the tree doctor had told her that at the center of every tree, the center of all those rings, there was a core of dead wood. Surprisingly, it was good—necessary—for the tree's health: the dead part kept the rest of it alive. The dead part was called the heart.

. . .

Eva hadn't seen Eli since the fire. At first, in the wake of disaster—real disaster, the kind with sirens—certain problems had become laughable. Heartbreak? She could remember the agony of it, but only in a hazy, general way, like a movie she knew she'd loved or hated but whose ending she'd long since forgotten. Even when Eva had felt her worst, waterlogged with sadness, she was glad to finally see things in proportion, to look down on the small dimensions of her life and understand how tiny it was—especially when it was in pieces.

But her sense of scale hadn't lasted. Summer was over, and sadness became familiar. The thought of Eli bobbed back to the surface, mocking her for ever thinking that she could push it down. One evening in the middle of October, while she was walking home in the almost dark, Eli texted to ask if she wanted to catch up.

The clocks were about to turn back, which made daylight precious, dusk mournful. She walked everywhere, because she didn't really want to arrive anywhere; as long as she was in motion, she was sort of okay. That night, her walk took more than an hour, and every few blocks, Eva changed her mind about what she would text back. By the time she got home, she was two different people. The yes person and the no person, the person who cared about everything and the person who cared about nothing, the person gripping her phone, longing for it to vibrate again, and the person who wanted to throw it as far and hard as she could.

But she didn't choose between these two people, because as soon as she walked through the door, she saw that Molly was in tears. Eva had seen Molly get nervous and embarrassed and flustered, and once or twice she had watched her lip tremble like a child's, but she had never seen Molly cry. Her crying face looked raw, as if it were a face underneath her actual face. Eva put her arms around her. They touched all the time—Molly hugged her, massaged her shoulders, squeezed her hand with brief, maternal pressure that meant *I believe in you*—but this was something else. Now Molly let her whole body go, all her weight collapsing into Eva. Her forehead pressed hard against Eva's sternum. It kind of hurt.

"Why am I so upset?" Molly said, when she could finally say something.

Her tears left a Rorschach stain on the front of Eva's shirt, which Molly looked at uncomprehendingly. That afternoon, she explained, she had received a call out of the blue.

"No one ever calls me. Not like they call you. It felt like something from a movie." She wiped her face, her eyelashes wet and clumped together. "The past calling. That's what happens in movies, right?"

She hadn't heard from anyone in her hometown in years. No one blamed Molly's family for what her father had done, but they couldn't quite forgive them, either.

"The easiest thing was just to forget us."

The woman who called was someone Molly had known for as long as she could remember. They had never gotten along very well—they were more like sisters than friends, their closeness unchosen and uncomfortable—but after the scandal, when they had suddenly stopped knowing each other, it was as if Molly had stopped knowing a version of herself. You think your memories are yours, Molly said, but there are certain places that it turns out you can't go on your own.

The woman was calling because the church's new pastor, the first one since Molly's father, had killed himself. For reasons the woman couldn't or didn't explain, she'd been thinking about Molly ever since. Molly had even appeared in her dreams. (The woman wouldn't say what the dreams were about.) She said the pastor had been a kind man, though not as charismatic as Molly's father, which had seemed, on the whole, like a good thing; the congregation was wary of charisma now. The woman said the suicide came out of nowhere, an expression that had a biblical sound to it: something from nothing.

The shock was clearly still new, and the woman was soon left speechless. The phone call didn't last long.

"She just kept saying, *I needed to tell you*." Molly's face was less red now. "But why? Was it some sort of weird apology? I was the one who said sorry."

"For what?"

"For her loss, I guess. Something like that. I mean, I *am* sorry." For a second, Molly's voice sounded like her usual voice, full of pure, simple feeling.

Molly went to bed early, but Eva stayed up late. When she finally fell asleep, she, too, dreamed about Molly, a dream that slipped away as soon as she woke up. She was still in bed when Eli texted her again. *So?* She closed her eyes to try to retrieve the dream. She was pretty sure the woman from the church had been in it, too. Could you dream about someone you'd never even met? She opened her eyes and texted back. *No.*

No, she didn't want to catch up. No, she didn't want to keep up. Eva abandoned the dream and got dressed. As she was hurrying out of the house, checking her pockets for the familiar weight of her most important belongings—wallet, keys, phone—she realized that Molly had never told her the woman's name.

Eva rang Jess's doorbell. She didn't know how else to reach her. There was an official website for contacting her, where constituents were encouraged to ask questions, log complaints, petition for causes. Eva had paused over the form: a blank box, a blinking cursor. But what if Eli read it? What if no one read it? She wasn't even a constituent.

A dog barked inside—once, then again without stopping. Eva

didn't remember Jess having a dog. She thought about turning around. As the barking got closer, she could hear a voice, too.

"Please. Can you please be quiet?"

The door opened and there was Jess, bent over to hold the dog's collar. A medium-sized mutt, with terrier ears, one eerie blue eye, and a tail like a feather quill. When Jess looked up at Eva, her hair fell in her face. Instinctively, she reached up to push it away. She only let go of the collar for an instant, but an instant was all the dog needed. It streaked outside and was gone.

They chased the dog for nearly an hour. How it avoided getting hit by a car Eva could never understand. A few strangers joined the effort, and in the end, it was a kid, a boy wearing a plastic crown and wielding a plastic Excalibur, who caught the dog—arms flung around its neck, sword cast aside. Jess thanked him profusely.

"Where's my reward?" he said, his fingers like claws in the dog's thick fur.

"Your what?"

"My reward!"

Jess just stared. Eva ignored him. She gave the collar a tug—it jingled—and the boy let go. She picked up the dog, even though it was too big to be picked up.

"There isn't always a prize," Jess said before they turned back to the house, the boy glaring at them from beneath his crown.

Inside, Jess explained that the dog wasn't hers. Technically, it wasn't anyone's. She had signed up to foster rescue animals—dogs, cats, the occasional guinea pig—from a shelter in Alabama, even though she'd never owned a pet in her life. It was a ridiculous idea; she had no time. But her mother had suggested it, and her mother was hard to say no to.

"She says I need to be more nurturing."

They were sitting on stools in the kitchen. Eva's sweater was covered in dog hair, and she could taste a few strands in her mouth.

"Why?"

"She already had a baby at my age. Two, actually." They listened to the dog drink noisily from its bowl. "The women in my family are nurses or teachers or customer-service representatives. One flight attendant. You know, helping professions."

"Politics doesn't count?"

"She says caring about voters isn't the same as caring about people. She liked it better when I was a nanny. She even admitted I was a good nanny."

Jess had loose tea but no tea ball, coffee but no filters, so they drank water, like the dog. He watched everything Jess did, wagging his tail the whole time.

"He looks guilty, doesn't he?" she asked.

"You're projecting."

"Look," Jess said. And she really did look, even though most people didn't: she looked Eva right in the eyes. "We never slept together."

"Who?" Eva said. And then, "Oh."

"Isn't that why you're here?"

Eva looked around the kitchen. It was dirty and ordinary—abandoned mugs on the counter, coffee drips on the floor. The fruit bowl was empty except for onion skins, and all the knives were in the sink.

"The possibility arose," Jess said cautiously, when it became clear that Eva wasn't going to fill the silence.

"That's a weird way to put it." Eva said this calmly, observationally. She expected to be angry but she wasn't. "You mean, Eli wanted to have sex with you."

"No," Jess said, stroking the dog absentmindedly. "I wanted to have sex with him."

The dog's hair came off in big gray tumbleweeds.

"And why didn't you?"

"He had lots of reasons. He was dating someone. I was his boss. I was lonely. I was *just* lonely." Jess laughed, a sad and bitter laugh. "Most of them were good reasons, but I doubt any of them was the real reason. There are people who deny themselves the things they want—"

"But Eli isn't one of them."

Jess smiled. (Sad, but not as bitter.) As soon as she stopped petting the dog, it looked up eagerly, whining.

"That isn't why I'm here," Eva said. "This isn't about Eli."

She had said this sentence in her head many times, but it helped to say it out loud. She swallowed a dog hair. For a second, Eli was a presence in the room, right there with the panting dog and the humming fridge, and this made it possible for her to get rid of him, as she never managed to do in her mind.

"Can I ask you my question again?" Eva said.

"Your question?"

"Who is it that you abandoned?"

"Oh, that question." Jess didn't stiffen or recoil. If anything, she looked more relaxed than before. "Everyone was worried about that question."

"How come?"

"Well, I didn't do the abandoning. I was the one that got abandoned."

They went and sat in the living room, so Jess could tell her the story. Eva slipped her shoes off and put her feet on the coffee table.

The man who abandoned Jess was the man she'd been planning to marry. They met on a blind date, shortly after college. Her first ever, but later she learned that he'd been on more than he could count. He liked anything with a risk. Over time, he'd taught her to like it, too. It was an exciting way to live—full of adventures. He took her rock climbing, surfing, foraging. They ate sorrel and wine-cap mushrooms from a park right in the middle of Brooklyn. On a frozen lake in Alaska, where he'd grown up, they cut perfect circles in the ice and came away with shimmering, wriggling fish. They got engaged, and when the time came to write her wedding vows, Jess used ice fishing as a metaphor for what she loved most about him: his belief in a world below the surface, his insistence on showing her just how deep you could reach, as long as you were willing to drop your line and wait.

But she never said the vows, because in the end marriage was one risk that he decided he couldn't face. Because the danger was not too much but too little, not calamity but boredom. Because the point was going not only below the surface but all the way to the bottom. Where was the thrill in that?

They canceled the ceremony and the party, and Jess returned the dress with its ridiculous, gauzy veil. If anything, the veil should have been the metaphor. All the rituals, all the clichés, had prevented her from seeing clearly.

"Afterward, everyone told me that he had a fear of commitment," Jess said.

The dog, who'd been lying under her chair, stood up suddenly and shook itself off. It disappeared into the kitchen, where they could hear the loud crunching of food between its teeth.

"They meant it as a bad thing, obviously, but the more I thought about it, the easier it was to forgive him. Why wouldn't you be afraid? Of all the things to commit to, why just one person?"

"Instead of many people?"

"Instead of many people or instead of a job or instead of a cause or instead of a movement." Jess sat up straighter, as if the idea itself had lifted her up. "Instead of all people."

"Is that possible?"

Jess's back slouched just slightly. "Am I getting idealistic?"

Eva shrugged.

"That's what Eli would say." Jess leaned back all the way now.

Eva didn't want to agree with something Eli had said, but she didn't want to disagree just because he'd said it.

"If committing to one person is scary, isn't committing to all of humanity even scarier?" she asked.

Jess considered this. "It's true, humanity will never love you back."

They were quiet for a while, both their feet on the coffee table now.

Was that why Jamie loved everyone? Why he protested for the 99 percent, why he prayed for the masses? *Bless them that curse you, do good to them that hate you.* Maybe it was safer, in the end, for him to love a stranger than a neighbor, an enemy than a friend.

Sadness broke over Eva like a wave. She felt the weight of it—couldn't bear the weight of it. The dog came back into the room, whining again.

"What is it?" Jess said, and it took Eva a second to realize that she was addressing the dog, not her.

The doorbell rang, and the dog cocked its head, as if locating a memory—the ecstasy of escape, the thrill of the chase—then started barking.

"Not again," Jess said, but she was laughing. "We won't let you go again."

Eva heard all the sounds, the ringing and barking and laughing, but they seemed far away. What *was* she doing here? The dog jumped onto the couch, paws all over her legs, fur in her face.

"No," she said, shrinking back. Panic pushed up her throat and she pushed the dog—a hard shove, harder than she meant. "No."

Instantly, Jess stopped laughing. She pulled the dog onto the floor, her face grave with concern, ignoring the tail that whacked her jubilantly on the side of the head, as if it were all a game. The bell was still ringing and the dog was still responding—*We're coming, wait for us*—and maybe it really was a game, because suddenly Eva was the one laughing. She hadn't thought it possible. She was sad but she was laughing—one laugh, which led to more.

As soon as Jess released the dog, he bounded toward the door, nails skittering on the floor. Through the front window, Eva could see the mailman, a thick stack of letters in his hand and more in his bag. Was that how people reached Jess? Eva never sent mail or received mail—nothing personal, at least. The electrical bill, a stack of coupons, a catalogue addressed to her apartment's previous tenant. Letters, in her mind, were for very old people or very young people (she thought of Gail's students), for people on vacation or people in prison.

The mailman, tired of waiting, was trying to wedge a package through the small slot in the door. The letters had already landed on the floor, spread out like a fan.

"We're coming," Jess called, grabbing the dog's collar.

Sadness was one wave and comfort was another. In her head, Eva started a letter of her own. *Dear Jamie.* It would take a long time to finish—to get right. She would put pen on paper, spit on an envelope. She would give it to one stranger, who would pass it to another and then another; Eva would never know how many people held it before he did. Before he turned it over, broke the seal, ran his finger over the words. His name in her hand. Ink that looked wet but was long dry.

Following the dog to the door, Eva repeated the promise: "We're coming, we're coming."

ARE YOU STILL THERE?

Working for the Wellness section didn't involve much work. One week, Eva edited an article about a nine-minute workout, and the next week, she edited another about a seven-minute workout. Both alleged to meet all your workout goals. On an especially slow afternoon, she watched a reporter watching a TV show at her desk about hoarders. This was research: the reporter was writing a profile of a celebrity who'd become famous by telling people to throw things away. She had already interviewed a doctor who said that, for certain people, this was impossible. It was more than a bad habit—it was an illness. They really couldn't let go.

All of Eva's co-workers were older than her, but most of them were still young. Most of them were women. They had good skin and nice clothes; they were recently married or recently moms. In the midst of these women, one stood out. Judy, who was in her seventies, had started writing an advice column decades ago, back when Wellness was called Lifestyle. She used to write it twice a week, but now she wrote it once a week, because another columnist had been hired—a woman in her mid-thirties, who doled out advice in a casual, funny tone. The new columnist had lots of range (sometimes she quoted Marcus Aurelius, sometimes she invoked astrology) and a significant social-media following. Eva observed the chilly relationship between the two women and felt sorry for Judy, even though Judy wasn't easy to feel sorry for. She was brusque and stuck in her ways. She wore pearls and pins, heels every day. But she needed help, and Eva decided to give it.

Judy hated computers. She missed the days when everyone wrote real letters, so Eva made her a proposal: every week, she would check Judy's inbox and print out the newest messages. That way, at least they would look like they were supposed to—the way Judy remembered. Then Judy would write out her responses by hand and return them to Eva, who would type them up to be published in the paper.

Eva didn't think these would be difficult or interesting tasks. At first, she only skimmed the letters: someone having an affair with her neighbor, someone wondering whether to tie the knot, someone tortured by a piece of gossip she wished she'd never learned. Eva couldn't imagine consulting an advice columnist and couldn't help judging people who did. But on days when nothing arrived in the inbox, she realized she was disappointed. She kept clicking Refresh. A new message would appear at last, and she would lean forward in her chair, reading it slowly, savoring every detail.

One evening, Eva stayed late at her computer and went through hundreds of old emails, reading letters that had already been answered—problems that had, in theory, already been solved. Most of them had never appeared in the newspaper, but as a matter of principle, Judy wrote many more responses than she had space to publish. She could have filled an entire section of the newspaper, she told Eva bitterly. That sounded like vanity, but she insisted it wasn't.

"If you ask, people will tell you that they read advice columns for the advice," Judy said one morning in the office kitchen. "They're wrong. They care about the questions, not the answers. All they're really looking for is someone who has the same problem they do."

Judy drank fragrant tea or hot water with lemon wedges, but Eva had never seen her eat. She didn't know where the lemon came from.

"I like the distinctive letters," Eva said. "The ones with crazy stories."

This was the kind of letter that the other, younger columnist selected. Like the one from a woman who worried, after her father's sudden death, that she'd accidentally poisoned him with old potatoes. They'd turned green on the sunny kitchen counter, but she'd cooked them anyway. Or the one from a newlywed who discovered, only after saying her vows, that her husband made twice as much money as she thought he did. They'd been splitting the check for years.

"No," Judy said. "No, no, no. Boring is better." She clutched her mug with bony fingers.

"But some problems are so common," Eva objected. "Like infidelity. Or your terrible mother-in-law."

"Common means *in* common."

To the anxious daughter, the second columnist had explained that solanine poisoning was rare, and usually preceded by symptoms that were hard to overlook, like lots of vomiting. To the angry wife, she advised a moratorium on date nights. Also, marriage counseling.

"People don't want to be entertained. What people want is—" Judy stopped to think. She brought the mug to her lips but lowered it without taking a sip. "They want to relate."

This sincerity surprised Eva, but then Judy laughed her usual sharp laugh and went back to her office.

Gradually, Eva started composing her own advice in her head. When she was lurching along on the bus or staring vacantly at her desktop or falling asleep, she let herself imagine the letters she would have written in Judy's place. After a few weeks of this, she realized that Judy was right: Eva, too, gravitated toward generic problems. A middle-aged professor wondered whether to reconcile with her dying brother. A young nurse debated whether to confront her volatile boss. Eva liked these letters because they sounded easy but turned out to be hard. Forgiveness. Bravery. These were words that could only be said with a certain fearlessness. They were so lofty, so earnest. What they meant was difficult to imagine. Once you said them—especially, she discovered, if you really thought about them—you felt a little bit exposed.

Eva's responses were simple. *Connect with your brother. Stand up to your boss*. She hadn't expected to be so decisive. She hadn't expected to believe her own advice.

The only person Eva told about her imaginary letters was Jess. The two of them took walks in the mornings, before they went to work. Eva had surprised herself by being the one to suggest this. She had worried, briefly, that compared with Jess she was too young or too boring—too regular—but then she stopped worrying. Not by trying; not by convincing herself that she was mature or interesting or in any sense unusual. It was easier than that, somehow—it was enough to realize that Jess was pleased to see her. The dog jumped up and pawed Eva's thighs. When she bent down, his tongue was rough and warm on her face.

Jess started work early, so they walked even earlier, watching the sun rise as they made loops in the neighborhood. Some mornings, Jess was already wearing foundation and pants with pleats, and those walks were short. Once or twice, they were tense. Afterward, Eva went home and checked the headlines for clues, because she took for granted that Jess was upset for newsworthy reasons. But other walks were long and unhurried. They wore sweatpants. Eva gave Jess advice about the dog: consistency, reinforcement, a device that made little, affirming clicks. She'd never actually owned a dog—Nick was allergic, Gail was impatient—but she'd looked up the basics online. Some dogs liked peanut butter and others liked salami. Some were motivated not by food but by affection.

Sometimes they talked about politics, but never about politicians. That was Jess's rule: no proper nouns. She said that turning congressmen into celebrities was bad for the country—for the people. Once, Eva asked about the senators-only elevator, and Jess seemed disappointed in her.

"What about it?"

Embarrassed, Eva searched for an answer that would prove she had a good reason—a serious reason—for wanting to know. But how to explain that she was after stories for their texture, not their substance? How to know if that was even true, or if she was a gossip like everyone else? She wondered who stood too close in the elevator and who stood scrupulously apart, who trailed a bitter citrus scent into the small compartment, who farted, who opened their phone and accidentally played aloud a video of a baby (the next generation, or the next next generation) learning to laugh for the first time.

"Enough about the news," Jess said. "Have you seen any good movies?"

She liked to hear about the new releases she wouldn't have time to see, and the not-so-new ones she'd missed. She asked Eva for TV and book recommendations, admitting that she had a soft spot for old, stupid sitcoms and the most commercial kind of fiction, both of which helped put her to sleep. Every night, she listened to the same audiobook, a detective novel that she could play over and over, because she was always missing the crucial plot twists, drifting off before the big reveal. She had other, more sophisticated-sounding tastes, but she talked about them with the same unfiltered enthusiasm. When a new exhibit opened at the National Gallery, she canceled a meeting to go; there was no substitute, she told Eva, for seeing colors up close. Back in college, she'd wanted to be an art major—she made big, elaborate sculptures—but she'd accepted that she wasn't good enough. She always thought her work was full of meaning, yet somehow she could never make anyone else understand what it was.

Whenever possible, Jess steered the conversation back to Eva, peppering her with questions. Soon she was referring to Molly and Judy and Lorrie by name, as if she'd known them for as long as Eva had, or even longer. She, too, wanted stories, and it was easy for Eva to give them—a shared pleasure that pulled them forward, like the dog (indifferent to clicks, even to treats) pulling on the leash.

"Judy almost only hears from women," Eva said one morning, a cotton-candy sky above them, wispy pink and blue. "It's so old-fashioned. What about the men?"

"Maybe it's like how men won't stop to ask for directions," Jess said.

"They can't admit they're lost?"

Jess nodded.

"Well, that's old fashioned, too," Eva said. "A myth."

The dog tugged, and they walked a little faster.

"No one asks for directions anymore," Jess conceded. "The GPS always knows."

"Maybe it's that men don't have as many friends."

"Is that really true?"

They looked it up. Eva was basically right: the percentage of men with at least six close friends had been steadily declining for decades. They were living with their parents, losing their jobs—lonely. They were less likely than women to tell their friends they loved them.

"Then shouldn't there be more men seeking advice?" Eva said. "They don't have anyone but professionals to ask."

There was even a clinical term, Jess read aloud from her phone, for men who couldn't put their feelings into words.

"A few months ago, a woman wrote to Judy because she was dying and she realized that her husband didn't have enough friends," Eva said. "She had everything else in order. Her finances, her funeral arrangements. She said she wasn't even that worried about her kids—they'd always been independent, and they were almost grown-ups anyway. But her husband was helpless. Ever since her treatment failed, she'd been teaching him the basics. How to preheat the oven, which kind of laundry detergent not to buy, mincing versus dicing, that sort of thing."

"He'd never done the laundry?"

"She admitted it was traditional. Nothing her daughters would have stood for. Nothing she would have *let* her daughters stand for. But she did it anyway. She made how-to guides and lists of emergency contacts. The problem is, how do you teach someone to make friends? He needed nonemergency contacts, too. Like, who to call when you need to get out of the house. Who to call when you want to hear about someone else's problems for a change. She said it would have been easier to find him a new wife than a new friend. There was even a woman in the neighborhood she thought might be a good match. She asked Judy if she should set them up."

"What's wrong with her?" Jess asked.

"A long illness. Cancer, probably."

"No, I mean, what's *wrong* with her? Why can't she just—"

Eva shook her head violently. "That's not how it works."

The dog, stopping to investigate a parking meter, got tangled in its leash, then wagged its tail obliviously while Jess tried to untrap its legs. Someone had told Eva that tail wagging wasn't really a sign of happiness—humans had just decided that it was, because it was convenient to believe.

"You can't blame her," Eva insisted. "At least, not directly."

"Sometimes direct advice is the best advice," Jess said, once the dog had been freed.

"Judy told her there's nothing harder than losing control. And for Judy, that's actually pretty nice."

Jess said that, if it were her, she wouldn't have pretended to have any of the answers. What did she know about matters of life and death? But she would have asked the woman, who'd spent so long thinking about how to teach things to her husband, to stop and think about what it was she might be trying to teach herself.

They walked the remaining blocks in silence. The dog, who by then had learned most of their routes through the neighborhood, always slowed down as they approached Jess's house. That morning, he sat on the nearest corner and refused to get up. Jess pulled, then pushed, and in the end just laughed. She had to admire his commitment. She sat down next to him, legs crossed on the sidewalk, reading through the emails that were already flooding the phone in her palm. Eva was about to leave—the ground was too cold for sitting—when Jess looked up.

"Do *you* have at least six close friends?" she asked.

Eva could have lied, but she didn't. "Of course not."

A few weeks later, right before Thanksgiving, the dog was adopted by a family Jess had never met. Someone from the agency handled the transfer, as it was called. When Jess pressed for details about the new owners, she was told that the agency had to respect the family's privacy. Jess cried as the dog was driven off in a minivan, but afterward, she insisted that the agency was being fair—she didn't deserve to know the dog's fate.

"Deserve?" Eva said.

"If I'm being honest, I never really loved the dog."

Jess kept staring down the street even after the minivan was out of sight.

"But what if this means you actually did?" Eva asked.

"How can you love someone without knowing you do?"

Eva thought about it. "Maybe you can only love someone without knowing you do."

Reluctantly, Jess turned back toward the house. Eva wasn't sure if she was still listening.

"Once you know," Eva said, "then it's something else."

In Wellness, the holidays were the most important time of the year. For months, they had been preparing articles about healthy eating and ethical gift-giving, about New Year's resolutions and how to keep them. Judy's inbox was filled with messages from people getting ready to see their families. Fear and dread and anger. Occasionally, reckless hope: why *couldn't* it be different this time?

For the final, chaotic weeks of December, Jess and Eva's walks became irregular. They weren't in the habit of texting or calling, so days passed in which they didn't speak at all. When they both went to New York for Christmas, they didn't acknowledge that they were going to the same place. For Eva, it was being somewhere old that made the new feeling—a surprisingly simple feeling—clear: she missed Jess.

In January, they resumed walking as if they'd never stopped. They went faster and farther now. It was warmer that way and, Jess said, more satisfying.

"I don't like strolling. Or maybe I just don't know how."

Efficiency was a skill that hadn't come naturally to her—she'd been a dreamy kid, wandering off, spacing out—but now that she'd acquired it, it was difficult to turn on and off. Most days, she had already chosen a route by the time Eva arrived at her door. Their destination didn't have to be anything special—no landmarks, no monuments. (The city was full of monuments.) It just helped, she said, to start with the end in mind.

One morning, Jess had a new project. Someone had shown her an app that mapped every tree on every street in the city. On her block alone, the map recorded three different species—twenty specimens in all. They started walking, Jess holding the phone out in front of them, zigzagging from one trunk to the next. The sky was barely light, the streets mostly deserted. Mounds of old snow were slowly melting, revealing flattened trash underneath. Without leaves, all the trees looked more or less the same: lonely skeletons with knobby arms and a mess of roots, reaching desperately in every direction. But the whole point of the app was to show just how different each one was. Eva and Jess looked from screen to tree and back again. Could you speak of a plant's individuality? Palms to trunk, they touched the bark. Rough, cold. They tilted their heads back. Black branches, gray sky. They repeated the names to each other. Bald cypress, red oak, ginkgo, pear, linden.

At the intersection of two quiet residential streets, they stopped in front of a London plane tree. Eva took the phone from Jess and read the important facts. Every year, the app explained, the plane tree shed its bark in big, gray-brown flakes, until a smooth new layer emerged underneath, pale green like an unripe banana. Even now, in winter, there were dappled patches of young bark and old bark, light gray bark and dark gray bark, like the pattern of sun and shadow dancing through the leaves, except there were no leaves and hardly any sun.

"This would be perfect for Jamie," Eva said, handing the phone back to Jess.

"Who's Jamie?"

For weeks, she had been on the verge of saying his name out loud. Jess grabbed a strip of bark peeling away from the plane tree's trunk and pulled. Eva winced, as if it were a bandage being ripped off her skin.

"I've never told the whole story," she said. "Only pieces of it."

She started at the beginning. The hospital. The black walnut: its teardrop leaves, its pungent fruit, the lightning bolt that had cracked it wide open. She explained the political stuff and the Jesus stuff, the tent, the warehouse, the phone calls that ended awkwardly or angrily or silently. The fear that he had left her behind, the fear that she was the one leaving, the fear that it didn't matter which. The fire. The police. The letter she was always writing—always rewriting—but still hadn't sent. The court date that never seemed to arrive.

When the story was finished, Jess stopped walking, but only for a moment.

"Oh, Eva," she said.

There were times when hearing her own name—a name so familiar that it was possible, the rest of the time, not to think about it at all—disarmed Eva completely. She brought her hands to her face and pressed hard. There was no way to tell the difference between what her hands felt and what her cheeks felt. When she spoke, she found herself repeating the same words that had been repeated to Molly: "I needed to tell you."

Jess was still holding the strip of bark, waving it back and forth absentmindedly. "Tragedies are like that," she said.

"Like what?"

"They make you want an explanation. They make you think you need an explanation."

The bark slipped out of Jess's hand.

"But there isn't one?" Eva asked. She was pretty sure she knew the answer, but it wouldn't help if she was the one who said it.

"Well, we could make one up," Jess said. "Plenty of people do."

They walked in silence, Eva considering and reconsidering what to say next. Now that she had told Jess about Jamie, she longed to keep telling her. There was so much to tell. More details, more stories. And what if she hadn't remembered the stories right? Had she forgotten to mention the roast chicken—its disassembled body, its questionable worth? What did the roast chicken *mean*?

They arrived at an unremarkable corner and Jess stopped. She checked the map on her phone, where the blue dot representing their location now hovered over the red dot representing their destination. There was another plane tree here, its mottled pattern no doubt different from the one they had studied before, probably even unique. They could have consulted the app for even more information: Latin names and historical data, all of it catalogued in a boldfaced section titled "Everything You Need to Know." Eva reached for the phone, but Jess was already putting it back in her pocket. They could have looked stuff up, they could have made stuff up: facts, stories, answers. Jess took Eva's outstretched hand and squeezed it. She was smiling up at the tree, its illusory pattern, its unreachable branches that seemed to scrape the unreachable sky.

"Okay," Eva said. She sounded resolute. Maybe she felt it, too. "Now what?"

Jess smiled some more. "Yes. That's the question."

WERE YOU AFRAID?

On mornings when she walked with Jess, Eva got to the office before everyone except Judy. Without meaning to, she had become someone who arrived early and stayed late. Her co-workers remarked on it. They said the same things her old boss had said: *Conscientious. Thorough.* Judy said nothing, but when it was just the two of them in the kitchen, she offered Eva tea or a lemon wedge. Several times, Eva encountered her alone in the bathroom, putting makeup on in the mirror, her face halfway transformed: one eyebrow undefined, lips still pale and chapped. Eva would avert her eyes, but later, standing at the sink herself, she would wonder what her own plain face was revealing every day.

Whenever the office was empty and no one could see her computer screen, Eva looked at Jamie's warehouse on Google Street View. The satellite image had not been updated: it showed the building as it once was, before it turned to crumbled brick, dangling beams, piles of ash. If she zoomed in, she could see the windows, steel-framed and small-paned, but she couldn't see through them; glass, in photographs, always turned opaque.

In the first weeks after the fire, Eva had thought about Jamie in brief, intrusive flashes—sudden bursts of memory and pain. She hadn't liked that, but it was worse, she discovered, when the flashes went away, when it was possible to go entire days without thinking about him at all. And so her visits to the warehouse, as she came to think of her googling, turned into a kind of ritual. They always started in the same place, dragging the cursor up and down the run-down façade, but then—slowly, almost naturally—they took her somewhere else. The past, of course.

She remembered a Saturday back in high school when they had walked all over Manhattan with a tape recorder. Jamie had found the device, old and clunky, at his grandfather's house. He'd never mentioned his grandfather before, but that day Eva learned that he and Jamie's grandmother lived in New Jersey. He was, or used to be, an oral historian.

"What does that mean?" she asked.

"Officially, he was a high-school teacher. Civics, which doesn't exist anymore. But he always had some other project, too, usually with the tape recorder. What he liked best was walking around, just asking people questions."

They were in Tompkins Square Park, and Jamie was holding the recorder over the fence of the dog run. One or two dogs stopped to investigate the outstretched device, panting straight into the speaker, but mostly they ignored him. Their owners watched him warily.

"Questions like what?" Eva asked.

"His main project was called *Where Were You When?*" A chihuahua came over and jumped up and down underneath the recorder, barking indignantly. "When we landed on the moon, when the Soviet Union collapsed—that kind of thing."

The chihuahua was old, eyes filmed with a bluish haze. Each time it jumped, it got a few unimpressive inches off the ground.

"He discovered that more people want to talk than you'd think. They want to confess." Jamie lowered the recorder toward the dog and it retreated in surprise, unsure whether to attack or defend. "One man told my grandfather that when Princess Diana died, he'd been in bed with his wife's best friend, the TV playing in the next room. Neither of them reacted to the news, or even acknowledged it, but the affair ended after that."

"Because it made them feel guilty?"

Jamie shrugged. "My grandfather didn't analyze the stories. He just collected them."

The chihuahua's owner was calling from across the lot. A young woman with frizzy hair and a denim jacket that looked new—stiff and unfaded. She walked toward them, apologizing as she approached, and when she was close enough to make eye contact, Jamie addressed her by name.

"Alice?"

She stopped. "Do I know you?"

"Jamie."

"Jamie," she repeated. The dog was barking and jumping again. "Oh my God. *Jamie.*"

She'd been his babysitter a decade earlier, back when she was a college student in need of extra cash.

"How could I have forgotten?"

"A lot has happened," Jamie pointed out.

"No, no," she said. "You were unforgettable."

She asked about his brother, his parents. Jamie didn't mention the drinking or the divorce. He said everyone was doing fine. Alice smiled, and Eva could tell that she was remembering something. She had the slack, absent look of nostalgia—of someone who is, however briefly, not really there.

Alice pointed at the recorder. "What's that?"

Jamie told her about his grandfather and his grandfather's questions. He told her about Princess Diana, but this time he said nothing about the man with the affair.

"One woman saw the newspaper headline at a gas station. She was buying a pack of cigarettes and a pack of Now and Laters. She broke a tooth on one of the Now and Laters, and had to get it replaced. She called it her princess tooth. She stopped eating candy after that, but she kept on smoking."

Alice laughed. "So what's *your* question?"

"I don't know," Jamie said. He turned to Eva. "What should our question be?"

Our question. This hadn't occurred to Eva. Until then, she had thought they were just collecting sounds: dogs, traffic. Jamie had bent over a sewer to capture the rush of water down the drain. Now he looked at her expectantly, and her mind went blank.

She asked where Alice had been on September 11, because she couldn't think of anything else to ask. Instantly, Eva saw that this was the wrong question. Alice's face stiffened.

"Never mind," Eva said quickly.

They stood there awkwardly for a few seconds, and then Alice bent down to pick up the chihuahua. Even in her arms, it kept barking, lunging hopelessly toward the recorder.

"He's afraid of it," she explained.

Jamie put the device in his pocket without turning it off. The dog barked a few more times, but they were quieter, confused barks—fear without an object. In the silence that followed, Eva stared at her hands, gripping the fence too tightly. Jamie had told her that what seemed like silence often contained the most valuable sounds.

Alice smiled when she said goodbye, but it wasn't the same smile as before. Jamie gave her his phone number and she said she'd call him—they'd see each other soon. After they left the park, Eva didn't ask Jamie any of the questions she wanted to: why he'd lied about his brother, what had happened to Alice that September. She didn't want to be the one to spoil the silence. She never found out if Alice called.

But now here it all was again, in Eva's head: the barking and talking, the little pauses in between and the long pause after. Unforgettable, apparently, though of course there was no way to know if she was remembering it right. She didn't have the tape. She wondered if Jamie had ever listened to it, if anyone would ever find it and play it back, or if by then the device itself would be truly obsolete.

In the satellite image of the warehouse, Eva could see a mailbox beside the grated front door. None of the men (not Jamie, not the dead men) would have received any mail there, because they had never officially lived there, but another Google search revealed that if they had—if their lives had been deemed official, which some lives were and others were not—they would have been in Jess's district.

This felt like a discovery. Eva called Jess right away.

"They're your voters!" She was triumphant.

"They're dead."

"Right. But you were their representative. You were their—"

It sounded too cliché to say *their voice.* Eva could have texted that—it was always easier to say things over text—and suddenly she regretted calling. She and Jess rarely spoke on the phone. When they did, it was usually about logistics: where to meet, who was running late. Someone was shouting Jess's name in the background.

"I'm walking into an interview," she said. "I'll call you back."

After they hung up, Eva looked back at the photo of the warehouse. Later, she'd be able to watch Jess's interview online. Most of the questions would be questions Jess had been asked many times before, but she was good at making each answer sound new. Eva clicked until the camera had rotated 180 degrees away from the warehouse—until she was looking at whatever Jamie would have looked at when he walked out the door.

Jess never did call her back. It wasn't until the following week, walking together down a street of elegant townhouses, that Eva returned to the conversation.

"What I meant to say, what I was trying to say, is—isn't your job to care about whatever your constituents care about?"

The street had been closed down for a TV shoot: a scene on a popular show in which women ran the country. "No Parking" signs were taped to all the trees. The only car left was a fancy SUV in front of a house with freshly painted white brick and recently trimmed hedges. The owner, still in his pajamas, had been summoned to move it around the block.

"It depends what you mean by care," Jess said. They stopped beside the SUV, which was sputtering and failing to start. "Take my mom. She'd say that caring means something personal. Like what an inspiring teacher does, or a doctor with a good bedside manner. She'd say it comes from the heart, but sometimes requires an advanced degree."

"We could give it a push," someone suggested. The TV crew all wore jeans and boots. The SUV owner wore a silk robe.

"But if you're a congressman," Jess went on, "maybe you think caring means passing laws. Or maybe you think it just means giving a good speech."

While Jess and Eva watched, the crew formed a line behind the car's bumper.

"One . . . two . . ." a man who seemed like the crew leader called out.

"And if you're you—"

Eva waited. This, she thought, was the ultimate form of suspense: to wait for the version of yourself that emerged from another person's point of view.

"Three," the man shouted. Everyone pushed. The car moved.

"If you're you, you try to distill caring to its purest, most abstract form."

"What's that?"

"That's what I want to know," Jess said. "You think caring is something you do in your head. You want, like, empathy in a bottle."

They walked alongside the car, staying even with the driver's window. The man looked uneasy with nothing to do behind the wheel.

"But even if you found it," Jess said, "even if you felt it—who would that help? Who except you?"

After they parted ways that morning, Eva killed time before going to the office. She arrived when everyone else did: a crowded elevator, a line for the coffee machine. She passed Judy on her way out of the bathroom, her face perfectly painted, fully composed. When their eyes met, Judy smiled. Eva didn't visit the warehouse that day, or the next. She stayed where she was supposed to be—where she actually was.

•

On a Saturday in February, Jess drove Eva to New York. Her car smelled like vinyl and dog food, even though she'd given all the dog food away. Jess had learned to drive right before she launched her campaign. She didn't really need to—in New York, she took the subway everywhere—but she realized that it had been years since she'd acquired a new skill. You learned to read, to ride your bike, to float on your back, to multiply by tens, fives, nines, to snap your fingers, to separate the yolk from the whites, to fold the fitted sheet—and then you stopped. You learned facts. What not how. You let someone else fix the sink, you forgot your mental math, you watched a child try to jump—he bent his knees, pumped his arms, but his feet stayed rooted on the ground—and it made no sense: how could he not know how?

It was terrifying, of course: the learning, the driving.

"You could die at any minute," Jess said, matter-of-factly.

Eva laughed. "Don't tell me that."

"I'm reassuring you, actually. You shouldn't get in a car with someone who doesn't understand that your life is in their hands."

Eva turned up the radio. Jess said she listened to a new station every time she got in the car. Pop and punk, traffic and talk. She paid attention to the slow, syrupy voices on Christian stations, rambling through prayers, and to the rapid, inhuman voices at the end of advertisements, racing through the fine print. Listening like that, she never got to know talk-show hosts or learned enough lyrics to sing along to the hits, but she didn't mind. It was like picking up new passengers along the way. Eva struggled to keep up as Jess continually scanned through the stations, unfamiliar voices starting and stopping in mid-sentence, but she admired the approach. Embarrassingly, she hoped they would land on the Top 40 soundtrack, where each song's climactic chorus sounded like the last.

Jess's staff didn't like her driving. For official business, they wouldn't allow it. She was supposed to sit in the back seat and make phone calls. Security followed in another car.

"Even now?" Eva looked in the side mirror.

"No," Jess said. "We're breaking the rules."

The *we* made Eva happy.

Jess's apartment in Brooklyn was cleaner than the one in D.C., but more cluttered. Her fiancé had moved in here, then moved out. Those were some of his books on the shelves. There were old holiday cards on the fridge, expired condiments inside the fridge. Eva marveled at all these artifacts. Since leaving home, she had never lived anywhere long enough to make much of an impression—nothing more than a few scratches on the walls that could be easily painted over.

They ate cans of soup and drank cans of beer. Jess answered a call from Reshma and flipped through a three-ring binder while they talked, nodding along. Eva couldn't make out exactly what Reshma was saying, but she could detect the authority in her voice. She wondered if Eli was on the call, too, but told herself it didn't matter. While they talked, Eva rinsed out the soup cans and crushed the beer cans into two flat discs. Lost in thought, she let the water run and was jolted back into awareness when it turned suddenly, scaldingly hot.

"Fuck."

Jess stuck her head into the kitchen. *Are you okay?* she mouthed. Eva forced a smile and waved her away. She turned off the water and found the recycling bin under the sink. If committing to a cause meant committing to Jess, she thought, maybe she could do it.

"I *am* working tomorrow," Jess was saying into the phone when Eva returned to the living room. Her voice sounded briefly childish, and Eva was surprised that she had to make excuses, that she had to answer to anyone but herself. "I'm going to visit some constituents."

This wasn't exactly true. Tomorrow wasn't Jess's idea, it was Eva's. No, more than an idea. Jess had been adamant that it couldn't just be an idea. Tomorrow was a plan. But now that it was about to happen, Eva wished that she had never made it. She didn't have a professional binder, didn't have an authoritative voice.

Jess hung up the phone and brought Eva a towel. They took turns in the bathroom. When Eva brushed her teeth, the mirror was still fogged up from Jess's shower, and she hesitated before wiping off the surface—it felt strangely intimate. So did her bare feet on the tiles, the strands of Jess's hair clinging to the sink.

"Is everything all right?" Jess called from the other side of the door. "Do you have what you need?"

Eva wiped a circle on the mirror and her face appeared. "Everything's fine."

By the time she finished brushing, the mirror was opaque again.

Tomorrow they would go looking for two dead men. For what they had left behind: one family without a father, another family without a son. Eva worried about what she would say to these families, but reminded herself that she shouldn't say much. She wouldn't offer condolences, because condolences sounded like black ribbon on an anonymous coffin, like a fake signature on thick, official stationery. The point, as Jess kept saying, was not to show that she cared—the point was to really care.

That night, Eva dreamed about Jess's dog. He'd gone to live in the suburbs, a yellow house with a green lawn. A forever home, it was called. But the dog was locked in the basement, and Eva was down there, too. The dog didn't sleep or eat, and he backed into a corner whenever Eva approached. The owners never appeared in the dream, but she could hear their every move through the ceiling, their footsteps back and forth, their voices back and forth. Everything about the way they sounded—that is, everything except the words themselves, which Eva couldn't make out—suggested that they were kind, calm people. They never yelled. She could hear the lilt of genuine, curious questions—the unhurried rhythms of real intimacy. Even the silences, she thought in the dream, seemed natural and pleasant. So why was she locked in the basement? She couldn't imagine these people, who sounded so nice, doing something so cruel. Was she being punished, or had she simply been forgotten? Which was worse? Eva had climbed to the top of the basement stairs and pressed her ear against the locked door when her alarm went off. Jess was already in the kitchen, and it was almost time to go.

Dear Jamie,

We looked for Luis first. At the apartment where his wife and three children lived, Jess and I sat down at the kitchen table. There were candles lined up on the edge of the table, and lots of dried wax stuck to its surface. Luis's wife looked like she was in her early thirties. She had shiny hair and shiny eyes. Her name was Carla. She brought cold sodas from the fridge and sat down across from us. She didn't say anything for several minutes, just looked at her feet. It was cold in the apartment, but she was wearing flip-flops. Her toenails were painted deep blue. Neither Jess nor I broke the silence.

When Carla started speaking, she told us that she'd lost Luis twice. First, she kicked him out and asked for a divorce. Then, six months later, he died. She had only just recovered from the first loss when the second one arrived. From her voice, I wondered if she was a singer. It was a nice, musical voice.

She told us that Luis was born in Arizona. He'd fallen in love with her on his seventh day in New York City, just as he was about to give up and go home. How he hated the desert! For a long time (but not forever), he'd said that she was his oasis. They got married and had three kids. He worked in a Mexican restaurant owned by Canadians. It should have been a joke but it wasn't. He had to keep reminding them he wasn't from Mexico. The days were long and the food was terrible. But Luis was an excellent cook if he was the one in charge. On weekends, he and Carla would bring chicken and corn and charcoal to the park and cook for people. For their friends, or just for anyone who was around. On those days, Luis was an entertainer. He opened bottles with his teeth. He chased the kids with corn silk, draping the sticky strands over their heads. The kids thought that was hilarious.

Carla didn't tell us the reason for their separation. She said profound things simply, without any trace of self-consciousness, the same way you do (or did). She said that an oasis was a place, not a person. You could bring someone water, you could even make them drink, but you could never quench a thirst that wasn't your own.

She didn't learn about the church until Luis was dead. For as long as she had known him, he hadn't believed in God. They'd baptized their first son, but they hadn't bothered with the others. They were too busy and it was too formal. Her parents were the only ones who would have cared, and they were dead by then. She couldn't imagine what had changed Luis's mind. Or was it his heart? Either way, it wasn't the first mystery that she knew she would never solve. Every person, she said, was their own mystery.

Then Carla seemed lost in thought for a while, scraping absentmindedly at the wax on the table. After a few minutes, she swept the shavings onto the floor and started talking again, as if she'd been in the middle of a story. The story was about how Luis taught himself to swim. There were plenty of pools in Arizona, but he'd never learned as a kid. By the time he saw the ocean, he was old enough to understand what its vastness really meant. How could you swim in it without being swallowed by it?

On weekends in the summer, the subways were packed with kids going to the beach. As soon as their son was old enough to learn, Luis panicked. Someone had to teach him. Carla didn't know how to swim, either, but she didn't care. She pointed out that you could go to the beach without swimming. Luis ignored her. He started going out to the ocean early in the morning, leaving the house while it was still dark. She had no idea what he did when he got there, because he wouldn't let anyone go with him. Once, when he'd been gone for hours, Carla convinced herself that he'd drowned. When he finally appeared, she was standing in front of the fridge, but she couldn't remember why she'd opened it. She was crying uncontrollably. He touched her shoulder and she jumped. For a second, she thought he was a ghost. Their faces were salty with tears and the ocean. A few days after that, he said it was time. They went out to the beach together and she watched him carry their son into the waves.

When Carla finished the story, she said she was done. No more talking. She showed us to the door. In front of the apartment building, her kids were playing on the sidewalk, pink-cheeked in the cold. They dipped plastic wands in a tray of bubbles and waved them in the air. They didn't look up as we left, mesmerized by the billowing, quivering shapes, tinged violet in the light. The bubbles stretched and stretched, until they popped.

It took most of the afternoon to find Alex. I had the wrong address for his mom. She had moved to Brighton Beach, to live with his grandmother. Not her own mother—Alex's father's mother, even though Alex's father was gone. (We never found out what kind of gone.) They served us fruit salad and glasses of water without ice. For a while, they wanted to talk about everything except Alex. They asked us about our families and our hobbies. Then his grandmother, who called him Alyosha, went to lie down in the next room and his mom stared out the window and told us what she knew. She was always aware, with Alex, of how much she didn't know.

From the beginning, his teachers said he was very bright. She had never really understood what that meant. *Bright*. It certainly didn't mean that he was good at school. He skipped a lot of it. He liked computers, but they didn't have one, so when he was thirteen, he tried to steal someone else's. There was more trouble like that: fights, punishments, fights over punishments. There were days when he didn't come out of his room. Then, when he was sixteen, he met a DJ, a man ten years older than him, from somewhere in Scandinavia. The man owned fancy sound equipment and fancy sneakers. He transformed Alex. Now Alex was making music. Mixing it, he said. He came home from parties at dawn covered in sweat and seeming ecstatic. He got paid. It was never ecstasy the drug, his mom said. She didn't worry about that, because he had promised her that drinking and drugs were just a distraction. He had a mission.

Or he would have, except he had a seizure first. The doctor said no more flashing lights, no more pounding beats. No more noise. Alex never forgot that, that the doctor had called it noise. The medicine made him heavy and sluggish. On a beautiful Sunday morning, he told his mom that it made him want to die. She always remembered that it was a Sunday, because it was Orthodox Easter. His grandmother had been on her way from church and everything had to be okay by the time she arrived.

He went back to music. His mom tried everything she could to stop him. Why was he throwing his life away? Alex shook his head. How else could he feel alive? They fought and fought. They fought so much he left. He would disappear for months at a time, then return without warning for a day or a night, never for long. She asked where he'd been and he changed the subject. His face was gray and puffy and he smelled bad. She tried to get him to stay by making him good food and pouring him all his favorite juices: cherry, peach, pear. He said that juice reminded him of childhood. The word *bright* made sense to her now. Back then, it had been possible to make his face light up.

She saw that light one last time. One evening, Alex was waiting outside her building when she came home from work. It was cold out, and he seemed restless, pacing back and forth and glancing over his shoulder. As soon as she gave him the money in her purse, he hurried away. It pained her to see him like that, but she was used to the pain. As she was unlocking the door, he suddenly reappeared, almost scaring her to death with his hand on the sleeve of her coat. This detail still upset her: she had thought her own son's hand was a stranger's. When she had recovered from the surprise, he told her there was something he wanted to show her. It was a song on his phone. She'd heard some of his music before, frenzied melodies in loops, or ominous beats echoing over and over again. If she was being honest, she had never really liked it. But that day he played her something new, which was actually something old. It was a Gregorian chant.

Like Luis, Alex had never talked to her about religion. He'd definitely never talked about God. Only his grandmother talked about that. That evening, both of them were lost in the music. The words seemed like they were coming from somewhere very deep in the earth or somewhere very far away in the sky. They belonged to a vastness that she would never see, only hear. Her key was turned halfway in the lock. Then the song ended and he disappeared.

When Jess and I left the apartment, we walked to the beach. It was dark by then. The water and the sky and the sand were all the same black. We went way down the boardwalk until we could see Coney Island. The rides were closed for the winter and the compartments of the darkened Ferris wheel were swaying back and forth in the wind. Jess said that everyone seemed to have a story about getting stuck at the top of a Ferris wheel. I didn't, because I've only ridden one once. I know it's a tame ride, but to me it was always one of the scariest. When you swing out into the sky, the wheel disappears behind you and the city expands in front of you, and even though you know you won't fall, you can't quite believe it. You can only believe it when you're on the ground.

While Jess and I stood there not speaking, I tried to bring myself to say what was on my mind. The boardwalk was empty and silent, and the ocean was huge and noisy. Jess touched my elbow. "Where did you go?" she asked. I wasn't sure, but her voice brought me back. I told her I wanted to see the painter.

She had also gone to jail, but not for long. Her lawyer might have been persuasive, but he didn't really need to be. No one had died in the painter's room. She wasn't the one who signed the lease or locked the doors, and she didn't object when you insisted that the space heaters and the paint tubes were yours. She said nothing when you insisted that the whole idea was yours, too. If it was your fault, then it wasn't hers.

I had found the painter's new address the same way I found all the other addresses. Databases at the office told me everything I needed to know. Using them for personal reasons wasn't explicitly against the rules, but I was nervous anyway. I worried that there was a record of all the names that I'd searched. I tried to imagine what someone else would think if they saw the list. Two dead men, a single mom and her three kids, an elderly Russian woman and her daughter-in-law, an artist from Colorado. They seemed like clues to something, but even I couldn't figure out what.

I hadn't looked carefully at the address, so it was only as we started driving that I realized we were heading toward my parents' neighborhood. The streets grew more and more familiar. There were childhood landmarks that I could have pointed out to Jess. The community garden where I'd once buried all my spare change in a flower bed, for safekeeping. The pet store where I'd longed for a yellow-and-green parrot perched in the window. The old, usually empty Italian restaurant where I'd once insisted on going by myself, without my parents, just to prove that I could. I'd clutched a borrowed twenty-dollar bill in my hand the whole time I ate. But we drove past these memories in silence. (The coins were gone when I tried to dig them up. One day, without warning, the parrot was gone, too.)

The painter lived on the parlor floor of an old brownstone, and I was surprised by how grand the place was. I had imagined something run-down, more like the warehouse. Standing on the sidewalk, Jess and I could see from the front windows all the way through to the back windows. Every single light had been turned on. The rooms were bare, but the walls were covered. There were at least two paintings on each and many more propped up on the floor. I could see a drop cloth on the ground and two chairs in the center of it, back to back. The chairs must have been for posing, not for sitting.

We rang and knocked and rang again. We went back to the sidewalk and watched, but no one appeared. I hadn't prepared for the possibility that the painter wouldn't be home, even though I had no reason to expect that she would cooperate with our plan. She didn't know there *was* a plan.

It was only when I realized how little I knew about the painter that I saw how much I had assumed I did. The picture of her in my head was fully formed: red hair, a dimple in her chin, sharp cheekbones, sharp collarbones. I have no idea where these details came from, but even now, some part of me wants to believe they're real.

I didn't picture her before the fire or during the fire. I didn't picture her painting or praying. I didn't picture her naked body wrapped around your naked body. I didn't picture her jumping out the window or landing in a twisted heap on the ground. I only ever pictured her after the fire, because she was the only one who got an after. Luis didn't and Alex didn't and no one knows, yet, if you did, or if you will.

I pictured her once her broken bones had healed and she could stand on her own two feet. Once she could go wherever she wanted. I had a hundred questions and they all started there.

Did she feel guilty or did she feel angry?

Did she have bad dreams or did she sleep through the night?

Did she have a boring job or a real career?

Did she still go to church or did she listen to pop songs instead?

Did she see a psychiatrist? Did she think she should see a psychiatrist?

Did she believe in being grounded? In being centered? Did she take each day as it came? Did she have at least six close friends? Did she believe that life goes on?

Did she still believe in an afterlife, the one she was living?

I had counted on her having the answers. I stepped closer to see the paintings more clearly. They were almost all the same. The only colors were orange and red and yellow, like Rothkos but busier and denser. The easiest thing to say was that they were paintings of fire. Of *the* fire. But they had to be more than that, didn't they? The shapes could have been figures. Or were they just shapes? I started to panic.

"Oh," Jess said.

I wanted her voice to bring me back again. I wanted her to tell me what the paintings were, and what they meant.

"Oh," she said again, and this time I heard her disappointment. "They're not good. Not good at all."

Jess and I got back to Washington after midnight. Technically, it was already Monday. For the last hour of the ride, she turned off the radio and said she couldn't talk. She needed to think. In the morning, she had meetings to go to, decisions to make.

What did I have to do?

The next day, I woke up early but decided to be late to work. If anyone noticed, no one said anything. At my desk, I read through a profile of a celebrity that I'd finally finished editing. The newspaper had sent a photographer to take pictures of the subject, a woman who told people they could clear out their lives by cleaning out their homes. In the image that had been selected, she stood in the middle of her house: one big room, with no walls and nothing out of place. Her billowing dress matched the billowing curtains. I wrote a note to the photographer with feedback. I said it was a good, sharp image, but it was missing an element of surprise.

When the Wellness staff gathered for our afternoon meeting, there were leftovers from the previous meeting on the conference table: other people's half-eaten sandwiches and half-empty soda cans. For a few moments, everyone just stood there staring at the food, looking confused and offended. I could hear the sputtering inside the cans. Then Judy sat down at the head of the table, picked up one of the sandwiches, and took a bite. The woman next to me gasped, but Judy ignored her, smiling strangely to herself. She finished chewing and looked up impatiently, so we all hurried to take our seats.

After lunch, I went back to my desk and checked Judy's inbox right away. I felt a sense of excitement: suspense, even. I was sure that something would be there, even though Judy had warned me that the first months of the year were bad for advice giving. The new year brought a surge of self-confidence, or at least self-discipline. For a few weeks, everyone was sure they could do it all on their own. But I was right: a message was waiting on the otherwise empty screen.

The letter came from a woman who said she had lost her daughter. She knew that she wasn't supposed to use the word *lost*, because her daughter was still alive and healthy, but grief really was what she was feeling. A few years earlier, her daughter had gone off to a big school in an even bigger city, and now when she came home, to their small house in a small town, the two of them had nothing to say to each other. It wasn't that they'd ever been friends. The woman didn't believe in that kind of parenting. But they had respected each other and understood each other, or so the woman had thought. Now her daughter was like the heroine of some coming-of-age story, who'd gone off to discover the world and forgotten that her own mother was part of it. *Coming-of-age stories are good for the heroines*, the woman wrote. *But what about the people who stay right where we've always been?*

When I had finished reading, my first reaction was disappointment. The letter was not as remarkable as I'd hoped. It came from a woman with a name so common she might as well have been anonymous. I printed out the letter and brought it to Judy's office. She was standing in the middle of the room, just as the celebrity was in that photograph. Her office was as clean and elegant as the famous woman's house, but that afternoon I was unsettled by the feeling that something about it had changed. While she was reading the letter, I scanned the shelves for signs of what it might be and found nothing. I thought of her eating the sandwich, the first time I had seen her eat anything at all, crumbs falling off her bottom lip, lettuce caught between her teeth. I turned to leave, but she stopped me.

"Why don't you try this one?"

She handed the letter back to me. I looked at her blankly.

"Yes," she said, as if I had asked a question. "You can do this one."

I took the sheet of paper back to my desk and reread it several times. I wondered if it was a test. If it was, it didn't seem like a very challenging one. In my response, I started off by expressing sympathy. This wasn't disingenuous: I really did feel bad for the mother. But then I told her that she couldn't just wait around for her daughter. If she wanted her back, she would have to go out and get her.

I thought that Judy would admire the firmness of this advice, and I returned to her office feeling pleased, even a little proud. This time it was empty, so I left my response on her desk, which was mostly bare. For as long as I'd known her, she'd never had any picture frames or decorations, none of the things that people call personal effects. Back at my computer, the photographer had emailed me with a few more shots of the celebrity. The new images looked exactly like the old images. Was I missing something? I stared at them for a long time. Just as I was about to give up and go home, Judy appeared beside the low wall of my cubicle. Her makeup had faded over the course of the day, and I could see the creases in her forehead and the grooves at the edges of her mouth. She handed my letter back to me and we said good night. She had never told me where she lived, or with whom. I pictured her in an apartment as spare as her office, leaning over a sink, washing her face until it was clean and old.

On her copy of my letter, Judy had used Wite-Out to erase entire sentences. Her own words were written in cursive, in the dark blue ink of a fountain pen.

When you say that you've lost your daughter, you assume that she's the person you want to find. I can see why you might think so. To be lonely is to doubt that you are enough.

I looked up from the page. My computer screen had gone dark. I kept several notebooks on my desk, all of them blank.

But might you be the one you're looking for?

I sat there for a long time, listening to the sounds of the office emptying out, until I was alone in the middle of the floor. I opened up one of the notebooks and wrote you this letter. I've written many versions of it before, and none of them have seemed quite right. They had too many questions: Where are you, Jamie? Who are you, Jamie?

Why, Jamie? This one might be wrong, too. I know now, and maybe I have known all along, that I won't send it. I'll keep reading it. In some places, my handwriting is bad enough that even I can't decipher it. For now, I can read it because I remember writing it, but someday I may forget.

Love,
Eva

DID YOU KNOW?

Months later, when Jamie was finally, officially cleared of all charges, Eva had moved to Los Angeles. She lived in the room that Simone, the ink-haired woman, had abruptly vacated, after a fight that none of the roommates would talk about. Lorrie's room was down the hall. Eva had learned to drive before she left the East Coast, because she wanted to get to California by car. On a plane, you watched two movies, fell asleep, and woke up with a view of a whole different ocean. If she was going to move across the country, she told her parents, she should move through the country. She saw St. Louis and Las Vegas, the Rocky Mountains and the Utah desert. She took a twenty-minute nap in Kansas City, Missouri, and spent six hours crossing the whole length of Kansas itself. There were long days of driving in which she didn't say a single word until late at night, when she rang the bell at the front desk of a motel and cleared her throat, waiting in giddy suspense for a stranger to appear—waiting for the sound of her own voice.

Eva was done with newspapers. In California, she got a job as a babysitter for two divorce lawyers, friends of Lorrie's parents who had twins. They were extremely friendly—paid her extra for gas, asked her questions about her life, stocked the fridge with expensive, out-of-season berries—but she could tell that their friendliness had nothing to do with her, that they were simply outgoing people. Maybe it was better that way. If they had seemed to take a particular interest in her, she would have had to prove that she was interesting. If they had seemed to see something in her, she would have had to show them something.

The lawyers had warned Eva that the twins, an eight-year-old boy and girl, could be difficult. Eva made snacks that were begged for but never eaten, cleaned up toys that were scattered everywhere but never used. She played games that she pretended to be bad at, until the twins were more outraged by being allowed to win than by being made to lose, and then Eva had to really concentrate. On some days, she was dismayed by how immature they were: they stole her phone and took pictures of their butts, they shut their bedroom door in her face and laughed maniacally. But on other days, she was taken aback by how adult they could be. Whenever their friends came over, the other kids wanted to play soccer but the twins wanted to play a game they called Cult. In one version, they built a bunker out of couch pillows and waited for the apocalypse. In another, they poured Gatorade into cups and told their friends to drink up. "Now die," they instructed. The Gatorade, they patiently explained, was poison.

One afternoon, the mother of a girl who had refused to stage a dramatic death called to complain. Eva was mortified, but the twins' parents were nice about the whole thing. The kids must have watched them watching a Jonestown documentary. They told Eva not to worry. They told her it was their problem, not hers.

Eva called Jess from the car that evening, as she did most evenings.

When Eva was first learning to drive, she had developed the habit of putting Jess on speaker phone while navigating daunting routes. She was especially afraid of the freeway, but Jess told her that highway driving was the easiest kind: straight and fast. Eva had conquered that fear and the calls had gotten shorter—Jess was working nonstop—but they still talked nearly every day.

"Their problem, not mine," Eva repeated on the phone.

"Good," Jess said, approvingly. "A lot of people would blame the babysitter." She had told Eva stories about her own nannying jobs, which seemed like a lifetime ago.

"I know they were trying to be nice—"

"They let you off the hook."

"But that's the thing," Eva said. If at first she had needed reassurance while driving, now—she relaxed her shoulders, she only sometimes used a map—she called Jess for company. "I think I want to be on the hook."

Lorrie worked long hours on a movie set and came home exhausted. She pretended to be curious about Eva's day, but Eva could tell that she wasn't. She didn't blame her. Eva's job would never turn into a better job. The twins would get older and smarter, both more and less difficult—but she probably wouldn't be around to see it.

Lorrie watched one feature film every night, because she said it was the best way to learn. She had a lot of ideas for her first movie, but she hadn't decided on one yet. Success, she told Eva, was about climbing a ladder and also about building a web. You had to know the right people. You didn't have to like them.

Eva wanted advice, but not this advice. She started reading Judy's columns again, hoping she would find in them whatever it was she wanted to hear instead. Usually, she read them online, which Judy herself would have disapproved of, but every now and then, Eva printed a column out and taped it to the side of her bookshelf—the side you couldn't see from the doorway. Judy signed every letter *Yours.*

But then, one week in the middle of summer, she was gone. Twice in a row, the younger columnist dispensed her wisdom: a bit of Shakespeare, a bit of tarot, a brief summary of Maslow's hierarchy of needs. Maybe Judy was on vacation. Eva waited for her to return: one week and then another. She had rarely read the younger woman's columns, but now she pored over them, as if for clues. *Love is not love / Which alters when it alteration finds.* (Was that true?) In tarot, cups stood for feelings. (You could fill them up, pour them out.) She stared at Maslow's pyramid, its sharp and unattainable point. After three weeks, she googled for obituaries. After four weeks, she picked up the phone.

Judy answered just as Eva was about to hang up. She wasn't dead, she was just retired. She lived in Los Angeles now, right nearby; she had been meaning to call. Eva was too confused by all this to ask questions. Judy was in the car with the windows rolled down, traffic and the traffic report in the background, heading to the nursery for soil and a couple new plants. By the time Eva got off the phone, she had agreed to meet her there. This didn't make any sense, either; Eva had never gardened in her life.

She found Judy in the backyard of the store, surveying the many colors of impatiens. She was wearing sneakers, not heels. She was holding an enormous bag of mulch by herself.

"Here, let me—" Eva took one end of the mulch, which was even heavier than she expected. They rested the bag on a bench and sat down, so that Judy could explain herself. In the life of another woman her age, the facts would not have seemed remarkable: she had decided to slow down, to get some perspective. She had moved to Los Angeles to be closer to her granddaughters. They were almost teenagers.

"They won't be interested in me for much longer," she said.

Eva had never imagined Judy having children. Certainly not grandchildren. "I would be interested," she said.

Judy laughed again. "They'll have their own lives."

She said that she rarely missed the newspaper. There had been no farewell party for her, no acknowledgment that she had been working for longer than some of her co-workers had been alive. On her last day, someone had passed a drugstore card around the office and delivered it to Judy's desk at five o'clock. Everyone's message was a version of the same message (congratulations, good luck, bon voyage), but she kept the card anyway, because it came in an envelope—the last real letter she'd receive in that place.

"No hard feelings," she said.

She spoke without a trace of her old bitterness, but Eva wasn't entirely convinced. Judy was wearing a sunhat and sunglasses, dark enough that Eva couldn't even see the shape of her eyes. Maybe she didn't want to be convinced.

"I still get emails from readers, asking if I can give them one last piece of advice," Judy said.

"How do they find you?"

Judy shrugged. "People want help. People always want help." She stood up and smoothed her pants, leaving faint streaks of dirt down her thighs. "But I don't have time."

For the next hour, Eva followed her from one aisle to the next, pushing a wheelbarrow that got heavier and heavier as they went. She would never have guessed that there were so many types of soil: garden soil and topsoil, something called lawn mix.

"You should try it," Judy said, pressing a finger into the dirt of a potted monstera, a strange and sickly-seeming plant, its leaves scattered with oblong holes.

"Try what?"

"Growing."

Maybe Eva sighed.

"Not like that," Judy said. "The metaphor is easy. The rest is hard. Light, water—the necessary conditions."

The holes in the monstera's leaves were something of a mystery, she explained, but they weren't a sickness. Some people thought they might be designed for withstanding strong winds, or for maximizing sunlight. As they walked into the shade, Judy carefully returned her sunglasses to their case, and Eva was glad to see her usual glossy mascara, each eyelash like a delicate insect's antenna. In the parking lot, Judy insisted that Eva take a box of impatiens—Divine Red—home with her.

"To get you started."

When she told Judy she'd consider starting a garden, Eva didn't think she actually would. But within a few days, she was reading online forums with elaborate instructions, then pulling up weeds in the backyard for hours at a time. It was the same backyard where, two years earlier, she'd lain on her back and closed her eyes and fantasized about Eli's betrayal. Two years was a long time that would become a shorter time. When she looked back from some distant point in the future, those years would collapse into each other, the labyrinthine course of days compressing and straightening into a simple passage, then to now. This was a habit of hers—looking ahead to looking back. Sometimes it brought comfort, and sometimes it brought pain.

She went back to the nursery by herself. She learned to check for healthy foliage and damp soil. Online, she had been advised not to be tempted by flowering plants: flowers took up too much of a plant's energy. Leafy ones were better, because they devoted their resources to their roots. Eva built a flower bed and admired the flat, bare surface, the sweet-smelling soil that crumbled gently in her hand. She almost couldn't bring herself to fill it in.

. . .

Eva was at the park, supervising the twins on the swings, when Judy emailed her. Judy had never emailed her.

"Watch this!"

The girl was pumping her legs, gaining height. The boy had his stomach on the seat of the swing and was slowly turning in circles, the two ropes above him twisting into a single thick braid.

Judy wrote with proper capitalization and punctuation. At the top of the email, she included the date, unnecessarily. *Dear Eva.* Earlier that week, she explained, on the same day that she had seen Eva at the nursery, she'd received a message from one of her former readers. Usually, she ignored these emails—she had always disliked her inbox, as Eva knew—but for some reason she kept thinking about this one. She kept thinking that Eva should read it. *Who knows,* Judy wrote, *you might find that you have something to say.*

"Ready!" the first twin shouted.

"Set!" the second shouted.

Eva looked up from her phone. "Go!"

The ropes untwisted slowly, then faster and faster, until the swing was spinning like a top. There was a split second when the two strands came fully apart and the swing was completely motionless, suspended in the air; then it reversed, spinning in the opposite direction, the ropes braiding back together. Soon the girl was on her stomach, too, the two of them spinning side by side.

While brother and sister twisted and untwisted, Eva read the letter. The woman writing it, who signed her message with the initial *M,* got straight to the point: her husband had left her. This was, she conceded, an unexceptional fate. It had happened to plenty of her friends and lots of her acquaintances—it had been happening for all of history. As a result, many people assumed that they understood what she was feeling. Mostly, they assumed that she was sad or angry, possibly both. Any extremity of these emotions, it seemed, was allowed: one woman told M that she had burned all her husband's clothes in the backyard, and another said that she had tried to kill herself. But M didn't feel sadness or anger or the urge to destroy things. What she felt was envy. Not because her husband had left her for someone else. That kind of envy—jealousy—might have been easier to endure: to wish for the particulars of another person's life could give you purpose. No, it was as if he had left her for *everyone* else. It wasn't the particulars she envied, but the pure and shining potential.

Is there any way, M asked, *to get it back?*

"You're not watching," one of the twins shouted.

Eva paid close attention for three more unravelings. When at last the twins stood up, they stumbled toward Eva in a crooked line. She put the phone in her pocket and steered them home, letting them exaggerate their dizziness, leaning into her for balance, gripping her arm harder than they needed to.

That night, Eva read the letter a second time and then a third, but she didn't respond. Not to Judy, not to M. She thought about telling Jess or Lorrie about it, but decided against it. What if they didn't understand the problem—or, worse, what if they did? What if they saw the solution that she could not?

Everyone on the East Coast had warned Eva that she would miss the seasons, but she surprised herself by not being homesick. She liked seeing it all from afar. Each transformation, arriving without the fair warning of changing temperatures, was sudden and stark: first, the obscenity of spring; now, the dignity of fall. Her mom texted pictures of the foliage beginning to change. At the beginning of October, she sent an actual leaf in the mail. It was brown and withered when Eva took it out of the envelope.

The presidential election was less than a month away. Everyone was rattled, even if they said they weren't. *Anything could happen,* the most rattled ones said. Or maybe they were the least rattled ones. Jess said that the people who were truly afraid held on the tightest to hope.

While she was campaigning—busy, worried—Jess had stopped picking up Eva's calls. This was understandable, which didn't mean it wasn't painful. For a while, Eva tried calling other people instead. Sometimes she talked to Molly, who still lived in their old apartment, whose optimism was alternately encouraging and annoying. She tried her mom, but Gail was usually getting ready for bed. Eva could hear Nick's electric toothbrush whirring in the background. Her parents were desperate to discuss the news, but they always said the same things. They talked about leaving the country, which Eva knew they would never actually do.

A week before Halloween, Eva was driving to buy fresh supplies for the twins' costumes when Jess finally called back. There were no good cult-leader outfits, so the twins were going as aliens. They had invented their own extraterrestrial language, which Eva wasn't allowed to learn. She was surprised by the sting of ignorance—what were they saying about her?—but their mom said the whole thing was developmentally important: they were creating a world all their own.

"I'm seeing someone." Jess was on speaker phone, her voice filling up the car. She said she was sorry it had taken her so long to mention it. "I never know how to tell people, but I want to tell people."

So it wasn't politics that had been consuming her; it was love. Of course. Embarrassment—why hadn't she known?—made Eva want to close her eyes, as if this might make her disappear. But you couldn't close your eyes while you were driving.

"Who is he?" she asked, hoping her voice sounded neutral, normal.

"Everyone thinks I'm private," Jess said, "and actually I'm just nervous."

He was someone from her past. Not a significant someone,

though: she wasn't exaggerating when she said that, in all the years since they'd last seen each other, she hadn't thought about him once. They'd taken acting classes together when they were kids. For Jess, the classes were fun, but for Isaiah they were serious. The point was to make it to Broadway—and he almost did. He got a string of important child roles, and then, just when he was old enough for the real, exciting parts, he quit. His parents said he was missing his big chance, but what about everything else he'd already missed? He'd never been to a regular school, or cut his hair just for fun. He had a résumé—his own name at the top, followed by the names of all the roles he'd learned to play—but no one had ever asked him the obvious question, the one you were supposed to be able to answer with pure and wild fantasy: What do you want to be when you grow up?

Listening to Jess talk, Eva couldn't bear the thought of going home. There were too many hours before the twins were done with school. She pictured the garden, an orderly line of holes waiting to be filled, and felt only dread. She typed a new destination into the map on her phone.

"He's a history teacher now," Jess said. The school where he worked was in her district of Brooklyn, and one day twenty-seven letters had arrived at her office, one from every student in his tenth-grade class. Some of them requested bigger bike lanes and more trees on their streets, others cited statistics on food insecurity. Several had fathers or cousins in prison who deserved to be free. Jess responded to every letter and then she wrote one more: *Don't I know you?*

They had discovered, early on, that they had different memories of the acting class. Jess remembered the instructor as a young, glamorous woman; Isaiah insisted that she had been stern and middle-aged. He couldn't piece together exactly what she'd looked like or sounded like, but every now and then, the scent of a stranger's perfume overwhelmed him with the memory of what she had smelled like. In general, however, they didn't talk very much about the past. As a history teacher, Isaiah said, he did enough of that on the job. He had read that the average person spent 47 percent of the time thinking about something other than the present moment. Outside the classroom, he did his best to focus on the here and now.

"He sounds nice," Eva said.

For a few seconds, no one spoke. *Nice* wasn't always a compliment. Then Jess and the GPS started talking at the same time. The voice in the machine told Eva to take the next exit. She had to cross two lanes quickly, her neck twisting uncomfortably to check her blind spot.

"What did you say?" Eva asked.

"I said I might lose the race."

Eva climbed the exit ramp, raising her hand to thank the driver behind her. "How are the polls?"

"Isaiah tells me to ignore them."

"But isn't it important to know?"

"Know what?"

"What would happen."

"What might happen," Jess corrected. "The other guy in the race, the challenger, he has a new ad on TV. At the end of the ad, he says, *We are the future.* Now there are yard signs and T-shirts that say it, too."

"Hasn't someone used that one before?"

"Isaiah says it's ridiculous. No one *is* the future."

Eva pulled into a parking lot. The ocean stretched out in front of her. She was about to say she had to go, but Jess said it first.

The way the beach glittered—the ocean, too—made it seem as if she was seeing everything in all its parts, each grain of sand, each drop of water, each point of light. She didn't have a bathing suit, so she wore shorts and her sports bra. No shoes, no towel. That way, she wouldn't have to leave anything on the beach, wouldn't have to return to exactly where she'd started. She walked along the shore. The ground sucked her feet and the water surrounded her ankles. She pictured Jess lying in bed next to someone while her phone rang. She pictured them curled on their sides, turned toward each other, knees touching, mouths almost touching, just talking. Jess silenced the phone, then flipped it over, facedown on the bedside table.

On her way back to the car, when the parking lot came into view, Eva turned toward the sea. Cold knees, cold thighs, cold hips. She plunged her head underwater and the horizon disappeared.

AND THEN WHAT?

Jess won the race. Eva read about it in the newspaper, a minor story overshadowed by the major story, the only one anyone could talk about. The country was changing, maybe collapsing. Even the twins knew what was happening. They invented new games: Republicans versus Democrats, red states versus blue states. Their dad said it would be a bad time for marriages.

"A whole new category of irreconcilable differences."

Other divorce lawyers agreed, but his wife was skeptical. She'd seen couples endure clashes of beliefs that seemed much worse.

"They all get swallowed up by the bigger belief—that there's only one person out there for you."

A week after the election, with new explanations for the outcome emerging all the time—now that it had happened, everyone said they should have known it was going to happen—Eli texted Eva for the first time since she'd moved to California. She was standing in front of a stranger's house, admiring a window box of succulents. One looked like coral and another like a strand of pearls, dangling opulently over the box's edge. Eli said that he was in Los Angeles for his sister's wedding. Could they see each other?

When Eva put her phone away, avoiding the question, she realized with a start that there was a face on the other side of the window. An old man, who held up one finger: *Wait.* It took him a while to emerge from the house, but when he did, he was holding a pair of scissors. He snipped the head off a plant—"*Echeveria,*" he said slowly, waiting for her to repeat after him—and gave it to Eva with a long set of instructions for how to make it grow. The roots would look like delicate white threads. The leaves would look like strange tumors at first, but eventually they would look like a rose.

At home, Eva put the cutting on a kitchen windowsill and stared at Eli's text for a while, hoping to feel nothing. She'd been here before; she didn't want to be here again. She considered calling Jess—a month ago, she would have called her right away—but she stopped herself. Lorrie came into the kitchen and poured herself a glass of milk. A sudden wave of affection made Eva laugh. When was the last time she'd had a glass of milk? Eva showed her the text.

"You'll never feel nothing," Lorrie said, handing the phone back to her and taking a sip from her glass. "You'll just feel different."

"So I can say yes?"

"Don't ask for my permission."

She finished the milk in a few big gulps and put the glass in the sink, translucent white film slipping down the sides.

A few days later, Eva met Eli for dinner, at a restaurant that had been designed to look like a classroom. There were maps and old motivational posters on the wall: a famous actor from the nineties, with a mustache and a mullet, implored them to READ. The metal chairs were blue and maroon, like the ones she remembered from elementary school.

"Weird," Eva said.

On the menus in front of them, the dishes were listed like all the possible answers on a multiple-choice test.

"Maybe they ran out of things to be nostalgic for," Eli said. "That's the thing about the past. Limited supply."

He looked the same. She recognized his shirt. Since moving to California, Eva had thought hard about how to change her own style. She had bought a pair of baggy pants and boots with platforms, because they seemed out of character. The first few days wearing the shoes were uncomfortable: blisters, self-consciousness. By the time she saw Eli, they seemed old and familiar, but in his presence, she remembered their newness.

The food at the restaurant was all comfort food. Eva ordered chicken nuggets. They drank beer in frosted glasses, and Eli told her that his sister and Coco were getting married on the beach. They'd planned the wedding in a rush, to make sure it happened before wildfire season started. The fires started earlier and earlier every year.

While he talked, Eva pictured the two brides on the beach, white dresses that would never be worn again but would never be thrown out, either, collecting dust as they had once collected sand. Once a year, the couple would take them out of the closet, for the sake of reliving the day in their heads. Most memories didn't obey the calendar like that. Eva still thought about Coco sometimes, but never when she planned to. For a while, Eva had convinced herself that she'd kissed Coco first; then she'd changed her mind and blamed Coco. But neither, of course, was really true—that wasn't how kissing worked. She wondered if Coco had told anyone about it. It wasn't really a big deal—it was just kissing—but Eva found herself hoping that she had.

Eva asked Eli if Reshma was in town, too. He shook his head. "We broke up."

"What?" Eva took a gulp of beer, watery and bad. She made herself swallow it. "Why?"

For a moment, the taste of the beer transported her to college. Not to the parties themselves; to the next day, when the smell of spilled drinks and scented trash bags seemed to trail her everywhere. But she wasn't in college. She wasn't there, she was here, drinking a beer in a classroom from her youth. The whole situation was absurd, crossing wires in her brain, scrambling memories. She imagined the twins holding tall glasses of beer, the foam clinging to their upper lips. That maniacal laughter.

"She cheated," Eli said.

The waiter arrived with their food.

"It was her college reunion. Some guy she used to date. She said they had history."

There were three miniature hamburgers on Eli's plate, and he ate the first in two quick bites. For a moment, Eva's old fantasy returned—the discovery, the shattered phone, the hoarse voice, the vindication—along with a surge of anger. *She* cheated on *him*?

"So you ended it?" she said.

"*I* didn't." Now he sounded angry, too. "I told her I could get over it. I could move on."

Eli smeared a bouquet of fries through ketchup. He was about to put them in his mouth but then he stopped, looking at them as if they had suddenly reminded him of something. Whatever it was flickered across his face—a flash of tenderness, a glimpse of a wound—then disappeared.

In many years, which one of his faces would Eva remember as his face? *This one,* she said to herself, even though she knew it was a promise she didn't get to decide whether to keep. He pushed the plate toward her.

"Here, have some."

Eva thought about saying, *I'm sorry,* so that maybe he'd say, *Me, too.* Her own plate was empty, but she was hungrier than she'd thought. She reached toward his.

"Thanks."

When she got home, Lorrie was sitting on the couch in the dark, Greta Garbo's face filling up her entire laptop screen. Lately, she'd been watching a lot of silent films, which she said were essential to understanding visual language.

Eva sat on the other end of the couch and opened her email. Without looking up from her computer, Lorrie shifted, giving Eva room to stretch out her legs. She tucked her feet under Eva's arm.

Dear M.

The invention of the closeup, Lorrie had told Eva, transformed the emotional complexity of movies. For the first time, you could actually show what feelings looked like.

For weeks, I've been seeing you everywhere. First I convince myself that you're the woman next to me at the traffic light, mouthing lyrics to the same song playing on my radio. Then you're the woman in the produce aisle who tastes the grapes before you buy them, and also the woman in the hardware store who holds up two freshly cut keys to make sure their teeth match. I'm absolutely positive that you're the woman who stops short on the street, patting her coat pockets, but later I'm just as sure that you're the woman crouched over the sidewalk grate, peering down at something I can't see.

As the movie's score crescendoed, Lorrie brought her knees into her chest, the computer angling toward her.

I remind myself that this isn't possible, that you can't recognize some-

one you've never seen before. And yet each time I really believe it. There's a tiny chance, after all, that I'm right. A pop song can be grief and a piece of fruit can be desire. A forgotten wallet contains proof of who you are. A ring, a promise, can fall underground. For those brief moments, the secret life of the world appears to me. It contains exactly what you said you miss the most: potential.

The music in the movie was quieter now—some wordless drama resolved. Or maybe Lorrie had just turned down the volume.

You write that your husband left you for everyone. But couldn't you be anyone?

When Eva finished the email, she didn't read it over. She sent it to M and then, hesitating for only a second, she sent it to Judy, too. She looked up at Lorrie and their faces were mirrors, glowing bluish in the light of their screens, each of them crying over something the other couldn't see.

Eva decided to like her job. She always had, but it made a difference to say it—to herself, to Lorrie, to whoever asked. Who cared that it was just a job, not a ladder, not a calling? She used to watch the twins' games, but now she actually played them. She wielded a plastic sword, learned to shoot a rubber band without its snapping back on her wrist. She drank the Gatorade. She died a dramatic death.

In exchange for her enthusiasm, the twins gave her theirs. She brought them to her backyard and they helped finish the garden. Impatiens, not impatients, she explained. They let her show them how to pull up weeds by the roots, and they lay on their backs while she told them things about leaves—the things Jamie had told her. Crown shyness.

She thought, at first, that this was a polite trade, a matter of fairness, which kids were more attentive to than adults. She assumed that they were sharing her fun the same way they would split a piece of cake: straight down the middle. But over time she saw that it was more than that. When the three of them dug up an elderberry bush that needed more sun, the twins listened not just patiently but eagerly.

"See," Eva said, "you have to disturb the roots."

You had to be rougher than you thought, prying apart the tangled, stubborn mass, exposing the bright white coils to their first-ever sun. The twins didn't usually mind being rough, but they did this solemnly, deliberately.

During the day, Eva gardened, and at night, she wrote emails. Neither M nor Judy had ever replied to her letter, but now the messages arrived regularly—Judy forwarded every single one she received. The advice seekers wrote for all kinds of reasons. Some of the reasons were, as M would have said, unexceptional. Deaths, divorces. A fork in the road. Others were so strange they were unbelievable: surely impossible coincidences and seemingly unforgivable betrayals. But Eva always did believe them. That came as a surprise, even to her—to realize that she didn't care if they were telling the truth.

Over time, people began writing directly to Eva. They usually explained how they'd gotten her email—M had sent L, who sent W, who sent J—but beyond that, they offered little preamble. Eva could have looked them up: most people's email addresses contained some version of their names. She could have found out where they were writing from, how old they were, what they did for a living. Their pictures were probably out there, on corporate websites or personal blogs, but she never looked.

The more messages Eva received, the more they came to seem like part of the same conversation. Impossible, of course, that any single person would have so many problems, but that wasn't quite what she meant. More that it felt as if the letters were circulating in the same space, with no single *to,* no obvious *from*. As she wrote, Eva imagined herself in a big but quiet room, sort of like a library, with everyone bent over their letters, sealing and unsealing, asking and receiving, forwarding and returning.

In the middle of December, Judy invited Eva to come and see her garden. She drove across town with the radio off and the GPS off, because silence was familiar now—her calls with Jess shorter and less frequent than ever. Silence was comfortable now, too: ever since she'd started writing letters, there was always someone to talk to in her head.

Judy lived in a stucco house with two spindly palms looming overhead. She was waiting out front when Eva arrived, wearing a pair of rubber gardening shoes, bright red and ugly—something a child might have worn, Eva thought. Judy's face was speckled with age spots but it was tan, practically radiant. She took Eva around back before she took her inside.

"A winter garden!" Her delight, too, was childlike. "I'm the one who planted it, but I still can't quite believe it."

December, she explained, was good for harvesting leafy greens. So far, she had chard, kale, and several varieties of lettuce. Her beets hadn't worked out, but the kohlrabi looked promising. Purple lupines were thriving. Pink nasturtiums, baby blue eyes, and a delicate fuchsia flower that Judy identified by its Latin name, *Lamprocapnos spectabilis.*

"Also called bleeding hearts."

When they reached the corner of the yard, where a bird feeder dangled from a leafless trumpet tree, Judy turned to face Eva.

"So," she said, "you've become a correspondent."

Eva wondered if this was a joke. She had, of course, wanted to be a real correspondent—filing stories from halfway around the world, from foreign capitals, from conflict zones, from someplace where bombs were buried. It had not occurred to her to call her letters correspondences.

"What's this for?" she asked, to change the subject, bending down to inspect the trunk of a squat lemon tree that had been wrapped in newspaper.

Judy looked at her for a moment, as if deciding whether to permit this diversion. "To protect it from the cold," she said at last.

They continued silently along the perimeter of the yard. Judy occasionally spoke in order to identify plants—coffeeberries, monkey flowers—but she didn't return to the subject of the letters. Maybe she knew that Eva would return to it herself.

"I know how to give advice to people who ask," Eva said at last. "But what about everyone who doesn't?"

Judy shook her head. "I used to give it anyway."

"And then what?"

Judy stooped to inspect a cluster of lamb's ears, the ridges of her spine showing through her T-shirt.

"Did you know—" she began, but then she trailed off. Seemingly lost in thought, she stroked the plant's furry leaves as if it were an animal. After a few seconds, she started again: "Did you know that I met my grandchildren for the first time this year?"

She plucked one of the ears and stood back up. Her face was still bright, but it was also old. Eva studied her carefully, wondering what to say next. There was probably a long story: lost daughters, lost years, lost memories. There were probably many long stories. Judy held out the lamb's ear—a green so pale it was almost gray, covered in down.

"I had no idea," Eva said.

The skin of Judy's outstretched hand was thin and papery, but there were calluses on her fingers. Eva leaned her face toward the hand and felt the plant brush softly against her cheek.

The holidays arrived, and the twins went to visit their grandparents. Lorrie went skiing. For a few days, Eva was alone in the house. She had a ticket for a red-eye on Christmas Eve—the cheapest flight to New

York. It had been years since she'd cared about Christmas, since she'd inspected each present under the tree, shaking the packages to guess what was inside.

The day before she left, Eva was doing nothing when a text from Gail appeared on her phone.

Can I get your advice?

Eva laughed out loud. She was still laughing when Gail picked up the phone. It was an ordinary, difficult question: she had no idea what to give Nick for Christmas. Now that he wasn't painting anymore, all her old ideas were useless. For years, she'd been giving him oils and brushes.

"Is a hat better than a scarf?" She was at the store, holiday music playing in the background.

"He isn't painting anymore?"

"Nope," Gail said, as if this wasn't a big deal. "He says he's taking a break. He spends every weekend at the museum, just walking around. But don't call it wandering."

"I won't."

"He says he should have spent more time looking at art, learning about art, and less time making it. Some of the guards know him by name now."

It sounded nice to Eva—the walking. Even the wandering.

"And what about you?" Gail said. "What do you want for Christmas?"

"Oh, I don't know."

She could remember the long lists she'd once written. There were things she'd wanted because other people wanted them (a belly-button piercing, that pet-store bird) and things she'd wanted because they were in books (a four-poster bed, a petticoat) and things she'd wanted but couldn't explain why (a marionette, a geode sliced in half). She rarely got any of the things—Gail explained that a petticoat wasn't a kind of coat—and it hardly mattered. It prolonged the longing. She had gotten the geode, but she'd lost one half right away, which ruined the best part: the surprise of splitting open the rough, unremarkable rock; the dazzling purple secreted inside.

"There must be something," Gail said.

Doubt flickered in Eva's chest.

"Let me give you something."

Her mom's voice, which had seemed offhand at first, was urgent now. This happened all the time in the letters Eva received: the moment when she finally understood why someone was writing. She smiled, but she also could have cried.

"Okay," she said. "Maybe a scarf. A long, winding one."

She could picture Gail nodding gratefully, even though she couldn't see it.

The drive from the airport was deserted. It was barely light out, but when Eva let herself in the front door, Nick was already up, scrambling eggs in the kitchen. Unexpectedly, the sight of him undid her. His pajama shirt was thin, his stubble grayer than she'd remembered. His patience—low heat, gentle stirring—was eternal. Eva's chest clenched and heaved. She sat down in the chair that faced the living room, the chair that had always been and would forever be her chair, and wondered if she was going to weep. She'd been weeping a lot. Nick put the plate of eggs in front of her and put his hand on her back.

"You're okay," he said. "You're tired."

The day after Christmas was perfectly blue—not warm but bright. Eva went running in the park. There were bikers in skin-tight suits, babies in cocoons of blankets, dozens of people in the same puffy coat. No matter what you wore, only your face showed. And so when Eva recognized him on the path ahead of her, it was by the way he moved. Dangly arms, wobbly knees. There was a certain way he tilted his head toward whomever he was speaking to—she would have recognized it anywhere. He was running, too, and there was a man one or two paces behind him, his gait a little slower and more uncertain, as if he were running on sand. It was toward the man that Jamie's head was tilted. Eva didn't wonder if it was really him. She could see part of his cheek, pink in the cold, and the ends of his hair from beneath a hat, yellow in the sun. He was wearing an orange vest, the kind construction workers and crossing guards wear, which said GUIDE in big black letters. She stopped so that she wouldn't catch up to them, her heavy breath in her ears, the smell of cold in her nose. It took her a moment to understand that the other man was blind.

Eva followed them around the entire loop. They ran slow and she walked fast. She could see that their mouths were moving, and in her head she could hear his voice. She had been hearing it for so long. He guided them around the pond with the tied-up boats and through the pavilion with its empty grills. He told her what they were passing, where they were going. They crossed a bridge over water green with algae, so thick they could only guess what was underneath. They ran under an elm tree, gray and gnarled, that was older than anyone alive. He never turned around, but even so, as they reached the top of the final hill and the rush of traffic merged with a rush of wind, sound and sensation all at once, she did not doubt that he had seen her.

ACKNOWLEDGMENTS

All novels are a little hard to believe, but none more so than your own. Creating this one required many higher powers, faithful readers, and acts of grace. Bill Clegg convinced me I'd be able to make something out of nothing, then coaxed it into existence. David Remnick and Henry Finder let me go write the thing. Deb Garrison edited it with steady wisdom, sharp insight, and humor, too. David Wallace and Emily Rappaport read drafts at moments of great doubt. My friends and family gave me time and space and forbearance. They were kind enough not to ask what it was about.

Zuleima Ugalde, Amy Hagedorn, Elka Roderick, Kathleen Fridella, Terry Zaroff-Evans, Maggie Carr, Chris Jerome, and many others at the Clegg Agency and Knopf made it real—a book other people can actually read. Universal Music Publishing generously granted permission to reprint the lyrics of "Like a Rolling Stone." David Grann's *New Yorker* article, "Trial by Fire," taught me what I needed to know about fire investigators; I quote from it on page 189. T. M. Luhrmann's *When God Talks Back* was an invaluable resource.

The most incredible creators of all are my parents—the best people to talk to, the easiest people to trust. My mom's notes did to this book what she has done to my life: transformed it.

Eddie read and reread, and kept the faith. Our life is better than a miracle. It's the thing we make every day.

Thank you all.

A NOTE ABOUT THE AUTHOR

Clare Sestanovich, named a "5 Under 35" honoree by the National Book Foundation in 2022, is the author of the story collection *Objects of Desire,* a finalist for the PEN/Robert W. Bingham Prize. Her fiction has appeared in publications such as *The New Yorker, The Paris Review,* and *Harper's Magazine.* She lives in Brooklyn.

A NOTE ON THE TYPE

This book was set in Adobe Garamond. Designed for the Adobe Corporation by Robert Slimbach, the fonts are based on types first cut by Claude Garamond (ca. 1480–1561). Garamond was a pupil of Geoffroy Tory and is believed to have followed the Venetian models, although he introduced a number of important differences, and it is to him that we owe the letter we now know as "old style." He gave to his letters a certain elegance and feeling of movement that won their creator an immediate reputation and the patronage of Francis I of France.

Typeset by Scribe
Philadelphia, Pennsylvania

Printed and bound by Berryville Graphics
Berryville, Virginia

Designed by Casey Hampton